...at must be taken on her own te... ...e almost zen handling of voice is a joy.'
Janice Galloway

'How can Sybil's stint, indexing at the troubled Royal Institute of Prehistoric Studies, be so hilarious, so gripping, and so heart-rending? Because Ruth Thomas is a devastatingly subtle novelist – a quiet voice among louder ones, but, for me, a voice which says so much more about our crazy times.' **Alan Warner**

'A deeply involving novel about the end of a relationship, blended with a deliciously nutty confection of haiku and ancient history. The prose is sharp, witty and well observed – pitch perfect. Ruth Thomas has created an unforgettably nuanced central character, flawed and humorous with a fantastic sense of the absurd. It's like reading about a best friend – from the inside out. Resonant and romantic, sad but never sentimental and laced through with wicked shafts of humour.'
Lesley Glaister

'A very funny novel with a dark undertow. Ruth Thomas creates a world which is vivid, emotionally true and acutely observed. Sybil's voice is compelling – both knowing and unknowing – and the dialogue bristles with the unsaid. Wry, sharp and tender. A delight.' **Meaghan Delahunt**

'I LOVED IT! All the best bits of Barbara Pym, with a little Jane Austen – on speed.' **Sarah Salway**

Also by the author

Sea Monster Tattoo

The Dance Settee

Things to Make and Mend

Super Girl

The Home Corner

Ruth Thomas is the author of three short story collections and two novels, as well as many short stories which have been anthologised and broadcast on the BBC. *The Snow and the Works on the Northern Line* is her third novel. Her writing has won and been shortlisted for various prizes, including the John Llewellyn Rhys Award, the Saltire First Book Award and the VS Pritchett Prize, and long-listed for the Frank O'Connor International Short Story Award. She lives in Edinburgh and is currently an Advisory Fellow for the Royal Literary Fund.

The Snow and the Works on the Northern Line

RUTH THOMAS

SANDSTONE PRESS

First published in Great Britain by
Sandstone Press Ltd
Willow House
Stoneyfield Business Park
Inverness
IV2 7PA
Scotland

www.sandstonepress.com

ISBN: 978-1-913207-36-6
ISBNe: 978-1-913207-37-3

Sandstone Press is committed to a sustainable future.
This book is made from Forest Stewardship Council ® certified paper.

Cover design by Rose Cooper
Typeset by Biblichor Ltd, Edinburgh
Printed in the UK by Severn, Gloucester

For M.G.N.

Amongst the graffiti is the name of someone I love

Bashō

THE SNOW

1

The accident was one of those stupid ones. It was the kind you're supposed to laugh about later. It happened at Streatham Ice Rink; Simon had thought it would be fun to go there one evening, so that was what we did. Unfortunately, neither of us could skate; this had not occurred to us. Simon was better than me – he was able to stand upright without holding onto the side – but I did not enjoy myself a single minute I was there: my skates were as heavy as leg-irons, and the rink just seemed to go on and on: you could hardly see across to the other side. I was wearing a bobble-hat that my mother had given me one Christmas years before, and an over-sized Parka that Simon had lent me, and I kept wondering why on earth you were supposed to skate on single blades when two per boot would have been so much more sensible; I couldn't understand why no one in the skates business had ever thought of that. Looking up at one point I saw a blur of gold and silver tinsel draped around the crash barriers, and looking down I saw a large brownish-red patch beneath the surface of the ice. I thought: *that's someone's blood*. And I wondered how often the Management at Streatham Ice Rink thawed the ice so they could get rid of things like that, little signs of something that had gone wrong.

We'd been there for ten minutes or so, slogging around as people span and twirled about us when Simon said, 'Oh, look – isn't that what's-her-name over there? Your old lecturer? Who was at your Christmas work thing the other night?', and he suggested we push out towards the middle of the rink, to see if it was.

I glanced over for a second, at my one-time university tutor and new work associate, Helen Hansen. I couldn't imagine what she was doing there. It seemed enough that I was always bumping into her in the corridors at work. Her complexion was a rosy, athletic pink beneath her snowy-white hat and she was wearing a puffy, expensive-looking ski-jacket that looked as if it would have been better suited to the French Alps than Streatham Ice Rink. 'I'm not sure it *is* her . . .' I said. Because if it *was* Helen Hansen, I didn't really want to speak to her. There was a certain history between us, and everything on the rink was a blur anyway.

'It *is* her,' Simon said. 'We should say hello. It'll be easier out there, anyway. More space.'

'Will it?' I flicked a quick glance at the slab of ice beneath my boots. 'But do we want more space? I'm not sure I want to say hello . . .'

'What's wrong with her? She's perfectly nice. We had a good chat the other night.'

'*Really*?'

But because he was taller and broader than me I made the mistake of thinking he was also more stable on slippery surfaces, more dependable. I did not say, 'I think this is a bad idea; I once heard of someone leaving an ice rink minus half their fingers.' We just lurched out into the middle, towards Helen Hansen: archaeologist extraordinaire, rising businesswoman-cum-academic star, member of the Institute's Board of Trustees. It was a Friday night and the rink was packed with very tall fifteen-year-olds and couples who appeared to be so good on the ice that they were *snogging while skating*, and there was a soundtrack playing very loud and distorted from metal speakers jutting out across the rink – some Lionel Richie song I vaguely knew – and we were a long way out now, sliding like Brueghel's peasants towards her, when I misjudged some technique I'd adopted for staying vertical, and felt myself slip. And straight away I knew this was not going to end well. Moving

4

semi-horizontally, I reached out for Simon's arm – 'Wha—?' he said – then we were both on our backs on the ice, the air knocked flat out of us, and spinning like bottles.

I'm not sure what happened after that. There was a lot of whiteness and coldness, the whole ice rink upside down and lit up and moving in a rush of tinsel and jackets and faces. There were steel skates everywhere you looked, only now they were all at eye level, and Simon and I were rocketing towards the crash barriers, heading there fast, and I put my arm up to protect my head from the impact I knew was about to happen, and Lionel Richie was telling us it was quite a feeling, dancing on a ceiling and the fifteen-year-olds were braking all round us in a spray of ice-splinters and contempt. And for the briefest moment, I had a strange vision of my *grandfather*, of all people, who'd died a few months earlier: there was my *grandad*, as clear as daylight in my mind, and I thought: *well, if I'm about to die it'll be OK because Grandpa's here to show me the ropes.* Then we hit the barriers, head first, and for a while after that I was nowhere at all.

A little later I *was* somewhere, of course: I was not in heaven with my grandfather, I was still living and breathing in some ward in Dulwich Community Hospital. I was in the same old world and it was late December, and Simon was so unscathed he'd already left Outpatients and headed home on a bus. He'd gone with Helen Hansen, in fact. Because it *had* been her. And really, it was quite a miracle that neither of us was not more badly hurt. Helen mentioned this herself, when she put her head round my door at work a few days later; she'd turned up again for one of the Trustees meetings she kept going to.

'So someone was looking out for you last week, Sybil!' she said, in her sassy way. And she smiled that big smile of hers.

'Yes,' I said, 'I suppose they must have been.'

I looked down at my desk-top, and couldn't think what else to say. 'Anyway,' I added, 'thanks for coming to the hospital

5

with us, Helen. That was nice of you. As neither of us was particularly compos mentis at the time.'

Because I'd been brought up to be polite – even to people I didn't actually like. Then I smiled briefly and got on with my work, and everything around me had looked much the same, for the next few weeks. It all *was* much the same. I just hadn't realised it was about to look different.

I hadn't seen her for ages, before that. Not for nearly seven years. But whenever I thought back to those days, I'd remember how she had seemed to quite like me. She'd made a strange bee-line for me – something I'd never really understood. I'd been a young first-year student, awkward as a goat, and she was a glamorous academic heading towards a doctorate. I've since learned that some people operate like this. They like to bask in other people's reflected lack of glory. But I didn't know this at the time; I'd just accepted her attention with bafflement and a vague wish to get away. Two things stood out in my memory: once, during a tutorial on funerary urns, she'd flattened a wasp with a plastic Helix ruler, squashing the life out of it rather than simply letting it fly through the open window and, halfway through our first term together, she'd started calling me Sybil the Blind Prophet. This was, she said, an affectionate joke. 'It's meant to be a compliment, Sybil! It's because you know so much! You seem to know things by some mysterious osmotic process, and I can never work out how you do it!' I'd always thought that was peculiar, too. My ability to retain any information at all really seemed to bother her.

At the end of my university days I'd gone to Swansea to do a post-graduate degree in Norse and Celtic Mythology, and although I'd heard occasional news of Helen's starry progress through academia via a journal called *Archaeology Now!*, which my old department intermittently brought out and sent to me via my parents' address in Norfolk, I'd assumed our paths would not cross again. I was perfectly happy about this: quite content to hear news of Helen through the pages of *Archaeology Now!* It was, for instance, where I'd first learned of her unexpected departure from my old university in order to take up *an exciting new role as Director of the London Museums Interpretation Centre*, in Tooting. I'd opened that issue during a weekend stay at my parents' house, and there she was, in the centre pages, standing beneath the diplodocus skeleton in the grand hall of the Natural History Museum. She was clasping a champagne flute, her blue eyes flashing, her jaw set at an ever more resolute angle. *'I see my role as facilitating the various commercial opportunities available to museums and academic institutions in the twenty-first century, while remaining sympathetic to and respecting the core values and aims of historians and archaeologists . . .'* she'd proclaimed, in an interview beneath this picture. The London Museums Interpretation Centre (LMIC, for short) was, apparently, *a much-needed new umbrella group for smaller British museums, channelling funds, arranging networking events and reaching out to new audiences and consumer markets.*

'Well, *she* looks like a force to be reckoned with,' my father had observed, peering over my shoulder at the photo. 'Tooting, though? Seems an unlikely place.'

'But where's a *likely* place?' I asked. 'For someone like her?'

'I don't know, New York? Tokyo? Paris? Somewhere glamorous.'

'Oh.'

He glanced at the picture again. '*Helen:* the face that launched ten thousand ships.'

'One thousand,' I corrected him.

'What was it she used to lecture you on?'

'Beakers. As in The Beaker People.'

'Oh.'

He looked vaguely disappointed.

*

7

I had not done much myself during my years in Swansea, after the perfectly respectable 2nd class Honours degree I'd wrested from the jaws of the 3rd class one Helen had (as I later discovered) recommended. I'd read *The Mabinogion* and the Arthurian legends and written a dissertation on *The Book of the Dun Cow* (a book I'd initially assumed was about a cow: I was wrong.) I had fallen in love for a while with a long-haired Irish legends specialist who'd smoked a lot of weed, never got out of bed before 3pm and owned a lime-green mug that said *Time and Relative Dimension in Space*. I don't know why the memory of that mug loomed so large in my mind, it just did. Then I'd returned to London and had an unexpected fling with a Danish astrophysicist called Mats, before moving on to a bearded and more sensible man named James who was doing a PhD and had been doing so for years. I imagined he would be about forty-six before he submitted it. He used to make a lot of gnomic and profound remarks and he also sometimes made me laugh. But after a while his immense, serious wisdom had begun to weigh me down, the way too much snow weighs down a too-thin branch, and I moved on from him, a little sadder but, paradoxically, lighter of heart.

I was alone for a few months after that, and then I met Simon: we met one night in The Olive Branch, an Italian restaurant round the corner from my flat, where he worked as a chef. I had gone in alone, a young woman about town, and ordered salted cod by mistake, and after I'd returned it and he'd appeared at my table with a replacement bowl of *spaghetti al pomodoro* and said he'd made the pasta himself, not from wheat but from spelt, it was pretty much love at first sight; I suppose it was what is called a *coup de foudre*. Even though we were not actually alike at all, it soon transpired, and we didn't even like doing the same things. He was an active sort of person, whereas I'd always preferred observing other people being active. He liked driving his boss's Alfa Romeo around town, and I liked going to the

8

cinema and watching other people driving their cars around. He liked outdoor pursuits – foraging, hiking, wild camping – while I couldn't stand windswept walks up uneven gradients, or eating fungi that might kill you, or listening to disconcerting noises outside a tent at three in the morning. But love is not concerned with such differences, of course; love does not have motives or reasons or ambitions or even shared tastes. We'd simply fallen for each other: we were yin and yang, light and shade, Mr Sunshine and Mrs Rain in their little wooden house. It didn't seem to matter that he was pragmatic and I was a conjecturer; that he made things, and I wondered about them; that he was an outstanding and inventive cook, whereas I was mostly a compiler of sandwiches. At the end of the day I would turn the key in the lock of our front door (we moved in together less than a year after first meeting), and would feel happy if he was already home, frying shallots or chopping herbs from the little pots he kept on our kitchen windowsill.

Of course, I did worry from time to time about the ways we were different, and perhaps, it occurred to me later, I should have worried a little more as the months went by. Maybe if I'd thought, for instance, about his decision not to go with me to my grandfather's funeral that autumn because *he'd hardly known the guy*; or reflected on the camping trip we *had* gone on just two days later, because *camping was extremely important to him* – and how, although I loved the pine-scented woods and the craggy hills and the birds flapping around the sky, I'd felt a terrible, lonely ache in my chest, and it had been clear to me within five minutes of pitching the tent that he was going to enjoy himself a lot more than I was. He was in his element, striding around the fields in his North Face windcheater while I was only in my element in theory. I'd taken my guitar along to play a few songs, but even as I sat there, picking out Bob Dylan and Pink Floyd tracks on a slightly sloping patch of damp grass, I knew I could never be truly excited about a holiday that involved washing up in a stream with a Brillo pad and gathering sticks; I knew that, at heart, I really wanted to be at home, missing my grandad, and watching *QI* in my slippers. We spent a lot of our first day trying to work out where we were in relation to the nearest village (we were fourteen miles away) and boiling up farro grains in a tiny saucepan, the clip-on handle of which kept falling off. Then halfway through Day Two, scouting in the woods for a suitably private patch of bracken, I'd peered up to witness a farmer appear puce-faced over the brow of the hill on a quad bike, yell something and wave his arms, before a flock of about fifty sheep came careering into the field where we'd pitched our tent.

'The thing is,' I said to Simon that night, as we sat in the greenish shadows, 'we do actually *live* in the twenty-first century. So why pretend we still live in the Bronze Age?'

He looked at me. He looked very serious, almost sad, as if some fundamental truth had just occurred to him, about the many ways we would never understand each other. Maybe he was thinking: *If we were depending on you for survival we'd have another forty-eight hours, max.* But then he smiled.

'Come here, twenty-first-century girl,' he said, unzipping the sleeping bag which he'd bought especially for me, because it was a *4-seasons tog rating*, and I slid along the sloping nylon groundsheet towards him and slung my arms around his neck.

The thing is, we were not always on the same wavelength. But this didn't mean I didn't love him. It did not mean I didn't care.

Then, one afternoon a few weeks later – the same afternoon (it transpired) that Helen returned to my life – we had an argument. It had a depressingly trivial cause, as arguments often do: I'd suggested, as we were washing up the previous night's dishes, that it might save space in our tiny kitchen if we stacked all our saucepans under the sink with their lids inverted. And Simon had said actually, no, you should always hang saucepans by their handles from a rack above the cooker.

'If you stack them,' he explained, 'you have to dismantle the entire stack to use them, and *no* proper cook does that!'

'Oh, really! So are you saying *I'm* not a proper cook?'

'Well, to be honest, you *are* pretty crap at cooking!' He stared glumly down at the draining rack. 'Also, I was going to let this go, but why did you use my rice steamer to steam fish in last night?'

'What?' I said, blushing – because he was right, I *had* used his rice steamer to steam fish in, the previous night.

'The whole thing reeks of cod now!' he said. 'I'll have to throw it out and get *another* one!' And somehow, within about fifty seconds of my quite casual remark about saucepan storage, our disagreement had escalated into something a lot worse: something intense and loud and hurtful.

'It's clear to me you have no real interest in food!' Simon was saying now. 'I mean, all your cooking seems to be variations on a theme of *tomato sauce!*'

'Hah! Well, that's because I don't want to spend half my life *fluffing wild rice!*' I yelled back, aware of a strange, almost physical hurt – it felt like a big punch in the stomach.

We glared at each other. It was as if neither of us could imagine what we'd ever once admired. Then, sad and rattled at this new depressing turn in our relationship, I picked up my coat and keys and barged down the hallway out of the flat.

'Don't wait up!' I yelled (even though it was only three in the afternoon) and I slammed the door and hiked off up the road. I headed to the tube station, walking fast but directionless, aware of myself gulping at the air like a fish. By the time I was through the ticket barrier I already felt contrite, depleted, but despite this I carried on, heading all the way into town on the Northern Line, all the way up to King's Cross and out again onto the Caledonian Road, then up to the British Library, for some reason – and it was at this point, in the gathering gloom, that I first bumped into Helen.

'Sybil!' a voice called to me across the wet, paving-slabbed courtyard.

And I turned, and there she was: this woman, waving, beside the statue of Sir Isaac Newton. It took me a second, maybe two, to recognise her, to comprehend why I knew this impressive-looking person with the big smile and the blonde hair and the smart coat. Then, when I did realise, I felt something happen to my heart: a kind of jump, a sort of lurching.

Helen had already abandoned Sir Isaac Newton and his set of compasses by this point, and started walking across the square towards me. It was raining slightly and she was holding a navy-blue umbrella – one of those big expensive ones that does not immediately buckle in the wind, unlike the flimsy telescopic things I was always buying.

'Come under my brolly,' she instructed, and I did. I did as I was told. And I saw that she had hardly changed at all. Her hair was the same, and her smile was the same, and even the coat was like the one she'd worn around the corridors of UCL – although this one was new and even more expensive-looking. Also, she still had a very sassy walk and a confidence that seemed to flatten everything in its path. We smiled a little over-enthusiastically and gave each other a hug beneath the spokes of her huge umbrella and went into the library through the heavy glass doors. We bought two coffees in paper cups and sat down at one of the round white tables in the foyer, even though by now I was already wanting to go back home to Simon, to apologise, to be apologised to.

'So tell me what you've been up to all this time, since our cosy tutorial-group days!' Helen said, but I had begun to feel strangely pinioned by this point because I suddenly remembered just how un-cosy our tutorial-group days had been, and how much effort Helen had put into trying to scupper my 2:1. *A disappointing collection of un-referenced and historically inaccurate theories*, she'd called my dissertation (I found out later) – though oddly, she'd been in the minority with this opinion because it had been contested that summer by the head of department, who'd described it as: *A diverting and audacious comparison between the myths of Classical Literature and the facts of prehistory.* (He'd said this during an exam board meeting, and it was his opinion which had won the day. Even though, secretly, I suspected Helen had probably been right all along.)

'I mean,' Helen went on brightly, smiling across the table at me, 'where has life taken you, Sybil?'

'Well,' I replied, 'I hardly know where to start, Helen. Because seven years is a long time.'

'It is, isn't it?'

Then she embarked on what *she'd* been doing in that time: how she'd been briefly married and divorced; how she'd travelled to Beijing and Toronto and Tokyo ('So my dad was *right!*' I almost burst out); how she'd left the university and had recently become the director of a place in Tooting called the London Museums Interpretation Centre – ('Yes,' I said, 'I read about that!') – which was an exciting career move, Helen ploughed on, because not only was the work fascinating and fun, but the perks and the bonuses and the social life were excellent, and she could also wangle more funded conference trips to China and Canada and Japan, thereby enhancing her reputation as a Beaker People expert. Which was the real point.

'That sounds great,' I said. 'Getting the chance to, y'know . . . continue your research. And go to Tokyo. Wow! I've always wanted to go and see what—'

'Yes, it's great,' Helen confirmed.

I hesitated. I still felt oddly numb, after my argument with Simon. 'So you're still specialising in . . . ancient peoples . . . ?'

Helen gave me a funny look.

'Of course I'm still specialising in ancient peoples! Ancient peoples are my life. The Beaker People in particular. I'm pretty

13

much a world authority on them these days, Sybil. I've even recorded a TED talk recently.'

'Wow,' I said, even though I'd never been sure about TED talks; they'd always sounded quite overwhelming to me, like a cross between bears and Ted Hughes. Also, I was not convinced Helen *was* a world authority on the Beaker People, though I knew she'd always been ambitious. 'So what's it about? Your talk?'

'It's about the Beaker People in general, and, more specifically, about a discovery I made earlier this year, during a dig in Sussex.'

'Really? In Sussex?' I said, feigning interest.

'Yes, my team and I came across some extremely exciting pottery fragments there, in Winchelsea. I've called it the Winchelsea Hoard—'

'Wow, amazing! Like Sutton Hoo or something!' I said, trying to maintain the note of wonder. Somehow, though, the words *extremely exciting* and *pottery fragments* had never quite gone together in my head.

'Yes,' Helen said, 'we found a whole stash of Beaker fragments in a field just up from the beach. Analysis of which suggests that Beaker trade routes went much further into Southern Italy than we'd thought.'

'Italy? But I thought you found them in Winchelsea.'

'We *did*,' she snapped. 'But finding them *there*, in Winchelsea, has opened up a whole new set of ideas about their trade routes.' She looked at me. 'Because of the type of *grain residue* that was in them.' She paused, as if waiting for my slowly whirring brain to catch up. 'Hence my extended trade route theory. Which is what I talk about, in my TED talk.'

'Well, wow . . .' I said. I didn't know what else to say. It was like being back in one of her tutorials. There was the same desire to get away. 'So what were they? These grains?'

'A variety of *turanicum* wheat from Southern Italy. And as we know, or *thought* we knew – that's the only part of the

14

Mediterranean the Beaker People were not supposed to have lived in!'

Triumphant, she stopped talking, and waited for me to speak.

'Well, that *does* sound exciting,' I mumbled.

I thought of my dissertation again, in which I'd ad-libbed wildly on parallels between the Beaker People and *the mythic significance of goblets and chalices in Ancient Rome*, which was all a load of rubbish, of course; I'd had no evidence for this at all.

'So, when's it going out?' I asked. 'The talk?'

'In the spring. It's in post-production. I'm focusing on PR stuff now.'

'Right.'

'Yes, so what I'm doing at the moment – mainly to get LMIC's role more *out there*, in the public consciousness – is I'm developing a range of Beakerware kitchen products with my colleagues in Tooting.'

'Really? Beakerware?' I thought of the Tupperware my parents had always used to bring out on picnics when I was a child; of our serious little party of three, at the beach at Dymchurch or Camber Sands.

'Yes. We're going to sell a range of replica beakers – earthenware bowls and cups of different sizes – in various museum shops next summer. Even in places like the British Museum, if they'll have us. Eventually we're hoping to roll them out across Europe.'

'Roll them out?'

'Expand the market. Then we'll channel the profits back to LMIC. Via our own museums, of course.'

'I see,' I said.

'The thing is, small museums are hopeless at commercial enterprises,' Helen explained. 'So it's LMIC's role to get them on board. They get the money and we get the kudos. And museum shops are awash with idiots wanting to part with their cash.'

'Yes.' I thought of the occasions I'd drifted around museum shops with Simon lately, picking things up – pyramid-shaped pencil sharpeners, key rings in the guise of Viking warriors. 'Would you like some earrings in the shape of hippo gods?' he had asked me recently, holding one up to his earlobe.

'Probably they're just, you know, parting with their money because they're having a nice time,' I said now. 'Just being tourists. And feeling a bit flush because they're on holiday. And wanting some sort of . . . souvenir of their time.'

Helen smiled, as if I might be one of those idiots. 'The Beaker People never interested you much, did they?' she said.

'Not really. The thing is,' I added, making it worse, 'they just kept making *beakers* all the time! And I've never been all that interested in bits of broken pottery.'

Helen's eyes were a quite spectacularly icy blue.

'Do you know how many museums we have under our belt at the moment?' she asked.

'No.'

'Eleven.'

'Right.'

'And do you know how many we plan to have by the end of next financial year?'

'No.'

'Eighteen!'

'Right.'

'So, what are you up to now? By way of gainful employment?' she added, stirring sugar crystals into her coffee. So I told her that I was – funnily enough – working in a kind of museum myself, these days: I was cataloguing fossils and belt buckles and old clay pipes, amongst other things, in an institute.

'Really? But that's hysterical! That's hardly a million miles from bits of broken pottery, is it?'

Well, no, I confessed, it wasn't. It's just, there weren't any jobs, when I was looking, that required an in-depth knowledge of Persephone or Zeus or Apollo, or even *The Book of the Dun Cow*.

'So where are you doing this?' Helen asked. 'The cataloguing?'

'Greenwich,' I said. 'In the Royal Institute of Prehistorical Studies.'

'You're working at RIPS?' she burst out. 'At the Institute? With Raglan Beveridge? And Hope Pollard and people? How utterly bizarre! That's one of our museums! It's our latest recruit! So how come I haven't seen you there, because I go there most weeks!'

'Well, I only started there quite recently,' I said, suddenly alarmed, and wishing I'd kept shtum about the Institute and my opinion of the Beaker People. Or that I'd never turned around when Helen had called over to me from the Isaac Newton statue.

'So hopefully we'll be seeing more of each other,' she continued. 'Isn't that funny? Hey – we can go for lunch sometimes and bitch about Raglan!'

'Hmm . . .' I wasn't sure I *wanted* to bitch about Raglan Beveridge, because although I didn't know him well (he was, after all, the Institute's director), and although he was a big man in his fifties and perfectly capable of looking after himself, I'd noticed a kind of vulnerability about him sometimes that made me feel it was unkind to talk about him behind his back. It was something to do, somehow, with the very careful way he wore his suits and the fact he was invariably the last person left in the building when everyone else had headed home. Anyway, as my mother would have reminded me, if you can't say something nice about someone, don't say anything at all. And already something was telling me that bumping into Helen had been a more troubling thing than I might have anticipated, that it was stirring up some quite unwelcome memories.

Helen smiled.

'You know, I'm so glad you ended up with that 2:1 in the end, Sybil,' she said. 'For that dissertation you wrote. All those years ago.'

'Are you?' I asked, my heart thudding.

'I really am. You deserved it. Because clearly I was the one who got it wrong on that occasion, wasn't I? As it turns out.'

'Well,' I said, remembering the unseemly haste with which I'd cobbled it together, 'that's very—'

'I was too exacting. Not forgiving enough. It's easy to forget sometimes that your students are only just out of *school*! Barely more than *children*! And the thing is, it's important to own up to your mistakes, isn't it? If we never made mistakes, we'd never learn.'

'No . . .'

'Seriously, though, I suppose what happened, that time, was I'd discounted that pretty interesting correlation you made between the Beaker People and stories about Ancient Roman cup-bearers. That "everything is connected" idea. It was just that Ancient Rome was not my area, of course.'

'No.' I could hardly remember the correlations I'd made. They'd been a means to an end, conjured up out of thin air when I was twenty. I just wanted to return to my life now at twenty-six, and the people I knew and trusted in it – even to Simon, especially Simon, despite the ridiculous argument we'd just had. Because he was my lover, he was my friend and confidant, he was maybe even my husband one day and the father of my children. But Helen seemed to want to keep chatting, and it was hard to know how to get away from her. She was telling me now about someone at work called Ed whom she'd been seeing for a while but was thinking about leaving, and also about the man she'd been briefly married to, whose name was Doug. They'd never been compatible, though, because Doug was so *unadventurous* and had a secret liking for David Gray and Phil Collins and all sorts of other deplorable middle-of-the-road music—

'But I thought you quite *liked* Phil Collins,' I said, pulling my coat from the back of my chair and dragging it on. 'I remember you playing "In the Air Tonight" once, in one of our tutorials.'

Helen frowned. 'That was to explain a point. About carbon dating. Because, if you recall, I always tried to make my tutorials fun.'

'Oh, I didn't realise! I'd just assumed you liked—'

I trailed off. Helen was peering at me again in quite a disconcerting way.

'So, how's your love life?' she said.

'Sorry?'

'Got a significant other?'

So I sat there a few minutes longer, and told Helen about Simon: about, amongst other things, his strange enthusiasm for ancient grains, and the funny black-and-white checked trousers he'd worn in his first job as a chef, and his love of mushroom foraging and wild camping and listening to Bob Marley. I even showed her the picture I had of him in my purse. Then for some reason I also found myself telling her that he hadn't gone with me to my grandfather's funeral – a fact that had upset me quite a lot at the time, I went on – and also about the ridiculous argument we'd just had about saucepans.

'But then again,' I added, 'I think I probably overreacted. Because people respond differently to death, don't they? To grief. And I suppose it must be pretty annoying, if you're a professional chef, to see your rice steamer being used to steam fish in . . . And I *do* love him. And maybe arguments, if you resolve them, can actually be a testament to . . .' I faltered.

'To what?'

'A grown-up relationship.'

'Hah! Not in my experience!'

She gazed at me across the top of her paper cup. 'It's funny,' she said, 'because I never imagined you with an alpha male type, Sybil. I always thought you'd end up with some poetry lover, wafting around playing a guitar.'

'Oh, Simon's not an alpha male type, really,' I said. 'He's pretty much beta, in a lot of ways.'

'Trust me, a man who likes his woman in the kitchen with her saucepans is an alpha male type.'

'He doesn't want me in the kitchen with saucepans,' I said, exasperated. 'He actually wants me *out* of the kitchen! And if anyone's interested in saucepans, it's him – he's even got a little Trangia set for when he goes camping!'

Helen paused. 'How sweet,' she said thoughtfully.

I suddenly wished I hadn't divulged this information.

'I'm quite a fan of camping myself, actually,' Helen went on. 'Good-looking guy, isn't he?' she added.

I did not reply. I found it hard to imagine Helen Hansen sleeping under canvas, even if she was an archaeologist. And Simon *was* good-looking, but I did not see the need to share this insight with her. So instead, I told her a little more about his work: the pasta and the pizza doughs he made, the different types of grain he'd started experimenting with at The Olive Branch. Because, I explained, it was one of those very artisanal restaurants that seemed to be springing up all over the place. He had shown me a list of ingredients when he'd come home recently. '*Look at this,*' he'd said. There was buckwheat, spelt, brown rice, quinoa and amaranth; there was barley, freekeh and rye. '*Freekeh*!' I'd laughed. But he hadn't seemed to find it such a funny word as I did.

Helen glanced at her watch. 'Bob Marley was a fan of multiple relationships, wasn't he? So I believe,' she said, looking at me with her impressively blue eyes.

'What's Bob Marley got to do with it?'

'Simon likes Bob Marley, you just told me. Keep up, Sybil!' she said. Which was what she'd used to say to me sometimes, during tutorials. *Keep up, Sybil the Blind Prophet*! Although when I *had* eventually kept up, surprising everyone with that 2:1 and a personal little note of praise and apology from the head of department, she had said nothing to me at all.

'Do you remember that boy in our tutorial groups?' she said, as we stood up from the table. 'John Milton? Who wrote poetry?'

'Of course I do,' I said. 'Except his name was John Nelson.'

'He seemed more your type, I always thought. John Milton. I always thought you two might get it together . . .'

'John Nelson,' I tried again. But really, there was no point. Helen was not listening; she appeared, rather, to be working something out. I even mentioned this to Simon a few hours later, after I'd gone home and promised to buy him a new rice steamer, and we'd kissed and made up. Yes, I observed that evening as we lay in each other's arms, gazing through our bedroom window at the darkening sky, yes, there's something even *steelier* about her these days . . .

'Stealier?' he said, his voice floating up into the darkness. 'What's she been stealing?'

'Steelier.' I laughed, stroking the underside of his arm, where his skin over the muscle was so beautiful, so soft as silk. 'Steelier, with two es.'

Although, as it turned out, his interpretation had been the correct one.

2

Floor 0	Gallery
Floor 1	Reception
Floor 2	Offices
Floor 3	Offices
Floor 4	Offices
Floor 5	Archives

The Institute stood in the middle of Greenwich Park, half a mile north from the General Wolfe statue and half a mile east of the meridian line. You could place your feet on either side of the line and be in two different hemispheres at once. I did that sometimes, on my way up the hill in the mornings. It only worked as far as geography was concerned, of course; unfortunately it was not possible to do the same thing with time.

I'd actually used to wander around the park years before, as a child; I'd gone there with my grandparents who'd lived nearby, in Blackheath. We'd drive there in my grandad's Triumph Acclaim then walk slowly, slowly across the grass, down past the doors of the Institute and on, down Greenwich High Street, to look at the Cutty Sark. Or we would walk through the Greenwich Foot Tunnel, our footsteps echoing against the curved white walls. I'd walk between the two of them, holding onto their hands. 'A rose between thorns,' my grandfather used to say. I didn't know what he was talking about.

*

The Institute's full name was the Royal Institute of Prehistorical Studies but this was usually shortened to RIPS – an acronym even its first employees found amusing, apparently, when it was founded in 1908. The building itself was Victorian, and '*still a seat of learning and intellectual endeavour*' (as Raglan Beveridge had said in his latest Annual Report). In the 1950s its research remit had broadened to include historical as well as prehistorical artefacts: there were now some staff who studied objects left behind by relatively modern peoples – *peoples* with an *s* – though its focus was still mainly on ancient pottery and bones. It had fallen on hard times in the 1990s and early 2000s, suffering from a lack of *core government funding*, but more recently it had started to receive sponsorship from various commercial enterprises, in particular, from the London Museums Interpretation Centre. Yes, LMIC had swept in, with its youthful energy and its commercial chutzpah! – and these days, as Raglan had also said in the report, RIPS was *back on the map*.

There was still a fusty quality to the place, though.

I liked that. I liked its fustiness, and the way time seemed to move so gently there, settling in layers. A week or so after I'd first bumped into Helen again, there'd been a small fire in the roof space, and when the staff gathered in the car park, I was surprised to realise how many people actually worked there. I'd never even *seen* some of them before. They appeared to have spent so many years in their rooms analysing finds that, in the daylight, they looked quite preternaturally pale. They reminded me of some tinned hearts of palm Simon had recently put in a salad. Or the axolotl specimen that lurked, alabaster-white and rubbery, in the *Comparative Zoology Gallery*. I'd spotted Helen that day for the first time since she'd told me about her connection with the place, and my heart had sunk a little. She was hanging out with all the time-served old members of staff in one of the parking bays. She'd somehow looked about twice their height and a hundred per cent healthier and *in colour*, instead of black-and-white.

There were five floors in total in the building, six if you included the gallery in the basement. These were called *Primordial, Sedimentary, Sandstone, Igneous, Chalk* and *Shale*. A few of the Trustees still called them that, anyway; everyone else just called them *floors*. Each floor was composed of six large rooms and various smaller side-rooms. I worked on the fifth floor, where I had a view right across the park and of the beautiful silvery ribbon of the Thames. On the floor above mine were the Prints and Archives and the Special Collections Rooms, and at the bottom of the building was the Carbon-dating lab, and housed at one remove, in a large, converted ice house a few hundred yards away, was the Printing and Reprographics department. I'd quite often go upstairs to Prints and Archives and Special Collections, but I didn't go to Printing and Reprographics if I could help it, mainly because John, the man who worked in there, did not seem to appreciate too much interruption. I think it suited him to be alone. I hardly ever went down to the Carbon-dating lab either, mainly because there was a large sign on the door saying *Danger of Death*. And I didn't want to die. Also, I didn't want to go crashing in there at the wrong moment and wreck someone's data analysis. One of the palaeontologists, a rather baleful trilobite specialist named Professor Jeremy Muir, had informed me recently that even *breathing* could affect the date-reading of something. So another thing I did, if I ever ventured in there, was hold my breath.

One of the rooms that intrigued me most at RIPS was a largish office located on the second floor. Everyone referred to this as *Peter's Room*, because it had until quite recently been used by a member of staff named Peter Edwards. Peter Edwards had died though, shortly before I started at the Institute. He'd died while researching 'in the field' – a fact that always struck me as sad, whenever I went in there to look for a book or answer the phone that still rang sometimes on his old desk. There was something melancholy about that phrase 'in the field'. It made me think of Captain Oates, heading selflessly out from the tent into the Antarctic wilderness. *I am just going outside and may be some time.* Poor, noble Peter Edwards, dying for the cause! Dying for the cause of things that were, in fact, already dead. It seemed such a waste.

I suppose death was on my mind a lot that spring, though, and any room once occupied by a much-loved colleague was bound to have a stilled, regretful atmosphere. A collection of artefacts he'd found over the years still sat on the shelves – little clay figurines and amulets and necklaces and knives. They seemed almost to be waiting for his return. Peter Edwards had apparently been a world expert in early European civilisations – although, unlike Helen, he had not specialised in Beakers. He'd been more into Minoan culture: much more interesting as far as I was concerned, because at least Minoa was in the Aegean and therefore sunny, and also, the Minoans had made up half the stories I'd studied at university. There were some framed photos of him in the corridor outside the room, in which he appeared a good-natured man, urbane, nice-looking, late-ish middle-aged and usually wearing an Arran jumper. One day, when I had tentatively asked Jane Beauchamp, RIPS' long-serving receptionist, about his losing his life 'in the field', tears had immediately sprung to her eyes, and she'd whispered, 'It wasn't literally in the field, Sybil. I mean, not during a dig. It was actually when he was travelling back to the airport: he was on his way home to London, and he . . . he had a heart attack, on the bus . . .' – 'Oh!' I'd exclaimed, shocked, embarrassed as we stood together at the reception desk. 'I mean, it was a matter of moments, really,' Jane continued sorrowfully, '. . . and there was absolutely nothing anyone could have done. He'd hardly even have *suffered* really, poor love, or even *known*. I suppose that's one comfort. Oh, but he was a lovely man, Sybil! We all miss him dreadfully. A terrible shock for Raglan, particularly, because they'd been very close since student days.' She sighed.

'They *were* the Institute, in a way. We had a little memorial service for him a few months back – just a week or so before you joined us, Sybil – and Raglan read this little speech he'd written, about Knossos and them being students together, and we were all in bits by the end of it.' Her eyes filled with tears again.

'Well,' I croaked. 'I'm so sorry, Jane . . .' And I stopped talking, because I couldn't think what else to say. Besides, I *was* sorry: it was a pretty sad story. I even told Simon about it that evening, when I went home.

Anyway, I could have been in a much worse state myself, I knew, at the start of that year. Because even though I was missing my grandfather a lot at least I *hadn't* died at Streatham Ice Rink, and at least I had Simon (I thought), and an income and a decent job, and there were several aspects of it I actually enjoyed. For instance, I liked it when I had to show visitors around the Comparative Zoology Gallery, pointing out exhibits of interest (the hominid skeleton, the massive trilobite, the alligator babies, the carved palm leaves in the cornicing). I also liked it when the palaeontologists brought in fossils or bits of ceramic for me to catalogue – crate-loads of them sometimes, like trawler-men bringing in a catch. I'd get two little pots from the Resource Room in the basement – one of clear varnish and one of India ink – and write very neatly onto the finds what they were, where they were found and who'd found them. Then I'd put them in the accessions box. I liked the room I worked in, too, high up on the fifth floor: I had an old-fashioned Anglepoise lamp there and a computer and a phone, and my chair rose or descended at the pull of a lever.

Sometimes, though, I couldn't help wondering why I'd been given the job in the first place. I'd wonder why Raglan had not been more picky at the interview stage, especially when I discovered that part of my job was going to involve working on an in-house publication he'd written, called *A History of Trade;*

from the Neolithic Revolution to the Vikings. He'd asked me to do some checking of the index before it went to print – even though I had virtually no knowledge of either the Neolithic Revolution or the Vikings, and no idea how to index. It was not the most welcome assignment in the world.

Then one afternoon towards the end of January, the day I was due to start working on it and only a few weeks after I'd first bumped into Helen at the British Library, I received a call from her at work, and everything about my understanding of indexing – and everything else, for that matter – had gone into a kind of freefall anyway.

'Hi, Sybil!' Helen began lightly, her voice instantly jangling my senses. 'How are you?'

'I'm OK, thanks,' I replied, mystified. I wondered why she couldn't just have called round the next time she was in the building. 'How about you, Helen? How are . . . things?'

'Well . . .' Helen's voice was oddly high (normally she had a low, quite sultry voice). 'Well, I'm fine, thanks. But actually, I'm just going to cut straight to the chase here, Sybil.'

Now I sensed something really bad unfolding; the certain coolness that had always existed between us ever since university days was extending fast, like frost formations running across a windscreen.

'So what's up?' I said.

There was a short silence at the other end of the line. Then Helen said, 'So, it's about Simon . . .'

'Oh, yes?'

'So, it's about Simon . . .' she repeated.

'Oh, yes?'

And now Helen was speaking again, but my brain was not quite processing; she was saying something about destiny and fate, and about a *fondue party*, for some reason, and also about *betrayal*: how she had not wanted to *betray* me, given her status as my ex-tutor; given that, in some ways, she still had a *duty of* care . . . and yet . . . well, sometimes these things were simply meant to be. 'A *fondue party*?' I repeated, dumbly, because my brain hadn't caught up yet, but then I recalled Simon saying he'd been invited to some work-related fondue party a few weeks earlier, in some arty kind of warehouse in Shadwell. It will probably, he'd said, be just a lot of pretentious wankers waving skewers around. 'What—' I began, but Helen ignored my interjection. 'Oh, and it's been so tough,' she was ploughing on, 'but sometimes you just have to do what's right, no matter how painful the consequences; you have to act honestly, decisively, because that's actually kinder in the long run. And poor Simon is in such torment, he's really quite torn because he cares so much about you, Sybil, he cares so very much – it's just,' she said, 'he hasn't known quite how to tell you himself. He hasn't wanted to hurt you so he hasn't found quite the right . . .' But her voice was beginning to sound peculiar now, as if she was speaking through folded gauze, or an old sock, like a spy in a phone box. '. . . it was simply one of those things,' she was saying, as I sat there in my swivel chair, my heart already broken, pictures of the two of them trampling their way into my head.

There they were, smiling meaningfully at each other on a coffee-shop sofa! There they were, entwined in a bed, sunshine pouring profoundly through a window! Then I heard Helen's voice in my ear again. 'It's ironic, really, because I honestly didn't have feelings for him to start with, Sybil. It really only began,' she was saying, 'because I felt he'd be perfect for the marketing campaign I've been planning for the new Beakerware range.'

'A *marketing campaign*?' I said. 'For your *Beakerware*?'

'Yes, I just, I just thought at the time that he could, well . . . be perfect. He could be "the modern face of Beakerware". I thought he could symbolise the revival of interest in ancient grains, and artisanal cooking, and . . .'

28

She fizzled out.

'And to be honest,' she added quietly after a moment, 'it did seem to me – especially as you two hadn't been getting on recently – that you'd—'

'That we'd *what*?' I said. I couldn't stop thinking of Simon now as 'the modern face of Beakerware'. What on earth was Helen planning? What on earth had she already *done*? 'Anyway, who told you we weren't getting on?' I said. 'We were getting on perfectly fine, Helen. Until you decided to invite him to your fucking fondue party!'

Helen hesitated for a second. Then she said, 'I know this must be a very tough thing to hear, Sybil. But perhaps it's better to have heard it from me, than for him not to have even *told* you.'

I did not reply. I couldn't stop picturing Simon talking to Helen in the arty warehouse in Shadwell, the two of them waving two-pronged skewers over a vat of bubbling cheese. I imagined how she might have worn him down as the evening progressed: how, serpent-like, she might have flattered his ego, or implied that I was holding him back in some way from a glittering culinary career. '*And you say Sybil doesn't even appreciate your buckwheat galettes when she comes home in the evening . . . ?*' It was almost laughable. But I found that I was not laughing. My heart felt like a stone that has been dropped from a very great height. I shifted my gaze from the inside of the room and out through the window, at the distant skyscrapers of Canary Wharf and the great upturned cow of the old Millennium Dome, and was aware of a great pain beginning to bloom inside my chest. It bloomed and spread, like the bloodstain beneath the ice at Streatham Ice Rink. It was as if Simon was in the process of splitting into two people in my mind: he was simultaneously a person I loved and a person who'd started to cause me huge pain. A person who shared a bed with me and who was also capable of lying, and heading off on furtive assignments to the other side of town. Who appeared to have fallen in love – fallen in *something*, anyway – with *Helen Hansen*. I couldn't reconcile the two Simons at all. I couldn't even go home and ask for his advice; I couldn't say, 'Simon, what do you think I should do about this boyfriend of mine who's gone off with this awful woman called Helen Hansen . . . ?' And I wondered if all the blood that had previously occupied the chambers of my heart might rise up and choke me.

'Sybil?' Helen said.

There was another sound now, in the background of Helen's life in Tooting: a phone was ringing, and someone was coughing in the London Museums Interpretation Centre, where she spent her time working out how to *spark the imagination and business acumen of museum professionals*. I thought of a tin of cough sweets she'd had on her desk when I'd gone to see her there recently, trotting obediently round to deliver some more bits of old pottery for some production she was working on. It was a pretty, enamelled tin – black with French writing and a picture of cherries on the lid – *les cerises de Provence*. I'd picked it up and remarked that Simon had exactly the same one. I'd bought it for him myself when we'd been in Paris the previous year. I'd spotted it in a little market in the 5th arrondissement. And now I thought: *That's because it was: it* was *Simon's tin*.

'Well . . .' Helen breathed down the line. 'I'm glad I told you.'

'Yes. That's a weight off your mind.'

'And I just hope that one day, you and I might . . .' She paused.

'Might what?'

'Be friends again.'

I considered this, my heart racing.

'Well, I'm not sure about that, Helen,' I said, 'because I don't think we ever *were* friends, were we?'

And it was at this point that I hung up, on my old tutor, and new enemy. Then I slipped down from my ridiculous swivel chair and walked over to the kitchenette on the other side of the corridor. I didn't know what to do; which part of the room to stand in. I didn't know how to locate my body in time and space. I went to the sink and put my hand up to the shiny pink line that existed now just beneath my hairline after the accident in Streatham, and I looked down at a small Easter cactus in a yogurt pot which Simon had once given me, and a Nice Day calendar that someone had Blu-Tacked to the wall. The Easter cactus had one bright pink flower on it, and the calendar said that it was 31st January. The cactus and the calendar did not agree with each other. There was a plastic air freshener that looked like the gridded helmet of a Star Trooper, and a packet of lilac Post-It notes that had *The Past is the Future* printed on the front. It came from the London Museums Interpretation Centre: one of Helen's initiatives, along with her TED talk, and her terrible plans to foist clunky, artisan beakers on the world. Which had always looked like a massive sell-out anyway, as far as I was concerned: she was supposed to be a serious academic, for God's sake!

But then, I clearly didn't know Helen.

Just as I didn't know Simon.

And I tried to understand my own ignorance, to think of signs I might have overlooked when we'd skated towards her that day and I'd had that peculiar vision of my grandfather waiting for me on the other side. But I was finding it hard to think at all now; even my eyes felt useless, like something in an old fairy tale I'd read once, about a dog with eyes the size of teacups. *And what about Cornwall?* I thought. Because Simon and I had been planning to go to Cornwall at the end of May: we'd been going to spend a week in Tintagel, visiting Merlin's Cave and swimming in the sea and drinking Rioja, and eating squid he'd proposed catching off the side of a boat.

I went back into the cataloguing room, sat at my desk and looked through the great expanse of *A History of Trade* which I was meant to start checking that day. Then I looked at all the Fineliner pens and bottles of ink and empty sandwich wrappers

31

(it was against Institute rules to eat and drink at the cataloguing table, but I only ever obeyed this if I was dealing with mercury or radioactive rocks). 'Hi, my name's Dr Hansen,' I remembered Helen saying at the very first tutorial of hers I'd attended, seven years earlier, when I was not quite twenty and Helen was twenty-nine. She'd been standing glamorously in front of a floor-to-ceiling window, wearing flamingo-pink lipstick and a massive gold necklace: it looked like one of those necklaces that some tribespeople use, to extend the length of their necks. 'Hi, my name's Dr Hansen,' she'd said, 'but please just call me Helen!' and all the male students in the room had suddenly sat up straighter and looked a lot more interested in the idea of studying Archaeology, and all the female students had remained in exactly the same slumped positions in their chairs. At the memory of which, all the words in Raglan's book started spinning around, spiralling around in front of me, like snowflakes flying out of a great empty sky, and I had to go home.

SW left early for personal reasons, as Raglan suggested, in his dashingly awkward way, in the minutes of a staff meeting I missed that day.

AOB: Hope Pollard to attend carbon-dating symposium;
             Mary Anning event confirmed;
             Helen Hansen appointed as new Chair of Trustees.

Jane Beauchamp had shown me this when I went back to work the following Monday – distributing minutes being one of the perks of Jane's job.

'Are you OK now, Sybil?' she enquired, tentatively. 'After the little . . . turn you had?'

'Well, not entirely . . .' I replied, and I told her then about Simon and Helen, and why I'd had the little turn. Jane went completely silent for a moment: she looked at me with an expression of great sympathy and concern. Then, in a very quiet voice, she said, 'And you did know, Sybil, that the reason Raglan's index has to be re-done is because of the new bit Helen's written for the book?'

I stood absolutely still, aware of a peculiar kind of calcifying around the region of my heart. A petrification, in its truest sense.

'A new bit?' I said.

'Yes. She's written a couple of pages about the Winchelsea Hoard.'

'Has she?' I said. 'Well, no,' I added after a moment. 'I didn't know that.'

'Yes. It was a sort of "hold-the-press" situation, during a Trustees meeting last month. A sort of recent excavations *update*. She felt it was important to get something in at the end about her new . . . Beaker theories. She said it was the perfect tie-in with the TED talk she's doing, and all the Beakerware promotion, and it would get her work more . . .' she hesitated, '*known-about*, in academic circles. And Raglan obviously didn't feel he could say no,' she concluded, regretfully, her voice becoming even lower and quieter. 'Given the new sponsorship arrangements with LMIC.'

When I went home that evening, to the flat I was still having to share with Simon, we had another row, only this one was much worse than the one we'd had about saucepans, during the course of which he told me that I'd never properly appreciated how he was trying to make a name for himself, and how Helen just *did* – that was one of the things that was so great about her – she really *did* appreciate him and the plans he had for *his* career.

'She even thinks I'd be perfect as *The Face of Beakerware*,' he added. 'For her advertising campaign!'

'Hah! The Face of Beakerware!' I exclaimed. 'What are you, a Toby Jug?' And I started to laugh. Then I stopped laughing and informed him that Helen was just using him.

'She's just using you!' I shouted. 'To big up her dodgy Beaker theories! Just as she's using the Institute!'

'Well, at least *someone* appreciates me!' he retorted. 'Anyway, what makes you think her theories are dodgy? Have you got any proof?'

I went quiet for a moment. Because I didn't have any proof. I just felt it in my bones.

And a week later I moved, still numb, husk-like, into a new flat about four miles down the road in Stockwell, which I was going to share with an old university friend named Esther Maclehose, who worked for an upmarket bathroom design company and was the most exhaustingly robust and pragmatic person I'd ever known. I sold a pair of gold earrings Simon had once given me when he'd thought I was probably about as beautiful as he was handsome, and I bought a brand-new smartphone with the proceeds. But somehow I did not feel very smart.

And walking home across the park one evening about a month later I recalled something else Jane Beauchamp had told me, while we were sitting having our morning coffee and gazing out of the window. She'd said that the time I would feel worst would not be when I might have expected to – not, say, mid-February. No, it would be more like two whole months after the initial shock of betrayal. She'd read a lot of self-help books over the years, she said, so she knew about these things, these pivotal moments on the path to recovery. According to the Kübler-Ross model, she'd explained, there were five stages of grief. Which was, really, what I was going through: a break-up was a kind of bereavement, after all, and this one had bells on. In any case, I was grieving for something important that had not lasted, that had not stayed the course. The five stages of grief being denial and anger and bargaining, followed by depression and acceptance.

That old chestnut.

'Yes, I already know about the stages of grief,' I said, a memory suddenly coming into my mind of a jumper Simon had used to wear: this old blue thing which I would always picture him in and would presumably never see again. 'But where does bargaining come into it, Jane? Who do I bargain with? Do I bargain with *her*? With *Helen Hansen*?'

'You don't bargain with a person, Sybil. You bargain with the situation you're in.'

'But how am I supposed to bargain with a *situation*? How's that supposed to work?'

'You see,' Jane said, regretfully, 'I think you're still at the denial stage. Possibly moving on to anger.'

She paused for a moment, and looked at me with her kind, sad eyes. 'Have you thought at all about some sort of *creative outlet*?' she added.

'A creative outlet?'

'Like an evening class, maybe? Something like life-drawing? Or flower arranging? Or poetry? Because it can be very therapeutic, poetry . . .'

'Well, no, I hadn't thought about that,' I said, glaring down at a book that was lying open on my desk. It was called *Museums for Schools Groups* and it was written by a woman called Constance Johnson in the 1970s, an era that suddenly seemed infinitely kinder and simpler. 'No, I hadn't thought about that,' I said, 'but I will, now. Thanks, Jane.'

I imagined that I would store that particular idea in the small flip-top filing cabinet in the corner of the room (as Simon himself might have said). Because only about half of Jane Beauchamp's suggestions were ever good ones.

But the days came and went, and nothing was getting any better – nothing was coming to any good – and about a week after Jane had suggested a creative outlet I saw a sign pinned to a noticeboard behind the lending desk at North Brixton Library.

POETRY FOR THE TERRIFIED! (it said)

Ever wondered if you could pen a haiku or an ode?

**Want to know the difference between
a simile and a metaphor?**

**Come along to our poetry-writing
classes, and find out!**

(Fridays 6–8pm; full price £85, concessions £55)

So I signed up. Even though poetry had never terrified me so much as made me think, 'So?' and I did not really have £85 to spare, and my heart still felt like a huge, untethered balloon, and I was still working in a crumbling old institute in the middle of Greenwich Park and having to exchange social niceties with a woman I hated more than anyone else in the world – who was the reason I was contemplating poetry at all. On my way home that evening I thought: *I have never had an enemy in my life before, and now I do.*

It felt almost exhilarating, like a strange new project.

THE WORKS

1

Spring haiku #1

Here's a haiku
Thirteen syllables long –
Now what?

Spring haiku #2

Pterodactyl (4)
Is never easy to spell (7)
Neither's hyrachyus –
Jesus Christ

I had an optician's appointment on April Fool's Day – the date of my twelve-week *post-traumatic head injury check-up*. My head was not in a great state that spring, especially now I was working on the index of Raglan's book. But at least I was remembering my post-trauma check-ups. The optician was called *In Sight*. I wondered how long it had taken someone to come up with that. I supposed *Four Eyes* or *Blind as a Bat* would have been ruled out early. In the window display there was a picture of a beautiful woman wearing ugly, thick-framed glasses. As if buying a pair would instantly bestow immaculate cheekbones, great teeth, perfect skin. She looked quite a lot like Helen, I thought. But a lot of things I looked at that spring looked like Helen.

I didn't have to wait long before the optician called me in to his consulting room. I sat down on the shinily upholstered chair and he arranged a pair of glasses over my eyes, even thicker and uglier than the ones in the advert. Then he switched off the lights.

'Yes, so there's nothing here that alarms me unduly about the back of your retinas . . .' he observed after a moment, into the darkness.

'Great.'

'Certainly no obvious damage after your little . . . *mishap* in December. However,' he added, 'it's interesting that you're still experiencing visual auras . . .'

'Visual auras?' I asked, intrigued.

'I mean the little floating lines it mentions in your hospital discharge notes. The black dots and the white stars.'

I stared ahead at the illuminated screen ahead of me, at the little moving disc of emerald green.

'Is that something to be concerned about?'

'Not especially. Visual auras are not as exciting as they sound. Nothing to do with ghosts or premonitions, I'm afraid. Just something to keep an eye on.'

'I see,' I said. I felt vaguely disappointed, because it seemed it might have been quite interesting to see ghosts. Or even just to see what was ahead of me, in the here and now.

'Do you do a lot of close work?' the optician added, suddenly scooting up close on his castered chair and peering into my pupils with a little torch. 'Do you find yourself looking at things at very close range?'

I thought of a notebook I'd recently started scrawling my bad poetry in on Friday evenings in North Brixton Library. Then I thought of some *fun worksheets* Professor Muir had dropped into my in-tray at work the previous day, and of Raglan's *History of Trade*.

'Well,' I said, 'I suppose I have been doing quite a lot of close reading recently . . .'

'Any headaches?'

'Sometimes.'

'Front or back?'

'Back, mainly. And top. Also side.'

'Because that would do it, you see. Too much close reading, and peering at the small print. Have a break sometimes. Have a KitKat! Having said that,' he added, 'your eyes are generally in pretty good shape. Certainly nothing that alarms me, following on from the accident. Look here: look at this!' He tipped the monitor towards me, to reveal an image of the back of my eyeballs: mysterious orbs, pale orange with red lightning flashes running through them.

'See? Perfect eyes.'

'Great,' I replied, embarrassed. It had begun to feel like a peculiar kind of date now, sitting so near in the darkness while a man described the perfection of my eyes. In any case, I sometimes felt like kissing the first man, that spring, who showed me any interest. But then I wrecked the potential of the moment by saying, 'It's funny, isn't it, how people's eyeballs look like planets? How the inside of people's heads looks like outer space?'

In the half-light I saw a look of hesitation cross his face. *Some people's heads look more like outer space than others*, he looked as if he was thinking. Then he scooted away for a moment on his little wheeled chair before returning to balance a pair of even smaller, uglier glasses across the bridge of my nose. It took a while for my eyes to adjust after that. Particularly as the drops he had put in made my pupils dilate unnaturally large and just made me think of Helen's eyes, so clear and blue, and wide enough to drown any man foolish enough to look into them.

I blundered on to work and arrived shortly before eleven. 'Punctual as ever, sweetheart!' observed Danny the gallery attendant, as I walked in across the marble floor of Reception. 'I know! Just call me—' my brain stalled, '—late.' I hurried on.

The funny thing was, I thought, as I ascended in the lift, when I'd started my job the previous autumn I'd felt like a perfectly competent member of the RIPS team. I could see straight and had a functioning relationship with my new colleagues, and with words on the page. Now, my eyesight was all over the place and my intellect had gone AWOL; my mind, like Odysseus's ship, had got becalmed in the Doldrums. Raglan had asked me about the index as soon as I'd returned from my impromptu afternoon's leave in January.

'It really just needs a quick skim, Sybil,' he'd said. 'Just a question of pulling out the keywords from Helen's chapter and adding them to the list in the index.'

'Great – no problem!' I'd lied.

'Oh, and there'll be a new entry for the Winchelsea Hoard, of course,' he had added. 'But that can just drop in right at the end. I mean, it will hardly disturb the pagination at all . . .'

'Absolutely! What could possibly go wrong!' I'd quipped. But I don't think he understood the sarcasm – especially as I'd decided not to breathe a word to him about Helen's destruction of all my happiness – it would just have been too painful, and what good would it have done? I suppose what I should have said was, *Can't someone else do this, Raglan? Surely one of the archaeologists would be better qualified?* But I knew they were all busy with their own work, and besides, I wasn't brave enough to upset John's print schedule in the ice house. So I'd just peered at the index printout in front of me.

Ware (cookery)
Warp
Weft
Wind

Winding
Winnowing

'Yes,' I said. 'Obviously Winchelsea will need to go between Wind and Winding . . .'

Raglan considered this.

'Between Weft and Wind, surely . . .'

'Ah, yes. Of course!'

'OK. Great . . .'

And after he had left the room, a new look of mild anxiety on his face, I turned back to the screen to read Helen's insert (*Grains of Truth: The Winchelsea Hoard*), and just went to pieces. I'd been working quite effectively until that point, but my mind had suddenly seized up, and I'd had to put the whole thing aside for the rest of the day. And then for the rest of the week. Then for quite a large part of the following month. I just felt a peculiar resistance every time I looked at it, despite the deadline being 9th April – and now it was April Fool's Day, it was 1st April already! and I'd still only picked out a few keywords.

The lift doors opened and I got out.

I went into my room, sat down at my computer and regarded the typesetting, still there at the page I'd left it at the previous evening. Beside it was a sheet of paper containing my latest list of words:

Funnel
Conical
Husk
Glazed

The previous Friday, in an email to Raglan, I'd typed *Re: Helen's description of Comical Beakers* – and had realised my mistake about half a second after pressing Send. I'd put my hands up to my mouth in horror, but there was nothing to be done. It could not be unsent. 'Back to my favourite pastime!' I observed now to Hope Pollard, the Institute's resident

43

dendrochronologist, who'd emerged from a meeting and stomped along the corridor to make a coffee in the kitchenette.

'What did you say?' Hope yelled, crashing the kettle against the sink.

'The new Winchelsea section! My reading material of choice!'

Framed in the doorway, her frizzy hair illuminated by sunlight, Hope paused.

'What?'

I gazed down at the page I had reached. *'It is likely,'* Helen had written, *'that a type of porridge would have been eaten at this time, possibly flavoured with herbs . . .'* And it ought to have been quite interesting that the Beaker People ate porridge – it cast a little gleam of light into their otherwise dull and unknowable lives – but I wasn't in the mood to care.

'What did you say?' Hope yelled again.

I wondered if Helen was in the meeting. Probably. She nearly always *was*: her presence around the place was almost a daily ordeal to be endured, like the eagles coming to peck out Prometheus's liver.

'I'm talking about Raglan's book,' I said.

'Raglan and *Helen*'s book, you mean!'

I closed my eyes for a moment. They still didn't feel quite right.

'Is it Raglan and Helen's book now, then?'

'Yes, she's going to be named as co-author! Didn't you know? Raglan felt it was only fair, considering the new Beaker People discoveries she's made. And also bearing in mind the sponsorship arrangement with LMIC – without which we'd all be up the Swanee without a paddle. I'd have assumed you'd know that,' Hope added, coming to lean in the doorway. 'Seeing as you're working on the index. And Helen's doing the final read-through.'

'Is she?' I said. This was also news to me. I supposed it meant that I would have to communicate with her, in words of more than one syllable, when it was time to hand it over.

Hope hovered, as if she might have vaguely recalled something – some half-heard rumour, even though I knew Jane had never breathed a word about *the Helen situation*.

'Oh well,' she said. 'It's only a few extra pages, isn't it? It *surely* can't take that much longer!'

She plodded out with her coffee and headed back to the lifts. She took the larger, more functional goods lift. It was like something in a hospital. I pictured her in there, standing silently beside a megalodon thigh-bone which had been leaning against the wall for weeks. It weighed half a tonne – literally – and had put a strain on the lift cables.

ODE TO MY EX I
why (1)
why (1)
why (1)
why (1)
did you do that? (4)

ODE TO MY EX II
I miss those suppers
You used to make.
Even the pink lamb.
I didn't think I would.
But there you are.

ODE TO MY EX III
is she taking your picture
is she calling you handsome
is she saying you're the face
to launch a thousand Beakers

Jane was not in yet. I liked Jane, but her absence could sometimes be a relief. For instance, if I hadn't spoken to Jane a couple of weeks earlier, I would not have saddled myself with expensive poetry-writing classes, for which I was now even supposed to do *homework* in my spare time.

april is the cruellest month, I wrote in magnets on the fridge door while I waited for the kettle to boil. **never fly through windows** – I added, sliding the words around the big expanse of white. **hush cats birds are cool**

'Never fly through windows!' Raglan exclaimed, wandering in as I was putting up the final letters. 'Well, that's something I'd agree with, Sybil!'

'Ah,' I said, 'hello, Raglan.' And I blushed. I suspected Raglan knew something, too, about my crushed spirits that spring, but I certainly wasn't going to tell him why, any more than I would have told Hope.

'I'm practising my poetry,' I said, for want of anything else to say. 'I've signed up for poetry-writing classes.'

'Poetry-writing?'

'Yes. Jane suggested it. She thought it might be . . . So anyway, I saw this sign, the other week, in North Brixton Library. So I signed up. Although I haven't actually . . .' I glanced down at some of the words still lying in the tin, in my hands. 'You know, *written any poems.*'

winter brother, said the words. **life passes. moon bird.** They were more poetic than anything I'd come up with, even just jumbled together like that in the tin.

'So we're meant to be looking for found objects,' I added, remembering this, suddenly, because we *were*: we were supposed to be looking for *something that means something*, as our tutor had said, and turning it into a poem.

'Found objects?' Raglan said. 'Not unlike my line of work, then!'

We were both silent for a moment. I hoped he wasn't going to ask about my progress with the index – a subject that had grown more troubling in recent days, given the deadline and my reluctance to go anywhere near it. *Do you really have to be making quite such a meal out of it, Sybil?* a less charitable boss might have said, but he refrained. He sighed, and gazed down at the tin of words too. He'd brought it in himself, a few weeks earlier. He'd been given it at some networking function Helen had probably had something to do with, and perhaps he'd imagined it might be useful or entertaining in some way.

'Anyway,' I said, 'I've been careful not to disturb *your* sentences, Raglan.'

We regarded what he'd put up on the fridge a few days earlier.

to be or not to be
tender is the night
the sun also rises

Which had seemed a bit of a cop-out to me. 'I mean,' as I'd said at the time to Jane, 'he's not going to win any originality prizes with *those*.'

'Hush cats, birds are cool,' Raglan said.

He smiled, his expression a little wan. I found myself thinking of a sentence the Institute's cleaner had put up there, a few days earlier: **where is the flash**, it had said, somewhat bitterly.

'The one problem with this tin of words,' I said now, 'is, there aren't any punctuation marks.'

'Does poetry need punctuation, though? Does it even need capital letters?'

'Hmmm . . .' A vision was floating into my head of the class I'd signed up to, of the members of my new little Friday group all hunkered down over their notebooks, like people sheltering under a tree, waiting for a storm to pass. I regretted the loss of £85, now, on top of everything else.

'e.e. cummings didn't think so,' Raglan said.

'Sorry?'

'He was not a fan of capital letters.'

'Oh.'

'Anyway. Enjoyable, though, the classes?'

'They're great.'

'Excellent.'

'Yes.'

'Have you got your lanyard with you today?' he added, obscurely.

'It's in my pocket.'

'Better wear it, then. As you're now officially *in the building*. And we'll all have to start getting used to swipe access before long.'

'Will we?' *Is that another LMIC initiative*? I'd been about to ask. But he'd already turned and wandered off down the corridor.

I could never quite work Raglan out. He was a big-voiced, big-opinioned man, but also he could be very shy. He was old school but he also seemed to have a peculiar respect for all Helen's dire money-generating plans, and had now even appointed her as the Institute's new Chair of Trustees. So I couldn't start condemning her in front of him, especially as she was going to be foisting her hideous new Beakerware on the Institute's shop as soon as it had rolled off the production line – complete, I couldn't help imagining, with accompanying marketing material depicting Simon as *handsome artisanal chef and Beakerware enthusiast*. I wondered if she might even invite him to the launch party. It was not beyond the bounds of her own tactlessness.

'The thing is,' I said to Jane when she came up to find me a little later that morning, 'I really don't know what Raglan sees in Helen. Apart from the obvious.'

Jane sighed.

'I know Helen's hardly your favourite person, Sybil,' she said, 'but *Raglan* doesn't know what happened, does he? As you've decided not to tell him. And I'm afraid that's what some men *see* in some women, isn't it? The obvious. I'm afraid some men are drawn to some women, like moths to the flame.' She herself had been through quite a difficult divorce a few years earlier, which was what made her so well qualified to speak about men's duplicity, and their capacity to be drawn to the obvious in some women.

'But what about women's duplicity?' I said.

'Well, of course, that exists, too.'

I looked out of the window and noticed a couple walking hand in hand along one of the pathways in the park. They looked like me and Simon, from about two years before. It felt as if I was looking at the ghosts of us. The boy was Simon's height and build and he was wearing a coat that looked just like the one Simon had worn when we first met. The girl was wearing the same kind of coat *I'd* used to wear: my old black velvet one that I'd worn at my grandfather's funeral and had proceeded to give away to Oxfam (a decision I'd almost instantly regretted). She also had black gloves like mine, and big black bovver boots, and her hair was dark like mine. And maybe, if I could have heard her speak, she would have sounded like me, and maybe if the boy had spoken, his voice would have been—

'Ah, well . . .' Jane sighed, sipping her coffee.

—and I felt like getting up from my desk, hurtling down in the lift, rushing across the grass and hanging onto the two of us, as we used to be, and telling us not to change, not to alter, not to let Helen destroy us with her smile and her flattery and her dissembling sweetness—

'The thing is, I just feel very in the dark these days, Jane,' I mumbled, suddenly close to tears. 'I feel I've been asking all these questions, for weeks now, and nobody's been giving me any answers.'

'But who would give you answers, sweetheart? Sometimes I'm afraid there *are* no answers. There's no explanation. You just have to work things out for yourself.' She paused. 'So how are the poetry classes going, that you signed up for? Have they been . . . a help?'

'Haikus are not as easy as you might think.'

'You should stick with it, though. Poetry can be a consolation.'

'Yep.'

Jane reminded me a bit of an old English teacher I'd once had, a sweet-faced woman named Mrs Beeslack, who'd operated from a small, glass-doored classroom that seemed to double up as the school's stationery cupboard; sometimes you could hardly *see* Mrs Beeslack for box files. She'd always been keen, too, on the consolation that existed in verse. She'd talked a lot about line-endings and assonance and enjambments, and had said that the word enjambment 'comes from the French "jamb", meaning "leg"' – an anecdote that had eventually featured in a game my best friend Bethany Cowley and I made up, that we called *Leg Bingo*.

'I mean, anything's worth a try, isn't it?' Jane added, lowering her voice, in case Helen herself came catapulting into the room. 'It's at least a way to get your thoughts down, isn't it? If nothing else. The pen is mightier than the sword.'

'I wasn't planning to actually mow her down with a sword.'

'No, of course not,' she said, looking worried, as if maybe I *was* considering some kind of Samurai solution to the whole thing. 'I'm talking metaphorically, about *metaphorical* swords.'

My head had begun to hurt.

'Poetry as revenge, you mean?'

She didn't reply.

'I know it helped *me* once, anyway,' she said after a moment. 'Poetry. When I was going through a difficult time.' She peered at me. 'So are you still looking for some sort of . . . *object*? For these classes?'

'I'm still looking. But I'm not finding.'

'I'm sure something will leap out at you when you least expect it!'

'Yes. Like an assassin.'

'Sorry?'

'That's an example of a simile.'

'I see . . .'

'Really, though, Jane, most of my poems could just be crumpled up and put straight in the bin.'

'Well, if *I* ever find one of your poems crumpled up in the bin, Sybil, I'm going to take it straight back out and un-crumple it!'

'Ah!' I said, my sad heart swelling.

'Also,' Jane added, 'a simile is like a smile with an extra "i", isn't it? That's what *I* was taught.'

And shortly after that, we finished our coffee and went back to work. I returned to Helen's writing – a paragraph about Early Peoples grinding grain between stone querns, and another one about conical Beakers and another about chaff which, all by itself, created the need for six new keywords to be added to the index. There was nothing I could do about that, though, unless I wanted, ultimately, to lose my job – a luxury I could not afford.

I worked for the rest of that morning and into the afternoon, hunting for keywords. The columns of text looked like great, unyielding pillars. They looked like tower blocks. They looked like standing stones.

Beakerware (Bell)

Beakerware (Corded)

Beakerware (Funnel)

Beakerware™ (twenty-first-century facsimile)

I worked all through the Emergency Fire Drill and the meeting that was going on upstairs. I worked until tears began to line the edges of my eyes. I worked until mid-afternoon, then hauled up my bag from beneath my desk and took out the lunch I'd put in there earlier: a Tesco's salad box and a small orange that had been scudding around for the past fortnight in a fruit bowl in my flat. The salad box had partly exploded on my way in, that morning – an event which I'd decided to ignore until now. Taking out a Handy-Andy from a pack, I wiped the shredded carrot and beetroot and pinkish mayonnaise off my umbrella and purse and hairbrush. Then I opened up the box, snapped together the plastic fork, and began to eat. Technically, of course, I wasn't supposed to eat in the cataloguing room, but I didn't care. The side of my head throbbed and the sleeves of my shirt felt oddly short somehow, as if it didn't belong to me, the fabric rising up awkwardly as I bent my arms. *The ancient, wind-assisted method of separating wheat from chaff is called winnowing*, I read, as I ate, *a derivation of the Old English wind-wian, meaning wind. The resultant grains are called 'naked' grains.*

It was all very interesting, as the dying Lady Mary Wortley Montague said. Also, Helen *was* in the meeting upstairs, I realised, as I packed up my lunch things and returned to my work. It was definitely *her* voice I could hear through the ceiling. She was probably reminding everyone about her upcoming TED talk. Or maybe she was talking about future-proofing and display panels and the delivery of the new Beakerware range to the shop. *Helen Hansen stole my boyfriend*! I wanted to announce to them all at the top of my voice, rushing upstairs to crash unbidden into the room. *She stole my boyfriend just when I was at my lowest ebb, and turned him into The Face of Beakerware!* But I couldn't do that – half of them wouldn't have believed me anyway – and if there was going to be any kind of revenge, I knew it was going to have to be of a lateral kind, cold and lateral as the Milky Way. In short, I had no idea how I was going to exact it. The meeting went on for ages. I could hear Professor Muir droning on till gone four, and Raglan chipping in about funding streams, and one of the palaeontologists trying to get a word in edgeways about some dig they wanted to set up in

Pembrokeshire. Then, after another five minutes or so there was a scraping of chairs and clatter of feet, then the lift doors squealed open and all the Trustees traipsed out, looking drained (apart from Raglan, who was looking oddly energised, as if he'd been standing on a cliff-top on a windy day, and Helen, who was looking as if she'd just launched all the ships).

'Sybil! How goes it?' she enquired, sashaying past my desk.

I pretended I hadn't heard. I had still not come up with an effective way to communicate with her. Every time I looked at her I would remember something my mother had said when I'd last seen her, about *confronting her maturely*, and my heart would twist into a knot.

'So, what are you up to this afternoon?' Helen continued.

'What does it look like I'm up to?'

She peered down at my list of words.

'How's it going?' she persisted.

'Brilliantly, thanks.' I said. 'Really fascinating stuff, Helen. By the way, how's Simon?' I added, my voice a sudden kind of shriek. 'Have you two had the photo shoot yet? For your *Beakerware*?'

Helen looked at me.

'I don't think you really want me to answer that,' she said.

I did not reply.

'You could ask him yourself though, if you like. I mean, you've got his number, haven't you?'

I remained mute.

'OK,' Helen concluded after a moment. 'So. Onwards and upwards!'

I looked up. 'Actually, it's "upwards and onwards",' I said.

Helen regarded me.

'I think you'll find it's *onwards and upwards*. As far as I'm aware. You have to go *on* before you go *up*.'

'Really? Do you? Is that what *you* do, Helen? Do you go on before you go up!' My head had really begun to throb; I hardly

53

knew what I was saying. Helen was staring at me, her eyes rather pebble-ish.

'Do you sometimes find yourself thinking out loud, Sybil?' she said. 'Because I remember you doing that in our tutorial groups. Going off on those flights of fancy. It was really rather sweet.'

'Well, I suppose you'd know *all about* flights of fancy,' I muttered. I had become a mutterer. I glared down at the *fun worksheet* that Professor Muir had left in my in-tray days earlier: he often left me things he'd been assigned to do himself.

Dinosaur Alphabet!

the worksheet said at the top.

> Did you know there's a dinosaur for every
> letter of the alphabet! We've given you
> some letters for the first one as a clue:

> A---l--------a--------s----

> B
> C
> D
> E
> F –

'By the way, Helen,' I added, the thought suddenly occurring to me, 'weren't you planning to mention in your piece that the word *Beaker* comes from the Greek *bikos*? You know, as *I* did in my dissertation? I just wondered if you might like me to add that in?'

Helen cleared her throat. 'I won't dignify that with an answer, Sybil,' she said, moving out into the corridor. 'Only to say that the book's beyond the point of any further additions now anyway, isn't it? Or deletions. Without John having some kind of meltdown in the ice house!'

And she proceeded on. Onwards.

The building began to clear quite fast after the Trustees meeting had finished. It always did on Fridays. I waited in my room while the Institute regained its composure. Then I typed START FROM HERE at the page I had reached on the screen, and switched off my computer. It was not quite five yet, but I couldn't see straight any more, all the letters and brackets and page numbers having started to slide around again, like a lot of dying black ants. They did that, when I was tired. I had my poetry class to go to that evening, in any case: I was already getting up from my chair and picturing myself halfway there, hurrying dutifully across town in the direction of North Brixton Library, when Raglan suddenly put his head round the door— 'Ah, just before you set off, Sybil . . .' — and I practically leapt out of my skin.

'Jesus, Raglan!' I said. 'You made me jump!'

He looked momentarily dismayed. 'Sorry,' he said, coming in. He was holding a large Tupperware box. 'I've just brought you some cake,' he added, putting it down on my desk. 'Helen made it. She brought it in, for the Trustees, and she thought you might like a slice. Seeing as you weren't in the meeting.'

'Oh,' I said, caught off guard. 'Well, that's very nice,' I added, trying to picture Helen, baking. *And what about Sybil?* I imagined her announcing to the group. *Poor girl, sitting all alone out there like Johnny No-Mates!*

'So, are you having a slice?'

'Sorry?'

'Of cake?'

'Oh . . .'

I looked down at the cake. I wondered if it might be poisoned.

'The thing is,' I said, 'we're not supposed to eat in the cataloguing room, are we? And I've only just had lunch.'

Raglan looked at me. It was five-o-one. The Institute was already virtually empty.

'A small piece won't hurt, surely? It'll keep your strength up, before you head off into the fray.'

What fray? I thought. I'm only going to a poetry class. And poetry was not a fray, not in the usual sense of the word.

'OK, then,' I said, and I put my hand in and scooped up a small triangle of the cake. Helen had scattered around some artful pomegranate seeds – pretty scarlet jewels – which bothered me, given Persephone's troubles with them in the Underworld.

'She's a rather fabulous baker,' Raglan observed.

'Is she.'

I plonked the cake slice down onto a small Melamine coaster Simon had once given me, which said: *My other coaster's a nice biscuit*, and blinked over at my copy of *Museums for Schools Groups. Paint, or draw*, Constance Johnson suggested at the start of Chapter 3, *and colour with felt-tips a picture called The Gardens of the Sea. Include starfish, sea anemones and other marine creatures . . .*

'So I'll see you later, then . . .'

And when I looked up from my underwater world, he'd gone.

2

123
ABC
The cat's in the cupboard
And he can't see me

Tottenham Court Road
Contains five syllables
Stockwell contains two

Standing in the train carriage that evening, I thought my face looked quite composed in the black glass of the window, but my mind was all over the place. Or – more correctly – it was full of Helen: Helen and Simon, Helen with Simon, Helen engulfing Simon. I was on my way to my poetry class but no poems were forming themselves in my mind. No poetry as consolation. *In just over half an hour I'll be there*, I thought, *sitting in the library again with my notebook on my lap* – then I looked at my watch and realised, with a sudden flash of recall, that I was actually meant to be somewhere else completely. I was supposed to be *at a conference dinner on the other side of town*. I'd utterly forgotten – despite what everyone had been saying all afternoon about lanyards – which we were only ever supposed to wear, for the moment at least, on conference days.

Hot-faced, I got off the train when it stopped at Bank. Then I ran along the platform, headed out, up the escalator and descended again, to wait for a Central Line train. When it arrived I stood for most of the way beside an elderly woman carrying a gold handbag under one arm and a small dog in a gold jacket under the other.

'No rest for the wicked,' the woman lamented as the train rattled on.

'No.' I glanced at the dog. It looked almost interchangeable with the bag. I remembered something Simon told me once, about not looking into a dog's eyes for too long, in case it stole your soul.

'Never rains but it pours.'

'No.'

The train continued. I hung onto the handrail. *There was even a minibus laid on*, it occurred to me. *That would have got me there on time.*

As it was, I had to get out at Covent Garden and run.

The restaurant was just off Bedford Street. It was a large, French-looking place, visible from quite a distance. A lot of RIPS and LMIC people were hanging around the doors, several of them with canvas tote bags hanging from their shoulders. *The Past is the Future!* it said, annoyingly, on the bags. We'd all been given them a couple of days earlier, courtesy of LMIC, and I hadn't even bothered to take mine home – it was another of Helen's ideas, so I'd just left it hanging empty at the back of a coat cupboard in Reception.

'Oh – there's Sybil!' I heard Hope Pollard's voice proclaiming from some nearby huddle of palaeontologists, and I felt like turning straight round and heading home. But I could see that I'd been spotted by Raglan too, now: he was peering across at me from the crowd. So I waved briefly, ducked sideways, and found a place to stand between a board saying *Drop-off Point* and a small lemon tree in a pot. Helen did not appear to be there. Which was at least something.

Noticing a conference schedule lying on the pavement, I picked it up and straightened it out against my thigh.

DAY 3 (EVENING EVENTS)

17.00–17.45

BREAK-OUT EVENTS (VENUE: RIPS)

'The Possession of Feathers' (Dr Theo Gerard, Sorbonne)

'Beakerware™: Dawn of a New Trading Empire?' (Dr. Helen Hansen, Director, London Museums Interpretation Centre)

'Manna from Heaven: the benefits of commercial collaborations in museum work' (Prof. Raglan Beveridge, Director, RIPS)

19.00–22.00

Dinner @ Mitchell's Restaurant

'Sybil! Glad to see you finally got here!' Raglan said, breaking away from the little crowd he'd been standing amongst. 'What happened? Where did you go?'

'Yes – sorry I'm late, Raglan,' I said. 'I got a bit waylaid.'

'You missed my talk. And Helen's, I'm afraid. She's had to go now. She couldn't stay for the dinner. She was meeting her boyfriend somewhere.'

'Right,' I replied, my heart folding over.

Raglan sighed. His face looked oddly crumpled, I thought, like a slightly crushed bag of sweets.

'She was announcing her findings this afternoon,' he said.

'Who was?'

'Helen. Her Winchelsea findings.'

'Right.'

'So her talk was, to all intents and purposes, the main event.'

'Ah.'

'It wasn't obligatory to come down to the talks earlier, Sybil,' he added, 'but I'd rather hoped you might have been there to field some questions . . .'

'Yes. Sorry. I'm just not sure my questions would have been—' – I hesitated – 'anyway, how did it all go? I – sorry – I just . . .'

'It was all extremely interesting. Especially Helen's talk. Which was really . . . quite something. *Is* quite something. It's basically what she's going to be saying in the TED talk when it goes out in a couple of weeks.'

'Right.'

'It's her contention, of course, that the Beaker People might even have had some influence on Roman mythology. If they were trading grain in Southern Italy, as her discovery indicates. Excitingly, it rather suggests a connection with stories about early Roman cup-bearers.'

'Does it?' I said, suddenly alert. 'I wonder where she got that idea from?'

But before he could tell me, a waiter wearing a very long white apron came to unlock the restaurant doors. 'OK, folks, you can come in now,' he informed us, and the crowd of archaeologists and their helpmates began to move forward, into the darkness of the restaurant. I went with them, Raglan's words ringing in my ears. I couldn't help thinking now that, as well as making off with my boyfriend, Helen had also just stolen half the ideas from my old dissertation. 'Archaeologists' party keep to the left, please,' the waiter announced, in the semi-darkness; and we all began to move from the beautiful new spring light into a kind of cave.

'Personally, I was hoping we'd get to see the guy with feathers,' muttered a youngish man beside me as we all shuffled in.

'Sorry?' I said, looking round at him.

'The one doing the "possession of feathers" talk.'

I regarded him. He looked a little dishevelled, I couldn't help thinking. Possibly a few glasses of wine down.

'It sounded as if he might have first-hand experience,' he said. 'Of feathers.'

I felt suddenly quite speechless. I turned and continued through the doorway.

There were a lot of mirrors in the restaurant, and glittering surfaces. I sat down at the table I had been assigned, beneath a round white lamp that looked like the moon and opposite several people all wearing lanyards: as well as Raglan, there was a Mandy Smith from Wandsworth Council, a Jennifer Porter from the British Museum and two young men – a John Coombes and a Teddy Chambers. And Teddy Chambers – I realised with sudden alarm – I actually *knew*. I'd once known him, anyway, a long time ago, at secondary school. Then he'd turned up, oddly enough, at a wedding Simon and I had gone to, in Brighton, a couple of weekends before our skating accident. Teddy had been on the other side of a large pale green room in Brighton Pavilion. Fortunately though, Brighton Pavilion being such a big place, I hadn't had to speak to him.

'Sybil,' Raglan said, across the table, 'let me introduce you to Teddy and John. John's doing a PhD on the evolution of jawless fish.'

'Hi,' said John Coombes, his voice low and glum.

'Sybil's a former student of Dr Hansen, who gave the talk about the new Beaker trade routes theory. The one that's getting everyone so excited. She's also contributed an important new section to my book,' Raglan informed the table. 'Dr Hansen, I mean: Dr Hansen has contributed the section. Sybil here is my . . . right-hand woman at the Institute,' he added, with less conviction. 'She's working on the final dotting of i's and crossing of t's before it goes to press. And Teddy, Sybil,' he rambled on, 'is here this evening from the world of corporate sponsorship.'

'Yes, actually, Teddy and I already know each other,' I said, feeling it simplest just to own up to this fact. 'We were at school together.'

'Were we?' remarked Teddy, an expression of wonder on his face.

Yes, you once pushed me into a river during Activity Week, I wanted to add, *and put your foot through my guitar.* I picked up a glass of water that was sitting on the table in front of me and took a big swig. 'Teddy and I were classmates once,' I confirmed to Raglan. 'Before he left for a different school.' *A Young Offender's Institute, probably*, I thought. I unfolded a napkin the size of a small sheet, and placed it on my lap. 'So,' I said to Teddy, 'what aspect of sponsorship are you—'

—but then something strange happened: the room and all the people in it seemed to warp for a second, and move in and out of vision – the tables and chairs and light fittings and waiters and diners wobbled, darkened, grew light again—

'So what aspect of sponsorship,' I continued, sweating slightly, 'do you think might connect with archaeology?'

'Well, mainly the blah blah blah blah . . .' Teddy replied. I found I was not listening, the rational thought-processes in my head having been replaced by visions of the elephant statues at Brighton Pavilion, of carnations known as *buttonholes*, of a hired jazz band and the sound of a church organ playing Pachelbel's Canon, of me and Simon getting into the car we'd hired, ready for the drive home—' . . . and the blah and the blah,' Teddy was saying, 'and the . . . oh, are you OK?'

'Yes, I'm fine, thanks. So, that's very interesting,' I said. 'Although I think LMIC might have beaten you to it, as far as sponsorship tie-ins are concerned!' And I smiled and nodded and hoped I wasn't about to keel over amongst the place-settings. It occurred to me that all I'd had to eat that day was a small, dry orange, the contents of an up-ended salad box and a few crumbs of Helen's cake. 'Great to see money heading in the general direction of the Institute, anyway,' I heard myself continue. 'Because hopefully it means none of us will get made redundant now!'

'Yes, I gather the Institute was in rather a state before LMIC turned up.'

'It was, indeed!' I confirmed, nodding like an idiot. I poured myself another glass of water, and gulped, and waited for the world to become normal.

Teddy was looking at me.

'Come to think of it,' he said, 'didn't I see you at Iona Fraser's wedding last year? In Brighton?'

'Did you?' I said. 'Possibly, yes. Because I was there.'

'I thought so!' he said, as if he'd just found out some tremendous secret about me. 'I thought it was you!'

The waiter in the long apron appeared at my side and put a small plate down in front of me. There was something on it that looked like luxury cat food; it would be called something like *Tasty Cuts* or *Purrfect*.

'That looks fascinating,' Teddy said.

'Yes.'

'It's a *terrine*,' Raglan observed from the other side of the table. 'For the vegetarians. I believe the rest of us are having pâté.'

'Right.' I picked up my fork and sliced a small corner off the terrine.

'So do you still play the guitar, Sybil?' Teddy continued. 'Now I think of it, I *do* remember you at school. And I seem to recall you playing the guitar?'

'I do still play sometimes, yes,' I said. 'From time to time. Mainly an electric one.' *Try putting your foot through that*, I thought. I'd once imagined that one day, some time before I hit thirty, I might be able to converse maturely, socially, with people

63

I didn't particularly like. It occurred to me now though that I might have bypassed maturity and sociability altogether, and fallen into some other more complicated category.

'So,' Teddy said, squashing a small rectangle of toast around his plate to collect some bits of pâté. 'Married yourself then, Sybil?'

I swallowed.

'Sorry?'

'Married? Or a boyfriend? Or a girlfriend? Because, of course, one mustn't assume . . .'

'No,' I said. 'None of the above.'

'So the bloke I saw you with at Iona's wedding wasn't . . .'

'No,' I said, 'he wasn't. Excuse me a second.'

I wiped my mouth on my napkin, got up from the table and went to stand outside. I stood beside the restaurant's big *fin de siècle* doors, my ears ringing. I took my phone out of my pocket and looked at the last communication that had ever occurred between me and Simon, a couple of weeks earlier: *How are you?* he'd texted me on 15th March – the Ides of March – having asked me the same question in seven identical texts he'd also sent in January and February, those cold, sad, dumbstruck months, and I hadn't known what to think, what to feel, how to respond, how to—

What's it got to do with you? I'd texted back, after about twenty seconds' deliberation. And he'd never been in touch again.

A little boy and girl were standing a short distance away from the restaurant doors, beside the potted lemon tree. I supposed they were the children of conference delegates. They were talking quietly to each other, and the little boy was playing with a snow globe, holding it in both hands and shaking it to make the glitter fall. I could just make out the tiny model of a dinosaur in there – stegosaurus in the snow – and remembered something my grandfather had said to me once, when I was about their age:

If you could stand on a planet that was far enough away, he'd said, *and if you had eyesight that was strong enough, you could see the dinosaurs still roaming around on Earth. You could see the past still happening.*

I'd looked at him in wonder. I suppose it was the first time I'd ever made the connection between time and space. Or thought how every creature that had ever lived was, in some strange way, still alive. However much you could no longer see them.

I went back inside after a few minutes and sat down again at the table. Teddy Chambers' chair was vacant.

'Teddy's left,' Raglan informed me, unnecessarily.

'I expect he had to go and deal with some off-shore banking crisis,' I replied.

'He isn't that that kind of banker.'

'Isn't he? I wasn't sure what kind of banker he was.'

I put the napkin back on my lap, and when the waiter arrived I ordered dessert.

I spent the next half hour or so speaking to John Coombes about jawless fish. Then, after he'd got up to go and speak to a colleague, the young man who'd talked about feathers appeared from some unknown hinterland of the restaurant and sat down beside me. 'Great – a whole table's worth!' he said, and began folding people's place-cards into origami shapes. I watched him for a moment. Then I said, 'That's quite a skill.'

'Thanks.' He seemed to have sobered up a little now. 'I'm making frogs. I would have made dinosaurs,' he added, pushing his thumbnail against the card, 'only they have too many bones.'

'I know what you mean.'

'Whereas frogs, I could fold all day. I could fold frogs in my sleep.'

'Poor frogs,' I said.

He glanced at me. 'So what's with all the "Past is the Future" bags in here?' he asked. 'Do you know? What are they supposed to be marketing?'

I hesitated. 'Time?' I suggested.

'Time *is* money, admittedly . . .' He flipped a frog across the table, where it landed in Mandy Smith's empty wine glass.

When John Coombes returned from his colleague's table he looked quite forlorn, as if no one was taking jawless fish seriously enough. 'Yeah, so I was doing this research last year?' he began again as the origami man made room for him along the table, 'about a particular species called birkenia elegans?'

'Ah yes,' I said, 'I've heard of birkenia elegans.' Because I had: I'd come across it recently, in the middle of some rambling paragraph Raglan had written, and I'd thought it had sounded a bit like Jane Birkin.

'And the fascinating fact about birkenia elegans . . .' John Coombes said, and I gave up listening. I did not trust fascinating facts. I had a whiteboard marker in the pocket of my dress, and I was very tempted to get it out and start drawing on the tablecloth. Maybe creating a little pond for the frogs. Would anyone notice? Would anyone even care? 'So what is it about ancient fish that interests you?' I asked. 'I mean, what's so interesting about them?' I ate the dessert I'd ordered – *Morello cherries in kirsch* – and placed the stones in a neat little row along the edge of my dish.

The dinner continued till ten. There didn't seem to be a way to make it stop sooner. Raglan talked a lot about Helen's Winchelsea triumph and her facsimile Beakerware, and John Coombes talked about jawless fish. After a while the origami expert pushed back his chair, said, 'OK, I'm off, it was nice to meet you,' and left, abandoning seven paper frogs on a side-plate. Watching him go, I felt peculiarly alone for a moment. I flipped one of the frogs onto my side-plate and recalled *The Frogs*, a play I'd read during my undergraduate days. I thought of Dionysus travelling to the Underworld to bring Euripides back from the dead.

Eventually, after a toast to the host from a man called Theo, and another speech from Raglan about losing things and finding them again, I detected a lull in the conversation and grabbed my chance too.

'OK, so, bye then. Bye, Raglan,' I announced, getting up from the table. 'I need to catch my train.'

'Sybil,' Raglan whispered as I edged past his chair. 'Are you carrying on with the indexing on Monday?'

'I am,' I said.

'Not encountering too many more problems with it? Because Helen told me today you were still identifying keywords.'

'Did she?' *Well, that's just the kind of snake-in-the-grass thing she would say*, I wanted to add. 'It's OK, everything's fine,' I said instead, untruthfully. 'I mean, I'm well beyond *that* stage now!'

'Great. Thanks then, Sybil. Just checking. Because of – you know – the publishing schedule . . .' Then he turned around in his chair. 'Sybil's doing some indexing for me at the moment,' he announced to the assembled little group. 'And she's also a poet, these days,' he added, causing my heart to sink. 'In her spare time. She's quite a literary tour de force.'

'A poet? Really?' said Mandy Smith, fishing the paper frog out of her wine glass. She looked over at me. 'So what sort of poems do you write, Sybil? What got you interested in poetry?'

Betrayal, I imagined replying. *Sorrow. Rage. Revenge.*

But I just said, 'To be honest, they're not really poems at all, they're just lists of words.'

The little girl and boy had gone from the courtyard, I noticed as I headed out. They had taken their snow globe with them. On my way back past the lemon tree, I spotted a piece of paper on the ground, so I stopped to pick it up. It was a page from the minutes of a Trustees' meeting that had taken place the previous week. I recognised Jane's careful note-taking style.

. . . plans for gallery shop extension and opening hours. Trial 'Beaker' merchandise to go on sale shortly (£15.99 for small beakers, £19.99 for large, £39.99 for 'Beaker' mixing bowls)

History of Trade progress: – RB to keep eye on rate of progress. HH to do final read-through

AOB: Mary Anning celebrations confirmed. HH to announce LMIC sponsorship arrangements (posters, flyers, social media)

I felt a momentary blur in the brain, a strange flitting, like a bat, across my understanding of things. There was a way to seek my revenge, I knew – there was some sort of entrance, like slipping through a narrow gap into a huge, strangely lit cave – but I didn't know where the cave was located, or how to get through the gap. On top of everything else, it now seemed I might soon be confronting posters of my ex-lover all over town. I could imagine the tag lines: *Re-light your fire, with Beakerware*! Or, *Beakerware: Are you ready for the One-Pot Revolution*?

There was a busker with a guitar when I got to Leicester Square tube station. He was playing 'Subterranean Homesick Blues', very slowly and not very well. I gave him some money anyway, then carried on down the stairs into the main ticket hall and down again, for the Northern Line platforms.

And when I got to Platform 3, there was Raglan! He was no longer sitting half a mile away in the restaurant in Covent Garden – he was standing on Platform 3 of Leicester Square tube station. I couldn't work this out at all – though maybe, it occurred to me, I'd taken longer to get there than I'd realised; maybe I'd just been wandering aimlessly for the past half hour. I'd noticed myself doing that sometimes.

'Hi, Raglan!' I said, walking over to him – because there was really nowhere else to go, other than jumping down onto the tracks. 'How did you get here so fast?'

'Ah – Sybil – hello!' he said, an unconvincing note of surprise in his voice. 'Yes. I appear to have beaten you to it!'

I hesitated. 'So I'm sorry I missed the talks earlier this evening. I mean, it sounded as if some of them must have been quite . . .'

'Yes.' He looked down at his watch. 'Yes, indeed. I think Helen was certainly planning to raise a glass or two later tonight.'

Or a Beaker, maybe, I nearly said, but stopped myself.

'I'm usually home late on Fridays, anyway . . .' I continued, keen to head off the silence that was in danger of engulfing us.

Raglan glanced at me.

'So are Fridays . . . normally quite a *busy* night for you?'

'Well, yes, in a way, because of these poetry classes I'm doing at the moment.'

'Ah, yes, the poetry . . .'

I peered down at the yellow line on the platform edge, beyond which you are not supposed to stray. There was an advert on the wall opposite, for *Secrets lemon-scented freshening wipes.* I thought of a terrible well-intentioned book my mother had sent me recently, entitled *When Life Gives You Lemons*; and also of some secret I'd overheard Helen whispering to Raglan earlier that day, in the corridor outside my room. 'Yes, she's clearly been through the mill a bit lately, hasn't she, and I think because of that her work rate's perhaps . . .' she'd murmured, before gently closing a door. And it was funny, I thought, because you heard that expression 'through the mill' and you never knew quite what it meant. Also, you heard people whispering about you to your colleagues and you never knew quite what that meant, either.

'So, you're writing about found objects, in these classes?' Raglan said after a moment.

'Yes, we're writing haikus about them,' I said. 'And odes.'

'Odes? To found objects?'

'Yes, like teapots and stuff. Like, Oh, Teapot! And talking about a teapot's attributes or something.' I hardly knew what I was talking about now, I was just opening and closing my mouth and sounds were coming out. 'We're meant to be looking out for signs and symbols, anyway.' I peered up at the board that announced train arrivals. The lettering was a blurry orange. It looked as if there might be a train for Brixton arriving in two minutes but it could have said Service Cancelled Indefinitely, for all I knew.

'So have you found an object?' Raglan asked. 'That means something?'

'Well, I've found several,' I said. 'But none of them have led to anything you would call poetry.'

Raglan looked thoughtful. 'Not unlike a career in archaeology, then.'

'How do you mean?' I asked, alarmed at this frank admission.

'I mean, you can find a lot of objects over the years, but they're not necessarily going to lead to any . . . particular conclusions. Apart from the significance of the thing itself. I've come to realise that. Which is why Helen's discovery is so exciting, of course,' he added, hurriedly. 'In terms of what it really does suggest about Beaker connections.'

Yes, but I wouldn't trust that conjecture further than I could throw it! I wanted to burst out. *Because she stole half of it from me! And I was making it up as I went along!* And I felt a sudden, almost unbearable urge to howl with despair at the mention of Helen's name, and the terrible way she had trampled all over my life.

'So, we've also been reading people like Emily Dickinson and Christina Rossetti,' I said instead.

'Christina Who?'

'Rossetti? The pre-Raphaelite poet?'

'Ah, yes, of course.'

Raglan shifted his briefcase from one hand to the other. He looked as if he was trying to recall who Christina Rossetti was. As if he was thinking: didn't I write a paper once with someone called Christina Rossetti?

'Well, I don't know much about Rossetti,' he said. 'But I've heard she wasn't a laugh a minute . . .'

'She wasn't. "Does the road wind up-hill all the way?"' I replied, raising my voice as a Kennington via Charing Cross train came rumbling towards us. '"Yes, to the very end. Will the day's journey take the whole long day? From morn to night, my friend." I mean, that's a laugh a minute, isn't it?'

'It certainly is.' Silence fell. Somebody walked along the platform in high heels. A warm dry breeze blew along the tracks, smelling of poor plumbing.

'Although,' Raglan said, 'didn't she also write 'In the Bleak Midwinter'? Christina Rossetti? Which is actually my favourite carol. "Earth stood hard as iron, water like a stone . . ." I like that one. It's very – apt.'

'Yes, I suppose that *is* quite . . .'

'"Snow had fallen",' he continued, '"snow on snow, snow on snow. In the bleak midwinter, long ago".'

'Yes,' I said. 'I suppose she could be pretty descriptive when she wanted to be. Because that's not a bad description of winter.'

There was a pigeon walking along the edge of the platform, one of those pretty, brownish-pink ones with a death wish.

'Have you ever come across "Air and Angels"?' Raglan asked after a moment. 'That's a beautiful one, too. John Donne. Probably my all-time favourite poem.'

And without further preamble he suddenly launched into it, his voice strangely low and melodious, and almost sorrowful: '"Twice or thrice had I lov'd thee . . ."' he pronounced as the train rattled away. '"Before I knew thy face or name; So in a

71

voice, so in a shapeless flame/Angels affect us oft, and worshipp'd be . . ."'

'Yes,' I said, embarrassed.

' "Still when, to where thou wert, I came, Some lovely glorious nothing I did see . . ." '

'Yes,' I said again, feeling the strangest little chill running up the back of my neck, because it was a poem I knew pretty well, and the words *were* moving, it had to be said – but also, to my irrational mind, it seemed he was quite possibly thinking about Helen while he was saying it. It seemed all the susceptible men in the world might be thinking about Helen.

' ". . . But since my soul, whose child love is, Takes limbs of flesh, and else could nothing do . . ." ' Raglan went on, unabashed, as people near us on the platform turned their heads to look at him.

'Yes,' I concluded, as he reached the end of the verse. 'That *is* a lovely one. It's funny, though, because for some reason, that particular poem has always made me think of Angel Delight!'

Raglan looked at me.

'Angel Delight?'

'Yes. I suppose because of the title . . . and Angel Delight *is* a kind of glorious nothing, isn't it? Especially the butterscotch flavour.' I stopped talking; I felt I'd inadvertently ended the life of some beautiful, short-lived thing, like stepping on a snail.

'I *think*,' Raglan said, after a moment, 'it might be about the soul prevailing, in some way. About true love overcoming absence—'

'Yes, well, that would certainly be a better analysis . . .' I agreed, then fizzled out altogether. 'Anyway,' I resumed after a moment, 'we're meant to carry notebooks around with us, in case we get inspired. But I've only written one page so far. And that's just a list of words.'

'Oh dear.'

'It looks more like a shopping list . . .'

'Hmm. Well, that's—'

'I go down to the gallery at work sometimes,' I went on, 'and I write down some of the things in the cases. You know, the specimens. Danny thinks I've flipped.'

'Danny?'

'The gallery attendant?'

'Yes, of course. Yes, well, that's . . .'

'And it's funny, because my handwriting's gone weird these days, too. Sometimes I miss whole letters off the ends of words. Or I join the end of one word onto the start of the next one.'

Raglan was looking at me again, a searching expression on his face.

'Well, I believe that's meant to be a sign of intelligence,' he said. 'Your thoughts travel faster than your hand can write them down.'

'Really?' I felt quite touched, that he had attributed me with intelligence. That he did not simply regard me as Sybil the Blind Prophet, who knew things without understanding them. Also, that he apparently trusted me not to ruin his book.

'So, you're on track to finish up the index on Monday?' he asked, mind-reader-ish, once the correct train had rattled up to the platform and we'd squashed ourselves in.

'Hopefully . . .' I said, casting around for excuses, 'though I do also have to do some of those worksheets for Professor Muir. Those "spot the difference" ones that he's passed on to me.' Raglan looked blank. 'You know,' I explained, 'the ones with the stegosaurus with a fin missing, or—'

'Sail.'

'Sorry?'

'Stegosauruses had sails. Not fins.'

'Oh.' I was suddenly very aware of Raglan's tremendous knowledge of all things ancient and prehistoric, and also of his physical presence, as we stood there: his height, his stature, his noble, monolithic qualities: it was as if one of the Easter Island statues had got into the carriage with me. He opened his mouth as if on the point of speech. Then he hesitated. Then he said, 'That was a test, Sybil. To keep you on your toes.'

'Sorry?' I said, the tiny hairs lifting on the back of my neck. 'What do you mean?'

He paused, and smiled. 'Just kidding! As long as the proofs make it to the printers on time: that's the main thing!'

'Hah! Yes . . .'

The lights inside the carriage flickered and went out. The expression on his face fell momentarily into baffling darkness. I felt suddenly, inchoately nervous. I had been considering earlier whether to ask if a slight delay to the publication date might be possible. But, all things considered, I felt that it was probably not. The lights came up again and the train rumbled on, beneath the Thames and on towards Southwark. People got into the carriage and out of it, or sat clutching their belongings and staring at the adverts on the opposite wall. I turned and looked through the window, at the curved blackness of the tunnel. Reflected in the glass were two women sitting with shopping bags, and a tired-looking man talking to a tired-looking child. Standing a few feet away from them was a man holding a large plastic horse head in the crook of his arm. He was also carrying a mandolin. It looked like some kind of Mafia nightmare. The train pulled into a station, but I couldn't see which one it was. The man with the plastic horse head looked at me via the window's reflection – it seemed he did, anyway – and I looked away and smiled at Raglan as he stood there, his handsome head in half-profile, one arm outstretched to hold onto the handrail.

'So, nice weekend lined up?' he asked, after a moment. 'Getting up to anything interesting?'

'Well, yes, I'm probably . . .' I said, 'going to do some . . . nice things . . .' I paused. 'So how about you?'

'Yes, well, I'm off to Crete. In a few hours' time, actually,' he added, glancing down at his watch, as if setting off for Crete that night was as unremarkable as going to Tesco. 'It's going to be a bit of a lightning visit,' he added. 'I'm only staying one night. I'll be back on Monday.'

'So what are you doing out there that's so specific?' I asked.

'I'm giving a lecture on the finds Peter Edwards made last year.' He paused. 'It was going to be *his* lecture, of course. He was going to give a keynote speech on some particularly unusual little ceramics he found last year. Near the site of his famous Knossos dig in the eighties. There are some wonderful little terracotta goddesses that he was going to . . .' He hesitated. 'Tell people about.'

'Right . . .' Neither of us spoke for a moment. Then shortly afterwards, after we'd discussed the malfunctioning photocopier at work, and the fact that it was April already, the train stopped and a lot of people got out. 'Oh – there's a seat!' I said, pointing towards a moquette stretch at the far end of the carriage. 'Yes – and there's another one!' Raglan said, indicating one at the other end. And we moved off in opposite directions and sat apart for the rest of the journey.

Lying on the seat beside mine was a copy of *Watchtower*. It had a picture of a young bearded man on the cover – Jesus, I supposed. Though he also looked like a man who'd made me a cappuccino that morning at a coffee kiosk on Clapham Road. He'd been flirty and twinkly-eyed, which had made me feel quite good at the time, but now I felt slightly guilty that I'd been flirting with someone who looked like God's son. *Once a Catholic always a Catholic*, as Simon had used to joke. Although a guilty conscience obviously hadn't bothered *him* unduly.

There was a lot of reading material inside the magazine, and some of it seemed quite ordinary, like something you might find in *Marie Claire*, and some of it seemed quite weird. There was an article on how to get your work-life balance right, and another on the miracle of the human body.

A CONSULTANT SURGEON EXPLAINS HIS FAITH

Dr Nigel Wilkins works as a brain surgeon in Wolverhampton. For many years he believed in evolution. But later, through the Jehovah's Witnesses, he became convinced that the human body was designed by God. Here we print his story.

There was a photo accompanying the article, of Dr Wilkins wearing a casual golfing jumper and with a look of strained happiness on his face. There was his wife Linda, too. Linda Wilkins. Linda looked more doubtful than Nigel, though, and she was wearing a dress that seemed to be made out of sofa fabric.

My wife Linda began studying the Bible with Jehovah's Witnesses, who showed her from its verses that God does not torture people in fiery hell

Well, that's a relief, I thought. Because I always wondered that about you, God. I closed the magazine and glanced up at Raglan, sitting at the other end of the carriage. He was sitting absolutely still, inscrutable as a sphinx. I flipped the magazine over to look at the back. There was a photo of two women standing at a market stall, holding out some oranges. 'Wisdom is calling out' it said beneath the picture. 'Can You Hear It?' I couldn't work out what the oranges were supposed to signify at all.

Raglan got up from his seat as the train was pulling in at Kennington, and walked back past me down the passageway. 'I'm getting out here, Sybil,' he said on his way past, moving on to the opening doors. 'So, good luck with the found objects!'

'Thanks, Raglan, and good luck with—' I couldn't think what to say '—with Knossos,' I concluded, as he stepped out.

'It's called Crete these days,' he yelled back, raising his hand in valediction. I thought he looked quite sad, as the train moved on – vulnerable, almost, standing out there alone.

On my way up the escalator, I received three text messages. The first was from Raglan:

Sybil, forgot to mention: John from Repro rang for an update. I told him A History will be with him on 9th as agreed.

I decided it was best to ignore this for the time being.

The second was from my flatmate Esther:

Hey Syb! Want to see Get Over It @ the Ritzy next Sat?

I didn't know how to respond to this either: watching a film called Get Over It did not seem the most tactful suggestion, even for Esther. But she was such an upbeat person that I knew she was just trying to humour me: trying to drag me back into a world of kindness and hope. So I wrote:

Sounds interesting! Will let you know.

Then I read the final text, which was from Jane Beauchamp:

Hi Sybil – you left your sandwich box behind. Just FYI. I've popped it in your tote bag, in Reception cupboard. Have a nice weekend.

Thanks, Jane, I wrote back. *Have sieve for memory!*

Which was true: I did have a sieve for a memory. Or rather, it seemed I remembered all the wrong things and none of the right ones any more. I didn't add a kiss at the end of my texts to either Jane or Esther; I had stopped putting kisses on my texts and emails. I didn't trust them. When Helen had used to email me sometimes, after we'd swapped numbers at the British Library, she'd always put an x right after her name. Helenx. Which made her sound like some sort of medical aid, as I'd observed to Simon a few weeks later when I'd shown him one of her incoming messages on my phone. We'd been sitting in the Institute's boardroom at the time, waiting for the RIPS Christmas party to begin. It was mid-December and he had come straight round from work; he'd left The Olive Branch early and cycled all the way across to Greenwich on his blue racing bike, and it was the last day we'd been together like that, before Helen had intervened in our lives. The boardroom was festooned with garlands of tinsel, I remember, red and green and gold. Hope Pollard had had a field day draping swathes of it, uncharacteristically girlish, around the marble busts of various Victorian dignitaries.

'Do you think RIPS might ever consider employing a new caterer?' Simon had asked me seriously, lifting a cold sausage roll from a foil platter on the table in front of us.

'Personally, I think RIPS will go on offering up sausage rolls until the end of time,' I'd replied.

Then Helen had messaged me: RU in the boardroom? Helenx

'Oh, look,' I'd said, 'Helen wants to join us.'

'Really?' Simon had peered down at my phone. 'Helenx . . .' he'd said.

'Yeah, sounds like some sort of medical brand name, doesn't it?' I'd said. 'Some kind of surgical support stocking.'

Then Helen herself had arrived, emerging magnificently from the lift. 'Sybil! And this must be Simon!' she'd exclaimed from the doorway, striding towards us past the little groups of palaeontologists skulking un-festively around the trestle tables. At which point Simon and I had stopped talking about surgical support stockings and he'd stood up abruptly. 'Hey there!' he'd said – which was not a greeting I'd ever heard him utter before. Helen was wearing a dress that I hadn't seen her in before, either: it was pale grey, with little blue flowers, and she looked good in it. It made her look like a nicer person than she was – open-hearted and kind, like Spring running up to Venus with a blanket to keep her warm. Also, her hair looked freshly washed and brushed, unlike mine; my hair was not even particularly clean. I'd gone into the staff toilets after I'd finished work that day, and sprayed Battista Dry

Shampoo into it, which had made it go flat and smell of fake coconut.

'So, can I get you a drink?' Simon asked her, after we'd all stood around wordlessly for a moment, as if briefly struck dumb. 'I've spied a pop-up drinks bar over there, behind the bust of Darwin.'

'Darwin and pop-up drinks: sounds quite a mix!'

'Hah!'

Then they'd both headed over to the temporary bar that Danny was running in one of the tinselled alcoves. I'd sat and watched them go. After a while, as I waited for them to return, Hope Pollard had come over with some RIPS raffle tickets to sell (first prize, a weekend's white-water rafting in the Lee Valley; second prize, a hot air balloon trip over the South Downs – neither of which I wanted to win) and Professor Muir had roamed across, on an apparent mission to engage affably with the more junior members of staff – ('So, will you be going away for Christmas, Sybil?' 'Yes: we're spending it with my parents in Norfolk.' 'Hah! Well, no shortage of turkeys in Norfolk . . .') – and moved off again. Then Simon and Helen had finally returned, with a round of drinks in plastic cups: Helen had a G&T, Simon had a pint of IPA and I had a whisky mac. 'There's yours . . .' Simon had said to me distractedly, slopping my cup down onto the trestle table.

'How funny!' I exclaimed, picking it up, 'I'm the only one not drinking an acronym!'

'And there's yours, Helen,' Simon continued, ignoring this entirely. 'Gin, eh? Mother's ruin!'

'Well, fortunately I'm not a mother, Simon!'

'I'm glad I got you a double, then!'

'I'm glad you did, too!'

And I'd just sat there, with my thick little green drink.

*

I got back that night shortly after eleven. Before going to bed I looked through all my old university paperwork, rummaging through all the battered old files and plastic wallets I'd hung onto, until finally, a little before midnight, I came across my old dissertation, the one that had caused Helen such offence.

Their Cup Runneth Over: The significance of 'the cup' within Beaker People cultures
(Student Matriculation number: 20030671)

. . . in conclusion, then, could it be said that there are parallels between the humble 'cup' of Beaker People cultures and the significance of the various 'cornucopia' residing within the pages of Classic mythology? Could Homer have been tapping into some long-lost folk memory when he wrote of Hebe[1] bearing ambrosia to the gods via a cup? Might Ceres'[2] 'cup of plenty' even echo a more primal tale of food and survival to be found amongst the ranks of the Beaker People of mainland Europe?
1. Wife of Zeus
2. Ceres, Roman goddess of agriculture and grain

I could see why she hadn't liked it; it was still a load of old rubbish.

Though this was interesting in its own right, I felt. It was certainly food for thought.

3

Spelt, teff, amaranth;
quinoa, buckwheat,
emmer
At least two of these
look like typos
to me

I dreamt that night that she was the Cyclops – she was a vast, one-eyed giant striding around all the pretty parks and gardens of London, and I was Odysseus, sleek and cunning and fleet of foot. As Odysseus, I took a bus to Debenhams on Oxford Street and bought a pair of 15-denier tights, into one foot of which I dropped a large grey rock I'd come across. It was to be a sling-shot device: it was what *my* Odysseus would confront Helen's Cyclops with. Somewhere along the line, in this dream, I'd got David and Goliath in there too, I'd got Homer muddled up with the Bible. Then I woke up, and it was twenty to nine on a Saturday, and Esther and her boyfriend Paul were frying bacon in the kitchen.

Bacon

I wrote in my notebook, which I'd left open on my bedside table the night before. I could think of nothing I wanted to write, though, about bacon.

I had a party to go to that weekend in Colliers Wood, and I had also arranged to see my parents in Norfolk. I took the train there from Liverpool Street station quite late that morning. The journey took over two hours, the landscape outside becoming increasingly flat the further east the train went. I could not think what my parents were doing in Norfolk. If I could choose anywhere to live in the UK, I thought, Norfolk would not be the place I'd choose. My grandfather had driven me there once in his Triumph, a few months before he'd become ill and permanently weighed down, like a deep-sea diver, with an oxygen tank in Blackheath Hospital. We'd stopped at a service station called Fourwentways, which had seemed to us like a very complicated way to say 'crossroads'. We sat in the Little Chef there, and I had a bag of crisps and an apple, and my grandad had sausages and chips, and at one point he looked out of the window and said, 'Blimey, it's flat as a bloody pancake, Syb. What the blazes were they thinking, moving out here?' which were my sentiments exactly.

Sleet swept lightly past the train's thickened windows, and I pulled my cardigan more closely around my shoulders. *Spring*, I wrote in my notebook, and I added a few more lines to my growing list:

Toilet door swinging open. Lock broken. View of overflowing bin.
Man on phone. Keeps saying 'it's a glorified greenhouse, Martin'
Sign on platform saying This Way Out
Cows. Builders yards. Telegraph poles. Tennis courts.

Then I closed the notebook again and looked at the cover. It depicted a painting by Magritte – the famous one of the bowler-hatted businessman with an apple covering his face. I'd never liked Magritte much; I'd always thought there was something irritating about all those clouds and repressed-looking floating businessmen. I'd spotted the book in the Tate Gallery shop near the start of the year – it had been half-price in the January sales, and I'd actually bought it for Simon, because he did like Magritte. Magritte had been one of his likes, in common

82

with buckwheat and Trangia sets and copper saucepans and me, or so I'd thought. But before I'd had the chance to give it to him he'd got together with Helen, so there was no need any more.

My father met me in the station car park, in his big sensible car. There was an angle-grinder strapped into the front seat, like a kind of robot passenger. He often drove around with DIY equipment of some sort, meaning I had to sit in the back seat, the way I always used to as a child.

'Journey OK?' he asked me dutifully, as we set off towards the low-lying little hamlet where they lived. He rarely mentioned Simon these days, but he'd never mentioned him much when we were together. 'I've put a blanket down,' he added as we drove down the grey-ish roads to *Broadlands*, 'because of Diane Kimber's dog.'

'Who's Diane Kimber?'

'She's our new neighbour. She's moved in next door. Her Labrador sheds hair like there's no tomorrow, so I've put a blanket down.'

'What was her Labrador doing in your car?'

'We had to take it to the vet's. It was having an operation. It ate a chocolate bar, which can be fatal for dogs. And Diane's car was being serviced.'

'Right.' My parents' lives seemed hugely complicated these days, with incidents and small crises I was no longer a part of. Even with other people's incidents and crises.

'Brandy,' my father said.

'Sorry?' For a moment I wondered if the dog had been drinking, too.

'The dog's name,' he explained.

'Oh.'

Well, make sure you don't get too involved with Diane Kimber and her dog, Dad, or there's no telling what might happen.

'I'm going to hoover the upholstery when we get back,' he said.

'OK,' I replied, squinting out at the hedgerows. The sleet had turned to a hard rain. I thought of something I'd come across recently in Constance Johnson's *Museums for Schools Groups*:

Badlands

A type of terrain where sedimentary rocks have been extensively eroded by wind and water.

My parents had invited me over because they were going to Portugal for a fortnight, and wanted to see me before they left. My mother was worried about me after *what happened in January*: she often worried about me, but these days she looked at me and my Streatham-Ice-Rink-scarred forehead with more frequent expressions of concern. 'Are you really OK, love?' she'd say. 'Yes,' I would reply, 'I'm really OK.'

Which was a lie, of course, and in any case, she didn't believe me. Sometimes she would become so affronted at the way Simon had behaved that I practically felt like siding with him. 'I mean, maybe he actually did me a *favour*,' I'd said, the last time we'd spoken. Because if he wanted to be with Helen Hansen – a woman who talked about *future-proofing* and owned a make-up bag the size of a suitcase – well, clearly, I had never been the girl for him in any case: clearly he had done us all a favour.

We ate roast chicken for lunch, and apple crumble. We sat in the dining room, looking out across the mudflats towards Mundeley. In the distance was Stow windmill, its sails static.

'Grey day,' my father observed. 'Low tide.'

'That sounds like the start of a poem,' I said, putting a spoonful of crumble into my mouth. I chewed and swallowed. 'You could call it "Grey Day in Norfolk".'

'What's *wrong* with Norfolk?' my mother asked. 'I know you think Norfolk's beyond the pale, sweetheart, but we happen to like it.'

'I didn't say Norfolk's beyond the pale,' I said, putting my spoon back into the crumble.

'I think, to be frank, you've made your feelings about Norfolk rather plain,' my father said.

'I don't have any feelings about Norfolk,' I said. 'My feelings about Norfolk are completely on the level.'

Silence swelled outwards like a fog, across the table.

After lunch, while my father hoovered the dog hairs from the car seats, I sat with my mother in the living room and answered her questions. *The Spanish Inquisition*, as Simon had used to call it.

'So how's the editing going,' she asked, 'on your boss's book?'

'It's not editing so much as indexing,' I explained. 'I have to add new page references and stuff to the index. Because of this new bit about the Winchelsea Hoard.'

'The Winchelsea what?'

'Hoard. It's this new section that's gone in at the eleventh hour.'

'How very thoughtless. Who added that?'

'I don't know.'

She looked at me. 'You don't know?'

'No.'

She hesitated. 'So how long's the book?'

'About five hundred pages.'

'And you have to re-do the whole index because of the Winchelsea Hoard?'

'No, just add some new references. I mean, technically, I only have to worry about cross-referencing twenty keywords or so . . . I mean, it's pretty straightforward, really . . .'

'Because it's not as if numbers have ever been your *strong* point!' my mother carried on, affronted. 'You only just scraped your maths GCSE!'

Which did nothing to encourage me.

'So have you seen Simon at all?' she added after a moment, in a quieter voice. 'Since you . . . since he . . .'

'No,' I said. 'Not at all. I haven't seen him at all since he got together with Helen. Apart from in the distance a few weeks ago, when he came to the Institute to pick her up.' I raised my cup of coffee and took a sip.

'He came round *to pick her up from your work*?' my mother almost shouted.

'Yes. I see Helen quite regularly at work. And hear her,' I added. 'She's got a very loud voice.'

'The nerve of the woman!' my mother said. 'Throwing her weight around at your place of work! Especially after what happened at university.'

'I'm under no illusions, Mum,' I said. 'Sometimes I think it's *because* of what happened at university. I think it might be some kind of revenge. For showing her up.'

She peered at me, a look of sorrow on her face. 'Surely you could say something to her though, darling! Surely you could at least confront her maturely!'

'You've already suggested that, Mum,' I said. 'But I don't think she's all that mature.'

I continued to drink my coffee. I surprised myself sometimes these days, with my own emotional stillness. My sluggishly beating heart. My mother had cried like anything the previous year, when my grandfather had died; she'd cried and cried. But now she had stopped crying, she had dried her eyes and was back on some sort of even keel. It made me feel bad. Because I'd loved my grandad, too, a great deal, and I missed him. Only I'd never cried.

'That's a nice perfume you're wearing,' my mother said after a moment. 'What is it?'

'Lavender pillow spray,' I said.

She moved on from this troubling fact without further comment.

'So you're not ever planning to confront her, then?'

'No,' I said. 'I'm just planning to go into work and earn my money and go home again.'

'And you say Simon hasn't even been in touch?'

'Well, he's sent some texts.'

'And have you replied to them?'

'Of course I haven't! Why would I?'

'Well, you *could* . . .'

'I know I *could*, but I don't want to.'

'I don't suppose you ever see anything of James these days, either?' she carried on hopefully, trying a different tack. 'I don't suppose you've . . .'

'I have no idea where James even lives now, Mum,' I said. 'He's probably married with kids and living in Berlin or somewhere.'

'*Berlin*?'

'Or somewhere. And his wife might take a dim view of me just turning up out of the blue . . .'

'He has a *wife* . . . ?'

'I don't know. I was being hypothetical . . .'

My mother sighed.

'Well, I certainly thought it was a shame, when you two split up,' she said. 'You and James.' She had always liked James: she'd thought he was sensible and kind. Which he was: he was sensible and kind. But then, she'd also liked Simon. She'd liked the way he'd always let her walk through doorways first, and the fact that he'd grown his own herbs and made buckwheat crêpes without the slightest concern that he might be about to set the kitchen alight. She'd thought he was a catch.

I looked out of the window. My father was still out there, pushing the hoover's carpet-attachment around the car's upholstery. Every so often he would pause, and pull Diane Kimber's dog's hairs from the end of it. The angle-grinder was still strapped into the front seat, staring philosophically out to sea.

The thing is, Mum, what I actually want, I imagined saying, *is revenge. I want my own back. Pure and simple.*

But I couldn't say that; it would scare the daylights out of her. In any case, I didn't know how I would seek revenge that was in any way dignified, or would even give me pleasure. I'd read once about a spurned wife who'd sliced all her husband's business suits into lasagne-width strips. And about another who'd broken into her rival's house and sewn prawns into the linings of her curtains. But these had both struck me as quite cheerless tasks, and even had the potential to result in arrest. Besides, I was not insane.

My mother sighed again. She had been sighing a lot that spring.

'So how are the poetry classes going?' she asked, glancing out of the window, too.

'I skipped it yesterday.'

'Really? Why?'

'There was a diary clash. I had to go to a dinner. An archaeology thing in Covent Garden. So there wasn't time. Anyway, poetry's not doing much for me, Mum. It's stressing me out. Because now I have homework on top of everything else.'

'Don't give up on it, sweetheart,' she said, looking back into the room. 'It's worth persevering. I think it's one of the better decisions you've made recently.'

'Right.'

'Maybe you could go down to the mudflats this afternoon,' she added.

'Why would I want to do that?'

'Because you could take your notebook and write some poetry. Find something inspiring. If your tutor's asked you to look for found objects.'

'You don't really look for found objects though, do you? You just *find* them,' I said. 'And I'm not convinced I'd find anything much on the mudflats. The only things I ever seem to see down there are old pants and empty vodka bottles.'

'We could both go down there,' my mother said, ignoring this, 'if we put on wellies.' She fell silent. On the mantelpiece, my grandfather's clock ticked, resplendent with its seated little figure of Britannia that I'd used to want to liberate when I was a small girl.

'Anyway,' she said, 'if you don't look, you won't find.'

Outside, my father stopped hoovering the car, straightened up, then stood for a moment, looking seawards. *Sounds like a case of glad-handing to me*, he'd said earlier, when I'd told him about Helen's influence these days around the Institute. 'Bribery. Favouritism. Still, she's clearly got a talent for dodging curveballs, hasn't she? Because *you've* certainly been given a Sisyphean task!'

Sisyphus, of course, being the idiot who'd had to push a boulder up a hill for all eternity. My dad had always been entertained by my choice of degree subject.

'I've just remembered, I'm meant to be going to a party tonight,' I said to my mother, this thought suddenly cantering back into my mind like the Charge of the Light Brigade. 'So I should probably head off quite soon.' I glanced at her. 'But maybe we could go down to the mudflats next time.'

'It's a date,' she said.

'Yeah.'

Before heading back, I spent half an hour or so in the guest room. I'd told my mother I had a headache and wanted to lie down. Which was true: I *did* have a headache and wanted to lie down. And the bed was comfortable. I'd slept in that bed a few times with Simon, and we'd found the mattress far superior to our own in London. We'd had some nice times in that bed. There was a Constable print on the wall – a reproduction of *The Hay Wain* – and an unlit vanilla-scented candle, and there was a not un-picturesque view through the window of the estuary and various hopping seabirds – oyster-catchers or maybe lapwings.

> Long-legged birds
> In the mudflats

I didn't see a need to actually go down to the mudflats to write that.

I got up after a while and roamed around the room, picking things up and putting them down again: a small ceramic hedgehog I'd made with modelling clay and the use of a dinner-fork when I was eight; a black and gold money tin; a little autograph book I'd used to keep; a small picture of my grandparents in an oval frame. Charlie and Dorothy Constantine. The last of the Constantines, apart from my mum and me. The last of our little Constantine Empire. A few people had written in the autograph book: mainly my mother, or friends of my mother, and a few old schoolfriends.

If all the boys lived over the sea, What a good swimmer Sybil would be! Luv Bethany, 3rd February 1996.

By hook or by crook I'll be last in this book! Lots of love, Granny, 17th October 1994.

Oh no you won't! my grandad had written in the fraction of space beneath this. Four tiny words that, out of nowhere, suddenly brought a tear to my eye.

'We'll phone when we get to Portugal,' my mother said, as I got into the car late that afternoon.

'Enjoy the party!' she added, as my father turned the key in the ignition.

'Find some objects!' she continued, as we drove off.

> view from a train
> Upturned bath in a field:
> I thought it was a cow

My phone made its little incoming text noise as I was waiting in the queue in the train's buffet car, and, unexpectedly, heart-arrestingly, Simon's phone number appeared on the screen. There was no message from him, though. Nothing. I wondered if he'd been scrolling through his contacts list and sent me a blank text by mistake. Or, more likely, his phone had dialled my number from the depths of his rucksack as he'd cycled to work for the evening shift. Or from the midst of some embrace with Helen, his phone in his back pocket pressing against the range cooker, their heads knocking against the hanging onion plaits.

I tried not to imagine these things.

Unfortunately, though, I did imagine them. And then my imaginings would be joined by memories. They would come into my head from out of nowhere: small pictures, as clear and bright as little films. As I schlepped back from the station, a clonky old camera that Simon had owned materialised in my mind: it was called a Nikon Coolpix 900, and he'd sometimes taken pictures of me with it, and also sometimes of the dishes he'd cooked. I recalled, too, that his best friend at primary school had been a boy called Jason Murphy: he was the son of one of the dinner ladies, and when Simon had used to go round to his house for tea, Mrs Murphy had always yelled 'Mash yer potatoes into yer gravy!', just as she always did at school. She'd been quite a form-ative influence, Simon once told me, in his ambition to become a brilliant chef who knew how to treat potatoes. I also remem-bered, for some reason, that he'd once caught a trout with a hook and line from the River Avon; I remembered that the brand of soap he favoured was *Imperial Leather*, that his favourite child-hood TV programme had been *The Flumps*, that his own mother had the quite surprising middle names of Hephzibah Dominica, considering her first name was Lynne, and that her house had smelt of rising damp and dried roses. I also remembered the night we first met: after he'd clocked off from the restaurant we'd drunk Merrydown cider until gone midnight and talked about *The Flumps* and *Postman Pat*, and also a film I'd seen recently called *Leningrad Cowboys Go America*. And at some point in the small hours that night he'd given me a piggyback all the way down Clapham Park Road because I'd somehow managed to step onto some broken glass at a bus stop. I couldn't remember why I'd had bare feet that night and was carrying my sandals, the black leather straps of them tied together and dangling from my wrist like some kind of handbag. I thought of how cold the night had been, and how bright the moon, and how he'd run most of the way – charged – like an armoured horse with an injured knight on its back; and of how I'd laughed and laughed because I'd been half hysterical and already half in love, and he'd called me *Sybilla* – *Sybilla*, with two ls and an a.

But then it also occurred to me that he couldn't just have left me to *bleed to death* in Clapham that night, and maybe he'd only ever called me *Sybilla* in the weeks and months and over two years that followed because it was less embarrassing than having a girlfriend called Sybil. There were a lot of old lady names like Grace and Martha and Lily that were quite sexy in a way, but Sybil was not one of them. And maybe he'd had some sort of *epiphany* nearly three years later at the cheese fondue party Helen had invited him to; maybe he'd realised that she'd actually been the woman for him all along – a glamorous, career-driven woman who wrote academic papers and did TED talks – and not someone who drank Merrydown cider and watched *Leningrad Cowboys Go America*. And the only retort I had to all the sadness was *poetry classes*. It was like holding up a fluttering white hanky on a battlefield. It was unlikely to be much use.

The person who'd invited me to the party was a colleague at the Institute, a *tracks and trails specialist* called Graham who was usually to be found in some remote corner of South America, pouring plaster of Paris into dinosaur footprints. He'd said that he would call round to my flat at eight that evening – only by the time I got back from the station it was quarter past and he'd already given up on me and carried on alone (as Esther had explained to me in a little note). Which seemed fitting, some-how, for a tracks and trails specialist. By the time I did actually set off – having showered and dried my hair and got dressed and put on make-up and deliberated, and deliberated some more, and finally left – it was already gone nine. Also, the party was miles away in a part of London I hardly knew, though it struck me as I got nearer that it was really only a few streets away from the London Museums Interpretation Centre in Tooting. Perhaps *Helen* would be there, it occurred to me, a sudden chill entering my heart – perhaps even *Simon* would be. But then I braced myself and knocked on the door, because it would have been ridiculous by that point to turn round and go all the way home again – *knock and the door shall be opened unto you*, as the chaplain had used to suggest during my old school assemblies – and almost immediately it was opened by a middle-aged woman.

'Jesus Christ, it's snowing!' she said, looking over the top of my head.

'Yes,' I agreed. Because it *was*; it had been snowing for the past twenty minutes as I'd walked there; a light, unseasonal snow-shower flying around my head in the darkness. 'I'm Sybil,' I added.

The woman turned her gaze from the snow to me. She was wearing a tight silvery dress that made me think of Bacofoil.

'So do you have the gift of second sight, Sybil?' she asked.

'Not generally,' I replied. She seemed to be quite a strange woman. One of her eyes was more thickly framed with mascara than the other one. It made me feel oddly nervous. 'I work at RIPS with Graham?' I added, as if this might act as a sort of password.

She did not look any more enlightened.

'Come in, then,' she said.

'Thanks.' I smiled and stepped inside.

'So, most people are in there,' she went on, stopping mid-stride and pushing open a door adjacent to the front door. 'Maybe you'll find someone you know in there. I'm off for a spliff.' And she disappeared back down the corridor.

I approached the doorway and peered into the gloom. Graham from RIPS was not there. Helen was not there either, and neither was Simon. There was no one in there I knew at all. A guitar was being played – some terrible song about loss and longing – and four people were sitting contemplatively on a small Persian carpet as if waiting to be spirited away. A young-ish bearded man was standing beside a small upright piano, a china bowl in his right hand. He looked poised, alert, like some-one receiving secret radio messages.

'Hi,' I said. We were standing so close it would have seemed rude not to.

'Hi there. Want some spicy chickpeas?' he replied, leaning towards me and shaking the contents of the bowl from side to side. 'They're fiery, but moreish.'

'Yeah, like *you*, Dom!' drawled one of the women sitting on the carpet.

'Want some?' he persisted.

I glanced at the dried peas rattling around the bowl and thought of a party Simon and I had gone to once, where the hosts had served cat biscuits for a laugh and no one had even noticed.

'They look nice,' I said now, to the man, 'but I actually have a rare pulses allergy.'

And I moved across to the corner of the room, where I posi-tioned myself beside a bookcase and pretended to be interested in someone's CD collection. It seemed to consist almost entirely of broken-cased albums by Mike Oldfield and Level 42, and something called *Songs of Joy*, which said Copyright Neasden Girls Grammar School on the back and had a black-and-white picture of some schoolgirls on the front. *I don't know anyone in this flat*, I thought. *I don't know anyone in this entire part of London.* I felt quite dizzy again, as if I'd just plunged off a diving board into a huge dark sea.

'Wine?' asked the man called Dom, lurching towards me now from the other side of the piano.

'I'm OK, thanks,' I said, moving away again, and went to find the kitchen. There was no one in there at all, just a coffee machine making a hissing sound, some stacks of empty plastic cups and a lot of washing-up in the sink. I leant against a cupboard and peered at a small maidenhair fern in a pot that was perched on the draining board. It seemed a very serene thing, in the middle of all the noise. I pulled a celery stick out of a mug that said *Slam Dunk 'Em In Here*, and put it in my mouth. It tasted of marijuana.

'Still on your lonesome?' said Dom, appearing in the doorway.

'Well, I'm just standing here, eating some celery.'

Dom remained in the doorway. He looked a little put out. He was wearing a piece of white and blue tasselled fabric around his neck. It looked like a tablecloth.

'So what's your name?' he asked.

'Sybil.'

He considered this for a second. Then he turned and left the room.

After he'd gone I reached out to touch the leaves of the maidenhair fern, the tender green nothingness of them, and thought of a maidenhair fern my grandparents had kept in a blue and white pot at the end of their bath and which seemed to survive the entire length of my childhood; and of another fern that Simon and I had bought once in Homebase and which had lasted about three weeks before crinkling up and dying.

'So, Sybil,' Dom said, returning to the room. 'Do you have the gift of prophesy?'

'I knew you'd ask me that, that's for sure.'

Dom regarded me. He was carrying two opened beer bottles in his right hand. He passed one to me.

'I'm sure I've seen you before,' he said.

'Yes, about five minutes ago.'

'No, before that. I've seen you somewhere else. You work in North Brixton Library.'

He seemed so certain about this that for a moment I thought he might be right. Then I said, 'I don't, actually, I work in Greenwich. In the Prehistoric Institute.'

'Really? A prehistoric institute?'

'You might have seen me there, though,' I conceded. 'In the Library. Because I'm going to poetry-writing classes there.'

'Really?'

'Yes. We're writing odes at the moment,' I said, taking a swig of beer. 'To found objects. Things like salt cellars and pepper pots.'

Dom peered at me.

'Salt cellars and pepper pots?'

'Yes.'

'Is a salt cellar a found object, exactly?'

'Ah, well, you might have a point there,' I said. 'Because something's only "found" if someone finds it, isn't it? Or if they'd thought it was lost. So if it's not *found*, as such, does that make it somehow . . . I mean, does that make it . . .' – but my head was swimming now, and I felt suddenly dog-tired, so I stopped talking.

'So what brings you to the party?' Dom asked after a moment, deciding not to pursue that particular line of enquiry. 'Who do you know here?'

'I don't actually know anyone,' I said, taking another swig of beer. 'I only know the person who invited me. But he seems not to have turned up.'

'So I suppose that makes *you* a found object! *You've* been found *by me*!'

'Hmm . . .' I was not entirely sure I liked being called an object. Or that my existence had somehow been conjured up by a man meeting me at a party. But it was true that the only people I even vaguely knew in that part of London were some old friends of my parents, Clive and Wendy Wedderburn. I remembered that my mother and I had gone round to their house in Colliers Wood once when I was small, and eaten cheese and crackers on wicker chairs in their back garden, and we'd played a card game called *Kan-U-Go*, kan-u-go with a k, and the weather had been so warm that the Brie had melted all over the cheeseboard.

'My parents have friends who live round here,' I said.

And I pictured myself going round to the Wedderburns' when I left the party, ringing their Westminster Chimes doorbell, and asking if I could stay in their guest room for a while, the bedspread clean and white, the curtains drawn against the darkness.

'So what do you do,' Dom persisted, 'in the prehistoric institute?

'I put rocks in boxes,' I said.

Dom did not reply. I wondered if I might have become drunk, without realising it.

'What I'm doing at the moment, mostly,' I added in a more serious tone, trying to prevent normality and politeness slipping away from me entirely, 'is, I'm cataloguing artefacts. Also I'm working on the index of a book my boss wrote, about ancient trade routes. So I suppose at the moment I'm mainly an indexer.'

'You're *mainly* an indexer? Isn't that what you're supposed to be?'

'Does anyone know what they're supposed to be?' I said. 'Do you know what *you're* supposed to be?'

'Last time I checked I was a senior support worker at Haringey Council,' Dom said, a little rattled. 'What did you do to your arm, by the way?' he added, peering with a look of sudden

97

concern at a reddish mark on my wrist; I'd burnt myself on a hot glue gun a couple of weeks earlier while archiving prints. (Raglan had wandered into the room, uttered *How goes it with the Winchelsea pages?* and I'd jumped like a scalded cat.)

'Ah, well, that's the mark of an indexer,' I said. 'Didn't you know? We're all branded.' I snapped another celery stick in half and put it in my mouth.

Dom looked slightly appalled now. He glanced up at the other, more alarming scar on my forehead – my battle-scar – and seemed to compute something.

'So, I'm going to get a top-up,' he said, despite the fact that he was drinking from a bottle, and he turned and left the room.

I remained behind, eating celery. I thought: *I don't even care.*

I stayed at the party longer than I'd intended. Somehow I could not work up the energy to leave. In the early hours of the morning somebody started playing Van Morrison songs in the living room, and I'd never liked Van Morrison much, despite everyone telling me I should. I'd never even liked 'Brown Eyed Girl', despite having brown eyes.

The woman in the Bacofoil dress came into the kitchen shortly after one in the morning, grabbed a tea cloth and pulled a tray of charred-looking garlic bread out of the oven.

'Like one?' she said.

'No, thanks,' I replied, 'they look like lumps of coal.'

She regarded me. Sometimes, that spring, my own rudeness could take even me by surprise.

The room I found myself in after that appeared to be someone's bedroom. It was deserted apart from a black cat sitting on a windowsill, gazing out at the falling snow and the moon – a huge, completely full moon, I realised, as I walked across the room to look out – a supermoon, perhaps – the kind that my grandfather had used to look up at, proclaiming, '*It's a braw bricht, moonlicht nicht the nicht*', despite hailing from Bermondsey.

'Hi,' I whispered to the cat, and I put my arms around it. Its breath smelt of cat biscuits and its fur smelt of marijuana.

I left, finally, just after two thirty, with a marine biologist called Neil. We'd talked for a while about books: Neil told me he was reading *The Hitchhiker's Guide to the Galaxy* for the fourth time, and I told him I was reading a book I'd borrowed from the library, called *Roy G. Biv and the Physics of Light*.

'Cool,' Neil said. 'I like a woman who's into science.'

'So do you dislike a woman who's not into science?'

'Ha ha ha!' said Neil. And without further conversation, we got our coats. Neil had a big yellow waterproof jacket, the kind that a trawlerman might wear in a Force 9 gale, and I had the terrible ill-fitting raincoat I'd bought in the People's Dispensary for Sick Animals – a poor substitute for the black velvet coat I'd so rashly given away – and we headed out into the darkness and the silently falling snow.

'So, do you know why horses quite often die of colic?' Neil asked after a moment, apropos of nothing, as we trudged along.

'No, I don't,' I said.

'It's because they're completely un-evolved. Their stomachs are very basic. And the reason for that is because Early Man tamed them and put saddles on them, so they never had the chance to interbreed in the wild and filter out their own dodgy anatomy.'

'Why are you telling me this?' I asked.

'Because you work with Early Man, don't you?'

'In a manner of speaking,' I said. We carried on in silence, along the slushy pavements.

'But what about cows?' I added after a moment.

'What do you mean?'

'Cows have got four stomachs. But they haven't had much chance to interbreed in the wild, either. And they don't die of colic. Not as far as I know.'

'Well, I hadn't considered that.'

'I thought I saw a cow in a field today,' I added. 'But it actually turned out to be an upturned bath.'

'OK,' said Neil.

And after we'd been walking along a little while longer, he suddenly put his arm around my shoulders and turned my face towards his for a kiss, as if this was the best way to prevent any further conversation, about cows or anything else. But I moved away because I didn't want to be kissed by a strange man, or have his arm around me, and I didn't want to end up in his bed in the small hours of the morning. It was much too soon and too sad. Also, I realised, we were at that precise moment walking right past the gates of the London Museums Interpretation Centre: I could see the shape of it looming smug and malevolent in the half-light.

'I hate that building,' I observed.

'Wow! How can you hate a building?'

'Quite easily. If you hate someone who works there.'

'Do you hate someone who works in there? Really? How come?'

'Actually,' I said, 'I think I'd better not say.'

We stopped talking and continued on in silence. I put my hands in my pockets and looked down at my boots, which seemed to be propelling me along the pavement without me even asking them to. From the branches of an old tree, a bird began singing. I presumed this was the start of the dawn chorus – something I'd been hearing a lot lately, lying awake in the small hours.

'Blackbird,' I said.

'Sorry?'

'Blackbird,' I said again.

I looked at my watch. It was not quite three. *Make or break hour*, I'd once heard someone call it, the time when someone, lying awake in the small hours, decides whether to give up the ghost or to carry on. Or reaches some momentous decision about something – whether to betray someone, for instance, or to settle for a kinder, more principled life.

'What day is it?' I asked.

'Sunday.' He sounded a little depressed.

'Oh God, Sunday, already!' I said. 'And then it's Monday. And then it's the rest of the week all over again!'

'Yes.' Neil sighed. He looked pale in the moonlight, I thought, glancing across at him. Almost pale green. *And I'll have to go to work again tomorrow*, I thought. *I'll have to get up and go to work and carry on with those bloody page references, and—*

—and that was when I saw it.

There are sometimes advantages (it occurred to me later) to looking down. Archaeologists do it all the time, of course. I wasn't looking up at the stars anyway, that was for sure, or even at the moon, or the birds singing in the trees; I hadn't been lifting my eyes to the hills from whence was supposed to come my salvation. I was just looking down at my boots and, beyond them, at a stretch of low wall a few hundred yards away from the Interpretation Centre. And I suppose that was the only reason I paid it any attention.

It was a small china cup, glinting whitely in the moonlight, and perched in a gap between two bricks in the wall. It was really quite an incongruous sight, sitting there: it looked as if it should have been sitting on a table in some café or in someone's living room, not perched on a wall in the snow. 'Oh, look!' I said, and I went over and picked it up.

'What are you doing?' I heard Neil enquire behind me, but I didn't reply. I stood, and turned the cup round in my hands. It was a very ordinary little teacup. Not especially old: late Victorian, maybe. There was a small chip in the rim, as if it had perhaps been knocked against a tap while being washed – like half the cups I shared with Esther in our flat. But it was otherwise intact. On one side of it was a picture of a bouquet of flowers, and on the opposite side were four printed words: *The cup that cheers.* Which seemed such an optimistic little state-ment that it did actually make me feel quite cheerful. I turned it upside down, an inch of snow sliding from it like sorbet, and saw that on the underside of it, someone had written their own sentence: *My cup – don't nick it!* they'd advised, quite neatly, with a fine black marker.

I looked over my shoulder. 'It says—' I began.

But Neil had given up on me; he'd already gone.

I walked home with it in my pocket, anyway. Nicked it, despite its instructions. I slipped it into my big coat pocket and carried on walking, virtually halfway across south London by the time I arrived back home, around five, just as the sky was growing light. I suppose a more normal person would have put it back on the wall where they'd found it, and hailed a cab. But I don't think I was a very normal person, that spring. I'm not sure I was all that normal at all any more.

4

Helen had not been present at my job interview the previous year, of course. If she had been I'd have run a mile. The meeting was conducted by Raglan and Professor Muir. And although I'd still been quite ignorant, at the time, of people's capacity for dislike, it had struck me that Professor Muir and Raglan did not seem to like each other much.

'So, Miss Wiseman . . .' Professor Muir had said in a finishing-up kind of way about six minutes in, 'I wonder if you could suggest any techniques you'd use when handling finds? Any procedures to adopt, or things to bear in mind?'

He glanced down at the desk between us, on which someone – Jane, I discovered later – had arranged a pair of white cotton gloves, a magnifying glass and a large piece of quartz.

'Hmm . . .' I said. I hadn't known what to make of that quartz at all.

'Anything occur to you?' He glanced briefly across at Raglan. But Raglan appeared to have zoned out, and was staring vacantly through the window at the sky.

I looked back at the quartz and the gloves. I was suddenly reminded of a game I'd used to play once at Brownies: '*Go!*' Brown Owl would yell, clutching a stopwatch; and six competing Brownies would each dress up as quickly as they could in dozens of layers – shirt, jumper, jacket, coat, scarf – don a pair of thick woollen mittens and cut up a chocolate bar with a knife and fork. It had always struck me as the most pointless waste of time.

'Well . . . one thing you should do,' I said now, 'is: *always wear protective gloves.*'

'Hah! Really?' Professor Muir asked, his voice coming out in a sudden little bellow. 'Even if you're just handling an old rock? Which, to be honest, is all some finds are! Aren't they, Professor Beveridge?'

Raglan did not reply.

'I mean, even that piece of quartz, rather splendid as it is, is hardly rare! Hardly something to get worked up about, on purely aesthetic grounds! Or stage some ridiculous son-et-lumière number about!'

'No . . .' I agreed, startled. 'What I meant . . .' I said, 'is, I know curators wear gloves to handle old texts . . .' – I glanced across at Raglan again, but he was still staring out of the window, apparently lost in thought. '. . . so, I presume,' I continued, looking back at Professor Muir, 'that people who work in a . . . in an archaeology institute should wear gloves, too, when they're . . .'

'Hah! In case they cause more damage to an object than time itself!' Professor Muir burst out, scribbling down a note. 'Or fail to notice its potential as something to flog in the gift shop!'

Then Raglan had finally dragged his gaze away from the view of Greenwich Park, leaned forward and begun to speak in a rather low, fast voice.

'Of course, the conservation and study of ancient artefacts is what we're all about at the Institute, Miss Wiseman,' he said.

'And Professor Muir is quite right: because a rock is just a rock. Even if it's a rather beautiful example, like this piece of quartz . . .'

There was a pause. Briefly, Raglan closed his eyes, then opened them again.

'However, we also have to move with the times, and think about our funding streams, and the people who come to visit us. The "visitor experience". And RIPS is no exception. Museums were once all about labelling objects and sticking them in cases, whereas now we're moving into an age of interactive experiences and tie-in marketing and touch-screen information . . .'

Professor Muir snorted.

Raglan threw him a look. He picked up his coffee cup, took a sip, spilled some down his jumper and put the cup down again.

'Some people, of course,' Professor Muir said, 'might use the term "dumbing down". Or even "selling out".'

'Yes, and some people,' Raglan countered, 'might use the term "adapt or die".'

'Hmm . . .' I said, my hands clenched into sweaty fists in my lap. I felt I was intruding on a conversation that should probably have been held between the two of them, behind a door.

'So,' Raglan continued after a moment, a little more brightly, 'I noticed, in your application, that you studied classical mythology?' He picked up the form I'd filled in, and looked across at me.

'Yes, Classical Literature is really more my . . . specialism . . .' I said warily, 'than archaeology per se. I mean, when I was at university, I—'

But then I noticed a peculiar expression on Raglan's face – a strange, wistful half-smile – and I was so disconcerted by this that I stopped talking.

'So do you think, in that case, you might be interested in the more . . . *word-based tasks* we have to deal with?' he said.

I felt alert to something, some little inkling of trouble ahead. 'What do you mean, exactly?'

'Because sometimes there's an element of editing work with this job. With our own publications. For instance: at the moment, we're looking for someone who can help produce some visitor information sheets for us. Aren't we, Jeremy?'

Professor Muir appeared to find this sentence not worthy of comment.

'And we're also hoping the successful candidate will be able to undertake some proof checking on a book I've been working on recently.'

I looked at him. The job description, when I'd seen it in *The Guardian*'s recruitment pages, had not mentioned books. 'Well, I'd certainly make sure I got my facts straight if I was checking proofs!' I said. It was fine to be categorical about this, I felt, because it seemed pretty clear that I'd already flunked the interview.

Raglan smiled. 'OK! Good to know. So, anything you'd like to ask *us*, before we conclude?'

'Hmm . . .' I attempted a thoughtful expression. From the corridor outside came the sudden whooshing sound of a vacuum cleaner: it was as if we'd all been transported to the corridors of some motel off the M6. 'Well, let me think . . .' I mused – but I couldn't think straight any more; the only question I could imagine asking was: 'Yes, Professor Beveridge, why does your name sound like a cross between a Guernsey sweater and a drink from a vending machine? And what's this strange atmosphere between you and Professor Muir? Why do you annoy each other so much?'

'No, I can't think of anything at the moment,' I said. 'But I'm sure something will occur to me as soon as I've left the room!'

'Ha, ha! As is always the case!' Professor Muir interjected gallantly. 'But now, alas, I hear the wheels of Time's Winged Chariot fast approaching.'

I looked at him.

'Sorry?'

' "But at my back I always hear Time's Winged Chariot hurrying near",' he explained.

'Oh.'

Then none of us seemed to know what to do, so we all stood up and moved towards the door.

'Well, it was nice to meet you, Miss Wiseman,' Raglan said in the doorway, as if the three of us had all just been chatting at a drinks party. 'Do you have far to go?'

'Sorry?'

'A long return journey?'

'Not really. I just live in Clapham. Near the station.'

He seemed suddenly livelier than he had been for the whole interview.

'A friend of mine used to live in Clapham. Near Clapham Junction,' he said.

'Did they?'

'Yes. He lived in terrible old student digs at the time, just off the Clapham Road. Just down from The Swan pub.'

'Really?'

'We used to go there a lot . . . The Swan. For *the craic*,' he added, in a very un-Irish accent. 'And because it was warmer and generally less dismal than his flat.'

'Well,' I said. 'I've never actually been there myself. I've only ever walked past it. But I've heard it's pretty . . . you know, *Irish*. I think they have Irish theme nights there on Fridays.'

Then I nodded goodbye, picked up my bag and legged it to the door. Because it was clear to me, even then, that the Institute was a strange place full of odd people who arranged tableaux involving lumps of quartz, and droned on about Time's Winged Chariot and reminisced about the pubs they used to go to with their old friends. I was pretty convinced I hadn't made a great impression either; I couldn't imagine Raglan wanting me to work there based on that performance. The weirdness of the interview actually made me smile as I took the lift down – all the way back to Reception, past Jane Beauchamp, sitting there behind the desk like the Keeper at the Gates of the Year. I zoomed past the great opposing marble busts of Sir Arthur Evans on one side of the hall and Heinrich Schliemann on the other, through the Institute's noble wooden doors and into the park. Beautiful, beautiful Greenwich Park in autumn, before everything changed. *Bye, then*, I thought, *I won't be back here in a hurry.* Then the next morning the phone rang, and it was Raglan, saying how delighted he was to offer me the job.

I took the little teacup I'd found to work on Monday. Its presence in my pocket made me feel happier, for some reason. *The cup that cheers.* It seemed a sentiment worth holding on to. Also, I just liked it: it was nice to look at, chipped or not, and it was mine, despite what someone had written on it in marker pen. I hopped up the front steps with it and into the lift, and when I arrived on the fifth floor I took it out of my pocket and placed it on my desk, beside my pen-tidy: I thought I could at least keep paperclips in it, even if it didn't inspire any poetry.

'So I've finally found an object,' I said to Jane when she came up to my room a few minutes later.

'Oh, yes?'

'Yes. Look: here, on my desk. I'm hoping it might inspire a poem for my class on Friday.'

'Really?' She glanced at the cup sitting there, and then at all the other strange things on my desk, all the lumps of rock and bits of amber and small fossilised bones gathered around like strange pets. She walked over to my desk, and picked it up. '"The cup that cheers",' she read out. She looked over at me. 'Old-fashioned phrase. Quite old school.'

'I know,' I said. 'That's why I took it. It's part of its *foundness*.'

There was a pause. Jane tipped the cup over, and read the words underneath. 'Even though it says, "My cup, don't nick it"? Or did you write that?'

'No. Also, I didn't nick it exactly . . .' I said. Though now I wondered if that was precisely what I'd done. Maybe I'd nicked someone's precious possession: the thirty-sixth piece from a thirty-six-piece tea-set. Maybe some old lady had wandered out into Colliers Wood in her slippers in the middle of the night and put it absent-mindedly down on the wall, and now she was wondering where the hell it was. 'Anyway,' I said, 'it's not as if the archaeologists don't pick up the finds they come across, is it? And interpret stuff about them.'

'True . . .'

'I mean, maybe it's rubbing off on me, all this analysing of artefacts. And cataloguing bits of pottery. Also, I suppose I was a bit drunk when I first noticed it,' I confessed, now. 'I was on my way back from that party Graham invited me to, only he never showed up, and I was . . . I mean, by the end of the night I'd probably had a couple of drinks too many. And then I just saw it . . .'

'Yes . . .' Jane rotated the cup, reading out the words again. ' "Mine . . . don't nick . . ." '

'It just spoke to me, Jane,' I said, feeling myself blush. 'The way some things just *do*. Like a pebble, on the beach. Like some big grey pebble or something. I mean, some things are just waiting to be claimed, don't you think, by their rightful owner?'

I stopped talking and peered miserably out of the window. Helen was standing out there, I realised, with a little start of dismay. She was out there, in the car park, in her sexy trench-coat, talking to Raglan – newly returned, I presumed, from his keynote Minoan goddess speech in Crete. But what was she talking about? I wondered, my heart continuing its strange, unhappy somersault. About her dubious Beaker People theory? Or her conquest of my boyfriend? Whom *she'd* thought rightfully *hers*, in some way. I noticed, as she talked, that Raglan had a strange, sorrowful look on his face again. He also looked completely exhausted. Now, to my surprise, I saw Helen put her hand out and briefly touch his arm, as if she was perhaps comforting him about something. Or possibly – it suddenly occurred to me – *leading him on*. It felt vaguely horrifying. I looked back into the room.

'So anyway, I just liked it,' I concluded briskly.

'What?'

'The cup.'

'Oh.' Jane sighed. 'Well, I suppose some things *do* speak to you sometimes, don't they? A friend of mine was telling me the other day that he sometimes speaks to his cricket bat.'

'Does he?'

'Yes. If he ever gets bowled out, he gives it a good talking-to. He tells it not to let him down again.'

'But isn't that . . .' I said tentatively, 'a case of him talking to his cricket bat, more than the bat talking to . . .'

'Then I suppose there's what Raglan was saying in his talk last Friday,' she went on. 'He was talking about signs and symbols.'

'Signs and symbols?' I asked, glancing outside again. But Raglan and Helen had disappeared.

'Yes. He was talking about certain things taking on this sort of . . . significance. Because prehistory can't talk to us in the way history can, of course. It's all conjecture, isn't it, really? So the things have to speak to us themselves. I suppose he's quite into all that though, isn't he? He's quite alternative, really, in his own way. Quite yogic.'

'Yogic?'

'Yes.'

Picking up a stapler from the top of the filing cabinet, she moved rather abruptly towards the door. 'Oh well. See you later.'

'Yes,' I said. 'See you . . .' Then I just sat, in front of my little chipped find, and my empty coffee mug. Which was actually one of Helen's trial-run beakers: one of her £9.99 ones. It occurred to me, as Jane stepped into the lift and the doors closed behind her, that nearly all our mugs at work seemed to have been replaced by Helen's *Beakerware.*

> Office morning
> Where are the paper clips? (6)
> Also (2)
> Where is the hole punch? (5)
> 13 syllables

I spent the first hour that morning cataloguing some belemnites that a marine invertebrate specialist had left for me in the accessions box. I wrote directly onto the underside of them – just as the owner of my little teacup had done. I wrote like a vandal, with black India ink.

    Belemnitida, Jurassic
    Dorset (L.C.)
    K. Catto
    Acc: 4/2011

The L.C. stood for Lulworth Cove; K. Catto was Ken Catto, one of RIPS' palaeontologists; Acc: 4/2011 explained the month and year he'd found them. In the accompanying fossils database on my computer, I typed:

Location:	Royal Institute of Prehistorical Studies, London
Genus	Belemnitida
Common name	Belemnite
Period	Jurassic
Rock Unit	Bridport Sand

Once, in the days before RIPS, I had not known what a *Rock Unit* was. I might have thought it was a group of roadies touring with a heavy metal band. Or maybe some sort of trendy baby's cot. Now I knew better. Now I knew it referred to a broad swathe of sedimentary or igneous mud.

There were always a lot of emails on Mondays. Some new ones arrived in my in-box as I was rummaging in my drawer for a packet of Werther's Originals that I'd remembered stashing there the previous week. **Newsflash!** the first message was titled. For a second, guiltily, I wondered if it might somehow relate to my theft of the little teacup. But then I saw that it was in fact a missive from Helen.

'Look what turned up in the paper at the weekend!' she'd written to All-Staff@RIPS.org, and she'd stuck beneath this a paragraph from *The Daily Telegraph*:

'Last year a British archaeology team working with the Royal Institute of Prehistorical Studies uncovered a number of ancient Beaker pottery fragments containing remnants of burnt wheat husks originating in Southern Italy. While at first an apparently unremarkable find, data analysis of this particular wheat variety – known as *turanicum wheat* – now suggests that the Beaker People may have established more extensive trade routes across Central and Southern Europe than previously thought. Dr Helen Hansen, team leader – has called it "a massive thrill – the kind of discovery archaeologists usually only dream of". Meanwhile, Professor Raglan Beveridge, Director of RIPS, has labelled it "an extraordinary discovery".'

Extraordinary discovery, I wrote in my notebook, dropping the last remaining Werther's Original into my mouth. *Massive thrill*. Then I looked at the other emails that had arrived. Raglan himself had sent one early that morning – most probably, I imagined, while still eating porridge at his kitchen table. He had entitled it 'Weed-Out Wednesday':

'Following a recent suggestion from Helen Hansen, Chair of Trustees, about local area workspaces,' he'd written, 'please note that next Wednesday 13th April has been officially declared "Weed-Out Wednesday".'

I sat and regarded this. It took my brain a few seconds to process, and even then I couldn't work out what a local area workspace was. It did not seem a term that Raglan would be familiar with, either. I wondered what the boundaries of *my* local area workspace were, when they included a plans table and a guillotine, and shelves full of belemnites and broken pottery, my work sitting around me in stacks of A4, or blinking accusatorily at me from the screen. 'Tidy your desk' was what Raglan meant; it could have been summed up in three words. It was funny, because the previous email he'd sent round had been about the imminent expansion of the gallery shop, to accommodate its *increased range of merchandise* – Helen's Beakerware, as far as I could see – an event which was actually going to introduce *more* clutter, and would also mean some of RIPS' exhibits would have to be kept off-site, in a secure museum storage unit in Barnet.

'Yes, and of course it's debatable whether Schliemann actually *was* working on that assumption!' I heard Raglan himself proclaiming in the corridor outside, and I returned to the other messages in my in-box. The next one was from someone I hadn't come across before: Clive-the-detectorist@aol.com.

To: Sybil.wiseman@rips.org.uk

Dear Ms. Wiseman,
Re. Roman ballisters
I have recently found what appears to be a set of Roman ballisters in a small wooded area at the end of my garden. I wondered if these might be of interest to one of your colleagues at the Institute? If so, I—

I did not have the strength to read this further, so I clicked onto the next message. It was from John in the Reprographics department. He had typed it on Friday afternoon, hunkered down in his converted ice house on the other side of the Institute's grounds.

To: Sybil.wiseman@rips.org.uk
Re: HISTORY OF TRADE

Sybil – please confirm asap that HoT will be ready to go to print on 9th April as stated in your last email. We are holding a place for it in the schedule but need confirmation.

John

I didn't know what to think about that, either. Emails from Repro John (as some people called him) always struck the fear of God into me; I felt powerless when his queries came in, as if all my strength had suddenly deserted me. I decided to ignore this one too for the time being, and turned to the last email in the list. This was from someone called DrAppalsawmy@cam.ac.uk, who seemed a nicer man already than either John or Clive-the-detectorist with his annoying Roman cannonballs.

Dear Ms Wiseman,
Re: Research for an academic publication

I'm currently researching a book called *Origins* (to be published next year) and wondered if you might hold information on Peter Edwards' work on the Minoan people, and specifically, the terracotta goddesses he found on his last dig at Knossos. If you were able to track down any research documents relating to this, and any relatively recent photographs, I should be most grateful. The usual permissions etc. will be sought. With all good wishes, Dr Aziz Appalsawmy.

This would be easy enough to investigate, I suspected, terra-cotta goddesses from Knossos being pretty specific. Also, I knew the Institute kept a file on Peter Edwards' final research project upstairs, in the Archives. I'd never seen it, but I knew of its existence. It was only six months, after all, since he'd filed his last report.

Dear Dr Appalsawmy, I wrote, rattling the toffee around my mouth, I am sure this information is in our files. I should be able to send something to you by the end of the week. Best wishes, Sybil Wiseman.

Then I looked back at the request from John. This required a more abrupt tone, I felt – abrupt sometimes being interpreted as efficient.

Hi John! I typed, fast – mis-typing as I went and having to go back over my mistakes – Yes, the re-indexed proofs will be ready as scheduled. *Please note, however, that all kinds of catastrophes might happen in the interim*, I felt like adding, as a sort of disclaimer. *I mean, we could all be dead by then! Or cast aside by our lovers!* But he was a serious man, John, and the last time I'd gone round to talk to him he'd looked at me with eyes as bleak and fathomless as a well.

Dear Simon, I began next, unable to resist a sudden impulse to contact him, to ask him why: *why did you let Helen Hansen come crashing into our lives?* Then I deleted this, discarded the whole email and returned to my in-box. Dear Clive – Thank you for—

Then I got up from my desk and looked out through the window, as recommended by the optician.

I spent around ten minutes after that finishing a fun work-sheet for Professor Muir. It seemed a more fun thing than Professor Muir himself.

Dinosaur Mix-Up!

Hidden in this jumble of words are the names of eight
dinosaur species! Can you find them all?

```
IBRONTOSAURUS OTATEIKWNTYSTEGASAURUS
YMQTYASRTRICERATOPSJBBSHHE RATYR
ANNOSAURUSREXA PNEROHMYGODMEGALOD
ONNRDOPUSMENYY YYYVELOCERAPTORP
HPTERODACTYLIM DIPLODOCUSBXZAPATOS
AURUSIGHGHGJSSIDHDEJTPSOQWERTYMDNOKL
```

Then I spent the next hour trying to focus on the new Winchelsea
section in Raglan's book. Helen had certainly written a lot of
very boring sentences about Winchelsea. Her writing style was
just the same as it had been when she was my tutor at
university:

It is highly likely (at time of writing) that the turanicum
wheat fragments found at Winchelsea will build up an even
more complex trading picture of the people who lived in this
small Sussex-based community. The carbon-data readings
carried out on the fragments cast an intriguing new light on
the trading reach of some of Ancient Europe's most enig-
matic peoples. Perhaps it is not too far-fetched to suppose —

But I didn't care what it was not too far-fetched to suppose. I
glanced over at the little teacup, sitting there beside my coffee
beaker. I felt slightly sick. Shortly before one I stood up again
and went out for some fresh air: I took the lift down to Reception
and went outside, into the airy green of the park. Looking
upwards as I walked across the grass, I saw some tiny black
birds – swifts perhaps, or swallows newly arrived from Africa.
They were wheeling and whirling high up in the sky. *That's
early for them to be here already*, I thought – then I realised that

they weren't birds at all, they were just the little black dots that appeared sometimes in front of my eyes when I'd been staring at the screen for too long. The *visual auras* the optician had warned me about. The normal functioning of my optic nerve did appear to be under some kind of strain.

Whenever I went to the park I always tried to find a bench that my grandparents and I had used to sit on when I went there with them. It had a brass plaque on it saying *I wish I was facing the view*, which had always made us laugh. I'd never been able to find it again, though. Recently I'd begun to wonder if it might have been a complete figment of my imagination. I sat down instead on a bench opposite the Institute's sundial. This had been placed there by some Victorian dignitary in 1872, a few years after the Institute was built. A motto engraved on the sundial's face said:

LET OTHERS TELL OF RAIN AND SHOWERS
I ONLY TELL THE SUNLIT HOURS

Which I always thought was quite funny, too. Especially as it was nearly always raining.

My lunch that day was a pot of mandarin yogurt and two dry ends of a Hovis loaf, inverted and stuck together with peanut butter. I'd forgotten to go shopping the previous evening, so that was what I'd resorted to. 'That's the worst looking lunch I have ever seen!' Esther had remarked in the kitchen that morning, as I was packing it. 'Why don't you treat yourself sometimes, Sybil, and go to bloody Prêt?'

'Because I like sitting in the park with my sandwich. Because *I vont to be alone*,' I'd replied. Which was meant to be a joke, but had just ended up sounding true. The sandwiches had also become rather squashed, as I still hadn't retrieved my lunch box from my canvas tote bag, where Jane had left it for me the previous Friday: I just hadn't had the strength to confront that annoying *Past is the Future* logo swinging there so triumphantly when I opened the coat cupboard door.

A light rain began to fall as I ate. I looked at my watch and wondered where Simon was, and what he was eating for lunch and whether he was missing me in any way. I wondered what on earth it was he'd ever seen in Helen. Apart from the obvious. *Apart from the obvious, Sybil*, as Jane had said. What he had seen in me, I knew, was kindness and sanity. He'd told me that once; that he loved me because I was kind and sane. And now I wasn't even those things. I was the sort of person who stole people's property and tried to write poetry about it. *The face that sank a thousand hearts*, I scribbled down in my notebook. Then I crossed this out. On top of everything else, I was a bad poet. In the middle distance, a small boy with a football fell over and began to cry, and a large woman, lugging several shopping bags and pushing a buggy, went lumbering over to him. A little white terrier appeared in a fenced-off area of grass and began careering around in circles, barking and barking and nosing into people's bags. A second woman, wearing blue jogging bottoms and a fuchsia-pink sweatshirt, appeared in the fenced-off area and started calling out a name. '*Bastard!*' she was calling, '*Bastard, come here!*'

The-bar-king-dog, I thought, counting the syllables on my fingers,

Bearing your name/Suits you better than/The dog

Then I realised the woman was not saying *Bastard* at all, she was saying *Buster*.

Hope Pollard thudded past as I was embarking on my yogurt. She was probably on her way to some dendrochronology meeting or other.

'Monarch of all I survey,' she remarked, halting for a moment.

'Sorry?' I said, my yogurt spoon halfway up to my mouth.

'From "The Solitude of Alexander Selkirk".'

'Oh.'

'Who was the inspiration behind *Robinson Crusoe*, of course.'

I never knew quite what to say to Hope Pollard. She was quite a serious person. Though I had recently had a conversation with her about Stonehenge. 'You know, maybe Stonehenge never had anything to do with religion!' I'd said. 'Maybe it was just some huge prehistoric football pitch, for all we know . . .' She'd found *that* observation quite diverting.

'Helen Hansen's looking for you, by the way,' she said now.

'Is she?' I asked, a tiny wave of horror creeping over me.

'She was saying she wants to speak to you about Raglan's book. She seemed quite keen to get hold of you. She's worried about the timings, apparently.'

'Really?'

'Yes. So is John in Reprographics. Worried. I just bumped into him coming out of the ice house, and he said he and Helen were talking about it.'

I returned the spoon to my yogurt.

'That's quite funny, really,' I said. 'Considering Helen's Winchelsea breakthrough's all *about* timings.'

Hope did not speak for a moment. Then she said, 'Oh well. Can't stand here chit-chatting all day. People to see, trees to date. Maybe you should go and track her down, though.'

And she continued on down the path, in the direction of Greenwich High Street and the Cutty Sark, sitting landlocked in its dock. I sat for a while with my empty yogurt pot and teaspoon, trying not to think about Helen and why she might want to see me about *timings*. One of the things I had discovered at my desk that morning was that the correct timing of various Mediterranean grain harvests had been absolutely critical to the continuing existence of early European Beaker communities; also that, in Arabic, *amaranth* meant *Love Lies Bleeding* because of the way its bright red flowers spread so dramatically across the ground at certain times of year. As if some terrible spring-time crime of passion had been committed.

The sky, after a while, began to turn a pale, cloud-scudding grey. Perched on the top plinth of the sundial was a child's pink hair-bobble. I did not feel the need to note any of this down. Equally, I saw no need to go looking for Helen, as Hope had suggested. If Helen wanted to see me she could bloody well come and find me herself.

> Where did you go?
> And why did you go?
> The sky, endless,
> Will not answer my questions

Straight after lunch that afternoon I had to take a case of ancient ceremonial pipes across town to the British Museum. Raglan was lending them for a display on the early use of tobacco. He couldn't take the case round himself (he'd informed me on my answer-phone while I was out in the park) because he was *unfortunately in meetings all afternoon*. So he'd left them for me to pick up. They were behind the desk in the Comparative Zoology Gallery. *I hope they're not too heavy,* he'd added, in his message. They were, though: even ceremonial pipes weigh heavy when you're carrying them in large numbers.

'Another load for you to carry, sweetheart?' Danny the gallery attendant asked when I headed down for them in the lift shortly after two.

'I know,' I said. 'Just call me the Stretch Monster!'

He looked at me. 'Sorry?'

'I mean, I feel as if my arms have stretched while I've been working here,' I said, 'lugging massive rocks around. My . . . ex used to have this doll called the Stretch Monster,' I added, recalling this fact with a sudden rush of sadness. 'His dad brought it back from America when he was little. It was a kind of rubbery green monster. You could stretch its arms. Also its legs. It was fun. You could stretch them to over eight feet.'

'Well . . .' He seemed briefly lost for words. 'That sounds pretty handy,' he said, after a moment. 'You could have used it to go bungee-jumping.'

'We could have done.'

'Or to strap a suitcase to the top of your car!'

'Yes . . .'

'Or to strangle someone you didn't like much, ha ha ha!'

'Yes,' I said, picking up the case and heading out.

The tread of escalator steps
Like silver corduroy

What's with the feathers –
The possession of them:
Thoughts of Icarus

On the escalator at Holborn I put the case of pipes on the step ahead and envisaged it sailing off without me, into the blue yonder. *Sorry*, I would say to Raglan on my return, *they just disappeared. All your precious specimens.* Because they might be anthropologically interesting but they were also just bits of clay. It was like the little teacup I'd found: it had no doubt been worth something to someone, but it was also just part of some tea-set someone had churned out in a factory in Stoke at the turn of the twentieth century. Then in the past year or so someone had gone and scribbled across the bottom of it in marker pen. Meaning it was perhaps only of value to *them* – the person I'd nicked it from. *You can't take it with you*, my grandad had told me once. And he was right, of course. You could only leave it all behind.

*

121

'What have you got for us this time?' the security guard asked, when I arrived at the museum's little entrance table; he was used to my escapes from RIPS with cases full of fragments.

'Just a few ceremonial pipes today,' I said, casually, as if this was a perfectly normal sentence. I heaved the case up onto the table. 'I'm handing them in to Displays. For that exhibition you're doing, on tobacco smoking.'

But he wasn't really listening: he'd already opened up the case and was examining the pipes, cradled in their polystyrene compartments. He lifted one out and turned it round as if he was imagining smoking it. He held it delicately at its edges.

'Well, they all look shipshape and Bristol fashion,' he said.

'That's funny,' I said. 'Because these ones were actually imported *into* Bristol in the nineteenth century.'

'Really? Well, you learn something new every day.'

He put the pipe back and snapped the case lid shut.

'I found a little teacup myself the other day,' I added, for the hell of it. 'A little Victorian one.'

'On a dig?'

'No, just on a wall. It was just, you know, sitting there. On a wall . . .'

He looked enquiringly at me for a second. Then he said, 'D'you know, when I was a kid, I used to find all these bits of Victorian china in our back garden. All these little fragments.'

He stuck a label onto the case and handed it back to me.

'I thought I was making all these amazing *finds*. All these little blue and white bits. But they were probably just someone's smashed up dinner service, to be honest with you. They were probably my mum's.' He sighed. 'You live and learn.'

Most of the administrative offices were upstairs. I took the lift up, and handed the case over to an assistant in Room 11b (Curatorial and Displays). 'These are the ceremonial pipes for the tobacco exhibition,' I whispered to her, in the half-light of the corridor. 'Brilliant, thanks,' she whispered back. It felt as if the two of us were engaged in some kind of reconnaissance mission, some secret agent scenario requiring code-words. The girl was about the same age as me: the same age and height, and even with the same slightly hollow-looking eyes and worn-down expression. She didn't have an ice-skating injury on her forehead, though: I always felt slightly jealous now, of women my age who didn't have facial scars; it felt somehow like an unfair advantage. 'They're to go with the *On Loan* stuff,' I said. 'I'll come and pick them up when the exhibition ends.' I turned and headed down the corridor again.

Back downstairs I walked through *Ancient Greece and the Arthur I Fleischmann Gallery* – a large room devoid of visitors but containing a lot of Ancient Greek and Minoan artefacts in glass cases. There were strange winged lions and little bearded athletes, and tiny serene-faced cats, and horses with quite comical, cartoonish expressions. There were also, I noticed, with a tiny jolt of recognition, several objects that Peter Edwards had once found. It said so on a sign stuck to the glass.

I felt quite thrilled for a moment at the sight of his name – it was like bumping into a minor celebrity in real life. The finds he'd made were quite beautiful, too. In one case there was a little snake goddess he'd dug up in Knossos in 1988, and in another there was a golden bull's head, and a man leaping over a bull, and also a small terracotta couple sitting together – opposite each other – in a terracotta bath. I stopped for a moment to look at them. There was something very sweet about them, very human, despite the fact that they were thousands of years old and made from terracotta. The bath looked too small for them, like some bedsit bath in Dalston or Palmers Green and they both had to sit upright with their knees bent. It made me think of an evening when Simon and I had sat in the bath together once, in the flat we'd used to share off Clapham High Street. It hadn't actually been a very erotic experience at all – the bath was much too narrow for it to have been anything except funny. We'd sat facing each other bolt upright in the bubbles, laughing. And then I'd got out, wrapped myself in a bath towel, leaned against the side of the bath and washed his hair, dipping my cupped hands into the warm water to rinse the shampoo away. That *had* been erotic: that had been the erotic part of the evening.

I leaned in to blink at the note stuck to the back of the display case.

Excavations are always turning up surprises, but these finds were a particular joy, saying so much, as they do, about the people behind the objects – Peter Edwards

Carrying on through the main hallway, I turned left at the shop and headed towards the café. It was completely deserted now, apart from a middle-aged couple sitting at a table, quite demure and old-fashioned-looking, with two cups of tea and one slice of chocolate cake between them. They reminded me of the terracotta people I'd just been looking at and also, slightly, of the couple from *Brief Encounter*. They seemed perfectly innocent, but maybe they were in the middle of some profound and torrid affair. Perhaps they imagined the British Museum café at 3.30pm on a Thursday was the least likely time and place to be discovered. *Some people are going around leading secretly ecstatic lives*, I thought, sitting down at a table with a cup of tea and a dried-up-looking cheese scone on a side-plate. It was a realisation that came into my head sometimes, at odd moments.

I left the museum shortly before four, heading back through the big hall and down the steps. The sky had grown dark, a purplish-grey that made the streets around me feel quite submerged, the pavement almost subaquatic. Crossing Bloomsbury Street, I saw a man and woman wading blurrily towards me, arm in arm. They looked like an artist's impression of people walking down a street. From a distance, they also looked quite a lot like Raglan and Helen. The man was tall, late middle-aged, with the same tweed suit and upright, striding gait; the woman was younger, glamorous, and her clothes had an expensively thick quality, as if they had been constructed from artfully tailored felt squares. Then I realised they *were* Raglan and Helen. My heart flipped up, like a fish, and down again. There was nowhere to hide, though: no handy doorway to dive into, or tree to disappear behind, so I braced myself and carried on towards them. They were standing on the traffic island now, and Helen was in the middle of a sentence – '. . . honestly feel it would be best, at this juncture, if you . . .' she was proclaiming into the wind and the traffic noise.

'*Hi, Raglan! Hi, Helen!*' I said, feigning gladness as I joined them on the traffic island, and they both whipped round, immediately unlinking arms. 'I thought you were in meetings all afternoon, Raglan!'

'Ah, yes, well. They finished,' Raglan said.

I nodded. I didn't know what to say. The traffic roared. My heart felt wild – a great, un-moored expanse – like an over-filled helium balloon.

'So, I've handed in the clay pipes,' I said, continuing to smile at them: my boss, and my enemy. 'And I gather you were looking for me earlier, Helen?' I went on, hardly able even to look her in the eye.

Helen peered at me.

'I wasn't looking for you, no,' she said. 'What made you think that?'

'Hope told me.'

'Hope?'

'Yes.'

'Ah – it's the green man!' Raglan cut in, his hair blowing upwards in a sudden gust of wind. 'Better scoot, Helen, while we've got the chance. See you back at work, then, Sybil!' And

125

without further utterance the two of them hurried on across the road.

I waited for the next set of lights. Then I ran over to the other side of the road. When I got there, Raglan and Helen had already turned a corner and disappeared from view. *So you are working on him,* I thought. It was clear enough. I wondered for a moment if I should phone Simon to break the bad news: to tell him there was probably, already, another man in Helen's life. But then I thought that I wouldn't. Because it was too late now, and Helen had destroyed any nobler instincts I might once have had. Besides, knowledge was power.

The office was silent for the rest of the afternoon. I couldn't work out where everyone had gone. Even Danny was not in his normal location in the gallery. I was only aware of Hope Pollard when I returned. She was back again and crashing around the Carbon-dating lab; I could see the top of her head through the little half-window. Despite the Danger of Death notice, she was the only sign of life in the whole place. *Marie Celeste,* I wrote in my notebook, on my way up in the goods lift. Then I drew a little picture of it. *Abandon ship,* I wrote beneath. *Abandon hope.* It occurred to me that I'd written virtually nothing else in my notebook all week, apart from

Elephant heart

Hermann's tortoise

Exploded sheep's heart

(which I'd jotted down in the Comparative Zoology Gallery), and

Umbrella

Sundial

Crow

which I'd scribbled down in the park at lunchtime. The little teacup certainly wasn't lending itself to poetry, as I'd imagined it might: it was just sitting up in my office, storing paperclips.

cool birds hush cats

I wrote on the fridge door when I went into the kitchenette, rearranging the magnets on the shiny white surface. Then I returned to my office, sat down at my desk and read something Helen had written about pollen analysis – a crucial part of the Winchelsea Hoard findings, apparently – and something Raglan had written about the kinds of flowers that Neolithic people would have scattered over the graves of their loved ones: *'Analysis reveals evidence not only of hollyhocks and flax,'* he'd written, *'but also of grape hyacinths, cornflowers and roses.'* I supposed it was quite touching that Neolithic people had mourned their dead and known about grape hyacinths – a flower I'd only ever associated with suburban front gardens and city centre roundabouts.

Quick query, I wrote, opening up a new message to Raglan in my email account. *Hi, Raglan – Nice to bump into you and Helen earlier. Just to say, I received a request today from an academic interested in Peter Edwards' last—*

But then I stopped, because it occurred to me that it might upset him to receive quite such a blunt enquiry about his old friend's final research project. It was not the most tactful email in the world. I suspected it might also be sensible to keep a generally low profile anyway, considering I was still nowhere near finishing the index, and both Helen *and* Repro John seemed to be on the warpath now, the publishing deadline being less than a week away.

It was almost five, anyway. A headache was curling itself around my temples: the same old dull ache. I spent the last twenty minutes of the day watching YouTube videos on my computer, the volume turned right down. I watched half an episode of *The Flumps*, then the start of an old *Countdown* show, then I clicked to a 1991 episode of *Murder, She Wrote*. I envied Angela Lansbury: Angela Lansbury, it seemed to me, led a sane and happy life.

On my way out through Reception I paused to retrieve my sandwich box from the coat cupboard. There were a lot more *Past is the Future* tote bags hanging in there now, redundant, like elephants gathering in an elephants' graveyard. The one hanging beside mine was Helen's; I knew this for a fact because it smelt of her perfume – a scent for which I had acquired a quite visceral dislike. Also, her annoying cardigan was in there, smugly folded and a horrible, green-eyed monster green. Averting my gaze, I put out my hands and sifted through the forest of canvas to reach my lunchbox. It was like Narnia in there: maybe, if I pushed on far enough, I'd find myself out in the open air, in some wintry forest. Maybe I'd be whisked off for tea by a faun. I could take my new teacup with me.

5

GREENWICH

We used to go to Crystal Palace,
and walk amongst
the dinosaurs
there was a gorilla statue too.
you took a picture
of me once,
sitting between his arms.

I'd never liked poetry much. I'd liked reading, just not poetry. The book I'd loved most as a child was *The Puffin Joke Book* – a bright pink paperback that my grandparents gave me one Christmas.

Q: How can you tell there's an elephant in the fridge?
A: Footprints in the butter.

Q: How do you fit four elephants in a mini?
A: Two in the front, two in the back

My grandfather had liked those ones. Also: *What's yellow and swings from tree to tree? Marzipan.* Also: *I'd tell you the one about the shark-infested custard but you'd never swallow it.*

I'd always preferred things that had a punchline. Unlike life. Life did not appear to have so many punchlines.

When I was ten or so I'd come across *Tales of Troy and Greece* by Andrew Lang, and *Heroes, Gods and Monsters of the Greek Myths* by Bernard Evslin, and also *D'Aulaires' Book of Greek Myths*, and I'd loved those as well, because Greek myths are pretty funny when you think about it and it was also nice that there were *people* in them – people with names, *doing* things, even if they were strange things, like running around labyrinths looking for minotaurs, or flapping out of high windows with makeshift wings strapped to their arms. I'd loved in particular the story of Patroclus and Achilles, those comrades against the Trojan army, who'd had a centaur for a tutor; and I'd liked Persephone and Penelope and Pandora, and all those other girls who'd had to turn into trees or stones or fountains to get away from some small-minded avenging god. I'd liked Sybil, too – because it was nice to know I wasn't the only Sybil around, and also she'd used to write her thoughts down on oak leaves that kept getting blown away by the wind, and I'd somehow related to that way of going about things.

The value of poetry remained a mystery, though. It was just too serious. There was too much in it that could bring you down. I was sorry now that I hadn't thought about this earlier, when I'd forked out £85 for the poetry classes in North Brixton Library. There was only one occasion when I could recall a poem ever having any real emotional effect on me, and that was because it had made me laugh. It had happened years earlier, when I was still at school. Our English teacher Mrs Beeslack had brought two poems into class that day, two different *treatments* (as she'd called it) on the subjects of Love and Betrayal. (*Because there's a lot of poetry, girls*, she'd said wearily, *about those particular themes.*) And we had all looked at the sheets in front of us. The first one was the love poem by Elizabeth Barrett Browning – that old chestnut that was always turning up on Radio 4 and in overpriced gift books:

How do I love thee? Let me count the ways.I love thee to the depth and breadth and height – etc. etc.

And the other was 'A Poison Tree', by William Blake:

I was angry with my friend/I told my wrath, my wrath did end.

Which had at least seemed a reasonable statement to me. Nobody else had seemed to like that one, though – they'd all looked up at Mrs Beeslack with a collective kind of indifference. Maybe it was because she detected some faint glimmer of interest from me that she'd asked me to read it out. 'So, Sybil, maybe *you* could do the honours?'

'All of it?' I asked, looking up from the desk I shared with Bethany Cowley. 'All the verses?'

'Please, Sybil!'

I looked down at the printout.

'And *while* Sybil's reading, let's all look out for any instances we can find here of *enjambment*,' Mrs Beeslack said, just as I was beginning to breathe out again. ('*Hey! Leg Bingo!*' Bethany whispered beside me.) I faltered and paused, a terrible urge to laugh building up low in my chest. Then, miraculously I controlled myself and began to read:

'"I was angry with my friend,"' I read, woodenly, '"I told my wrath, my wrath did end."' I paused. '"I was angry with my foe: I told it not, my wrath did—"'

'Yes, and I'll just stop you again a moment, Sybil, because another thing to mention,' Mrs Beeslack said, 'is the *theme* here. What can anyone tell me about the theme?'

She looked around, as if someone might be planning to enlighten her. They were not.

'Because it's certainly not *romantic love*, is it?'

Nobody seemed to know. I certainly didn't. But feeling a strange sense of duty – maybe because I was the one who'd been asked to read it out – I'd hazarded a guess. 'I suppose . . .' I said into the silence, 'it's about someone not saying something they ought to be saying . . . you know. It's about being silent, when you should actually *speak*.'

Mrs Beeslack turned to me, her mild floury face a picture of astonishment.

'It's about *being silent*?'

'*I* think so . . .' I said. Then, as if to prove a point, I stopped talking. I couldn't help noticing that Mrs Beeslack had also gone silent herself now. She was just sitting there. She drew breath. Then she said, 'But being silent is not a *theme*, Sybil, it's an *action*. We've already gone over the difference between themes and actions, haven't we?'

'But silence isn't an action either, is it?' I said. 'It's just a *thing*. A state. Anyway,' I muttered, sotto voce, to Bethany, 'I thought poetry was meant to be open to interpretation . . .' I looked down at the page again, as if concentrating hard on the words. But they were all wobbling now, they were going skewiff at the sudden unexpected fun there was to be had in contradicting Mrs Beeslack. I glanced sideways at Bethany, sitting there in her bendy plastic chair. She was sniggering into her hands by this point, because, really, it was pretty funny: the bendy chair, and that weighty old poem, and the atmosphere of incipient insurrection.

Mrs Beeslack had not thought it was funny.

'The prevailing *theme*, in fact, Sybil, for your education and delight, is *Anger*,' she said. 'Not "being silent". *Anger* is the theme here. We need to know things like this, people!' she added, her normally placid voice rising to a sudden, unexpected kind of bellow. 'It's one of Blake's most famous poems! And I'm going to let you in on a little secret: *it's going to be on the GCSE paper this year, and there are going to be TEN QUESTIONS on it*! So interpret your way out of that if you like, Sybil!'

I'd laughed even harder about that, because Mrs Beeslack really seemed to be quite angry herself now. She had been silent, and now she was being angry. Bethany had collected herself by this point, but I couldn't stop. So Mrs Beeslack sent me out of the room, to compose myself, and to *reflect*. I stood there for quite a while in the dank-smelling corridor, beside a greenish area of mould that was invading the doorway of the Modern Studies room, and a poster depicting teenagers in baseball caps, informing pupils to *Wise Up about drugs*. And I reflected for quite a while, until the reason it was so funny was no longer there.

I walked the long way through the park after work the following evening, down the hill, along the narrowly winding leafy paths, past the ice house and the Meridian Line and the old Altazimuth Pavilion. A cold white mist had begun swirling across the grass – it was like the mist that always seemed to hang around the Norfolk mudflats when I went to visit my parents. Or the fog that had used to skulk, beautiful and romantic, around Wandsworth Common when I'd walked there in the autumn with Simon. *Season of mists and mellow fruitlessness*, I thought. Even though it wasn't autumn any more of course – or even winter. There was pale pink blossom beginning to appear on the cherry trees, and a magnolia displaying its blowsy white flowers.

A puppy came bouncing stiff-legged towards me across the grass as I neared the gates, its tongue billowing from one side of its jaws, a big, mad smile on its happy face.

'Piss off, dog,' I said to it, and it went barrelling on, its carefree ears flapping.

Mist haiku 1
Boys in white hoodies
Looming up
Like icebergs

Mist haiku 2
Man on phone
In the whiteness:
I am reaching out to you

Mist haiku 3
Hello there Cutty Sark
Triangular, strange
Dry-docked and full of tea

It was cold again that evening. When I emerged from Stockwell tube station shortly after six, it looked as if it might snow. The whole sky was a pure off-white. It was like walking across a sheet of packing paper. *If your name is Lauren, come in for a free coffee*! urged a sign chalked on the window of a café a couple of streets away from my flat. The owner changed the name on a daily basis. I imagined parties of Laurens, all piling in for fun and free coffees. Once, it had said *Helen* on the window. It had even said *Hector* on one occasion, and also *Penelope*. It was funny, though, because I'd never seen 'Sybil' chalked up there.

I had been planning, that night, to watch *MasterChef*, a plate of cheese and crackers balanced on my lap, but Esther decided, shortly after I got in, that we should go back out again, for dinner. It would do me good, she said, phoning ahead to book a table, because I was looking as if I could do with a good meal. I was looking as thin as a rake these days, like death warmed up; I was looking like all these things it wasn't good to be. She was worried about me, she said. 'It's probably all those awful lunches you're packing for yourself,' she carried on, as she locked the door of the flat behind us shortly before eight, and we headed out again up the steps, into the sleet, 'and you're just sitting out there in the park in all weathers these days like some kind of loony.'

'Thanks, Esther,' I said.

'You're welcome, honey.'

'*Thin as a rake*'s such a funny expression, isn't it?' I added, plodding up to pavement level. 'Because who actually looks like a *rake*?'

She peered at me, the keys making a pretty, metallic sound in her hand.

'It's just an expression, Sybil.'

'Yes, but when you think about it, a lot of these expressions are quite . . .'

'Quite what?'

'Funny. Like *happy as Larry*. I mean, who was Larry? Or *drunk as a skunk*,' I added, suddenly recalling, for some reason, the man I'd met the previous week at the conference dinner, the one who'd made all the origami frogs. 'Because *drunk as a skunk*'s not even to do with metaphor, is it?' I said. 'It's just because it rhymes. And then there's *deaf as a post*, which—'

Esther put the keys in her pocket. 'You don't have to analyse it, Sybil,' she said. 'You're not at work now. Doing your indexing. Or at one of your poetry sessions.'

'No,' I agreed, rearranging my scarf more snugly against the cold.

She paused.

'I suppose one of the things about Simon was, he made really good lunches, didn't he?' she said. 'That was one of the good things about him, wasn't it?'

Esther had decided that we should go to a Thai restaurant she had recently been to with Paul. It was just a few minutes' walk away from the flat and it was great, she said, as we walked towards it along the wet pavements, it was great when she'd gone there with Paul. Fresh ingredients and friendly service. She'd had prawns in batter and Paul had had the chicken satay sticks.

'Well, thanks for introducing me to it,' I said, as we approached the doors, 'this is going be really nice . . .'

Even though I felt that it might not actually be very nice; I felt quite disconcerted after our oddly combative start to the evening, and Esther's mention of Simon and his lunch-making abilities. Which was clearly something else I'd failed to appreciate at the time. I liked Esther: we went back a long way, but sometimes her frankness could have quite a pummelling effect. And the restaurant, I realised, as soon as we walked in, was not going to make me feel any better because it was the sort of place more suited to lovers and first dates. It just made me think how strange it was that I did not see Simon any more, that he was no longer a part of my life, that we might sail straight on through our separate lives, into middle age, into old age, and eventually *die* without ever seeing each other again.

'We've got a booking for Maclehose,' Esther announced, and the waitress smiled and led us across the room to a small, candle-lit table for two. Esther followed the waitress, and I followed Esther, my heart thudding sorrowfully. There was a splashing motorised water feature involving plastic rocks, and a version of 'Let it Be' playing over a small loudspeaker above our heads. We sat down on either side of a white orchid in a vase and looked at the menu, and I felt pretty flat – not like a rake so much as a single sheet of paper or finely beaten metal.

'So how was that party the other night?' Esther asked after we'd ordered and the waitress had brought over our drinks and a little plate of complimentary snacks.

'Well, it was OK,' I said, pronging a small piece of battered tofu with a cocktail stick and putting it in my mouth. 'Only it turned out,' I added, 'that it was just round the corner from the London Museums Interpretation Centre. You know, where my nemesis works . . .'

'Your nemesis?'

'I mean Helen,' I explained, swallowing.

'Yes, I know you mean Helen,' Esther said. She frowned, picked up her glass of wine, took a sip and put the glass down again.

'Sybil,' she said.

I looked at her.

'What?'

She sighed, plucked a piece of carved, flower-shaped carrot from the plate between us, put it into her mouth, and began to chew.

'The thing is, you need to stop obsessing about her,' she said after a moment.

'What do you mean?'

'I mean, you're not behaving normally. You keep talking about her. You talk about her all the time. You're obsessing.'

'I'm not obsessing, I'm just upset about what she did,' I said. 'About the fact that she stole my boyfriend. And also, it turns out, half my old Beaker People ideas. And now on top of everything else I have to index her stupid writing!'

'Well, you need to stop being upset, then!' Esther said. She picked up a piece of battered yam, and crunched into it.

'I mean, how long's it been now?'

'How long's what been?'

'Since you and Simon split up.'

'Two and a half months.'

'That's not very long, I suppose...' she conceded. 'And I suppose it was pretty bad timing, coming so soon after your grandad died. Because I know you were quite cut up about him and all. I know he meant a lot to you. But, still: it is *two and a half months*...' She sighed again, and looked rather crossly down at the menu sitting in front of her. 'Pad Kapow,' she read out, 'Pad Lad, Pad Stay, Pad Wan, Pad Prik... they sound quite funny, don't they?' she said, looking across at me.

'They do,' I agreed. *They look like an account of my relationship with Simon*, I almost added, but decided not to.

Esther looked back at the menu. 'Quite like those lists of words you've been writing down,' she said. 'In your notebook. You know: the layout...'

'You mean my haikus?'

'Yes. Your haikus. Anyway,' she carried on, closing the menu and slinging it over onto the empty table beside us. 'So, Paul and

137

I were having this really deep chat about stuff the other night . . . about relationships and things. And I said to him, "What's the worst break-up you've ever been through?" And he said it was when his first girlfriend left him, about six years ago. They'd been together for a year, and then she went to work as a singer on one of those tasteful cruise ships.'

'A tasteful cruise ship?' I said.

'You know: those ships that stop off at Lake Garda and Venice and places? And take all these rich old people round the Adriatic and stuff? Anyway, he said he completely lost it for a while when this girl Julie left him. He just went to pieces. It was, like, he was staring into an *abyss*. It was just this kind of existential *nightmare*.'

I looked at her.

'I'm sorry,' I said, 'but what's that got to do with me?'

'The thing is, Sybil, he was in bits,' Esther said. 'Apparently.' She paused again, as if waiting to let this sentence sink in. 'And it's just,' she said more quietly, 'you seem really screwed-up at the moment about what this Helen woman did to you. And about Simon. And I was thinking about what happened to Paul, when Julie went to work on the cruise ship. Which wasn't something he could have done anything about, to be honest. I mean, she was just following her dreams. It was destined to happen. But for a while he honestly thought he was going to *die*.'

I peered down, and felt a lump in my throat. I couldn't work out what Esther was trying to tell me. Was I going to die? Maybe I was going to die! There was a piece of cucumber and a piece of lemon on the edge of my plate, and they were both shaped into flowers. Everything on my plate seemed to be shaped into flowers. I pictured Paul lying abject, heartbroken, on some bedroom floor in Rickmansworth, while a beautiful young woman called Julie stood on the deck of a cruise liner, singing arias across the Venetian lagoon.

'Anyway, what he did, eventually . . .' Esther continued, because she was clearly so in love with Paul that she'd reached the stage of wanting to talk about him all the time, even if the stories involved his old girlfriends. 'What he did in the end was, he phoned her on the boat one night, while her phone had reception, and he said, "It's OK, I forgive you".'

'Right . . .'

'And he said it was this amazing kind of . . . catharsis. That was all he had to do: just say, "I forgive you" and he felt loads better after that, and he was able to move on.'

'OK,' I said. I wasn't really listening any more. We had been in the restaurant for under fifteen minutes and I already wanted to leave. There was a clunky, jade green salt cellar standing on the table beside the orchid vase, and it made me think of Helen again, Helen with her ridiculous Beakerware and her desire to erase me from the scene. How could I ever have my revenge, though? How would I ever regain my equilibrium? 'I bet I know who'd approve of this salt cellar . . .' I began, but then I thought of what Esther had just said about *obsessing*, so I changed tack.

'The thing is, Esther,' I said, 'have you ever been left by someone you loved, for someone you never even liked in the first place?'

'No, I haven't, to be quite honest. But I don't think Paul liked the ship's band leader much . . .' She paused. 'Anyway,' she added, 'maybe it's better that you *didn't* ever like her. Because surely it would have been even worse if you *had!*'

'And another thing,' I went on, rattled, 'I'm pretty sure she's up to something with Raglan too, now. There's clearly something she doesn't want me to know about at work.'

'Up to what?' Esther asked. 'What do you mean?'

'I don't know,' I said, 'but I caught her walking arm in arm with him yesterday, outside the British Museum. And she'd said she wanted to speak to me earlier that afternoon, but when I saw her with him she clearly didn't want to speak to me at all.'

'Walking around arm in arm with someone is not a crime!' Esther retorted. 'Or proof of some passionate affair! She was probably just buttering him up about something. About these stupid beakers she keeps going on about. And I mean, if they were having an affair they'd want to keep it secret, wouldn't they? They wouldn't be prancing around in public like that!'

Which was a fair enough point. Then a waitress came and took away our plates.

'Was everything OK, ladies?' she asked. 'Did you enjoy the spring rolls?'

'Yeah, they were great. Fab,' Esther said, smiling regretfully up at her as if she would have made a much truer, saner friend than I ever would, nowadays. I dipped my fingertips into the little bowl of water in the middle of the table (it contained a flower-shaped piece of lemon), and wiped my mouth with my napkin. There was a faint ringing sound in my right ear: a high-pitched singing, like a malfunctioning telegraph wire or someone running their finger very fast over a wine glass.

'Well, I'm sorry if I've been acting strangely, Esther,' I said. 'I mean, if only Simon had left me to go and sing on a boat, I'd probably be fine by now!'

I picked up my chopsticks and levered a thick piece of mush-room from my soup. Esther ate, with far greater speed and agility, from her bowl of Green Thai prawn curry. After a while someone changed the soundtrack from Beatles covers to Abba covers. There was an instrumental version of 'The Winner Takes It All' and another of 'Waterloo'. We did not discuss Helen or Simon or Paul, or poetry or Beakerware; we hardly spoke about anything. I felt like weeping at my own rudeness, and the uncomfortable fact that I appeared to be losing all my remaining friends. Customers came and went through the door behind us, letting in blasts of cold air as they did so; there was only a thin little door and a bead curtain separating us from the pavement outside.

'Bloody freezing, sitting here,' Esther commented after a while. 'Paul and I sat at a much better table.'

Then we split the bill in half, stood up, pulled on our coats and scarves, and walked home in virtual silence through the falling sleet. *I am just going out now*, I thought, *and I may be some time*. And I thought, for some reason, of Peter Edwards. I wondered what kind of dining companion he might have made. It's funny how you can almost miss a person you never knew. How you can imagine the sorts of conversations you might have had.

6

what are you thinking?
cold night
wet pavements
old memories

> sweet jasmine tea to go –
> but the dregs taste bitter

I took the Tube most of the way to my poetry class the following evening. I still felt rattled after falling out with Esther the previous night but also, for some reason, keener to write a poem. I took my found object with me, anyway. My *cup that cheers*. I thought it might still be worth trying to work out what it was saying.

I got off the Underground at Westminster and took the 344 bus to Brixton High Street. Then, when the bus arrived at the top of the high street I stood up, clattered down the stairs and headed to the library. I was nearly fifteen minutes late.

'And a useful thing, as I've said before . . .' I could hear the tutor (a woman named Fleur Baird) saying as I hurried along the basement corridor, '. . . is to imagine yourself *as* the object you've chosen. What would your view be of the world? What would your—?'

She stopped and looked across at me as I pushed open the door.

'Hello?'

'Hi.'

She hesitated, as if she could not fathom, suddenly, why I was there. Why *any* of us were.

'So, come in and join the merry throng,' she said. 'We're about to do a quick-fire round.'

'OK,' I said, wondering what that meant. I walked across the room to an empty seat, took out my notebook and pen and teacup and balanced them all slightly reluctantly on my lap.

'Ah! And I think I can see something?' Fleur gestured to the cup. I pretended I hadn't heard.

'Hi,' said the woman sitting in the chair beside mine.

'Hi,' I replied, smiling at her, then glancing further along the row. Everyone appeared to be sitting in exactly the same places as at the very first session I'd attended, over a month earlier. Nothing seemed to have moved since then, not even Time. There was the same Shakespeare sonnet written up on the whiteboard: I suspected Fleur had used the wrong kind of pen and now it wouldn't wipe off. It was stuck there indefinitely, like the ever-fixèd mark Mrs Beeslack had once talked about in English lessons.

'So I've brought in a *lemon* as this week's prompt,' Fleur was saying, and I looked up to observe her placing a lemon in the middle of the teaching desk. 'I'd like you to think about all the things this reminds you of.'

We all regarded the lemon.

'Have a good old think and then, when you're ready, write your thoughts down.'

The clock ticked. From outside the window came the sound of children running along the pavement. I picked up my biro.

Yellow, I wrote, to show willing.

zest

smells nice

Then I noticed that one end of the lemon had a downward curving dent and two eye-shaped hollows, reminding me of Repro John's disappointed face the last time I'd gone round to see

143

him in the ice house. Then, surfacing into my mind, came a vision of the lemon quarters at my dinner with Esther the previous night; and now there was another memory, of an afternoon when Simon and I had made lemon curd once, one wintry evening: we'd gone to the greengrocer's at the end of our street and had bought a lot of fat lemons from Spain, then we'd stood in the kitchen, stirring lemon juice and sugar and egg yolks and butter round one of his big copper pans, and listening to his Bob Marley collection on the CD player. We'd played 'Jamming' three times, because it had seemed appropriate. Then for a while we'd just stood and kissed, as 'Jamming' had turned into 'Redemption Song', then into 'Exodus'. And I didn't want them to be in my head, those memories, especially not that one, but unfortunately they were, there was no way they were going to leave.

'I'm sorry,' I said as Fleur was going round the group, asking for our thoughts. 'I couldn't think of anything I wanted to write.'

'No?'

'No. Sorry.'

Fleur closed her eyes, as if doing so might remove her from the room entirely. Then she opened them again.

'Not to worry, Sybil! No problem at all! Brenda?'

And Brenda, who was sitting next to me, proceeded to reel off a great list of things that lemons were like. They were like sunshine and happiness and washing-up liquid and fresh paint and stars. They were like daffodils and chrysanthemums and the bedroom wallpaper she'd had as a child.

'Now: a useful approach, *I* find,' Fleur continued, after Brenda's list of lemon metaphors was exhausted, 'is to picture yourself *as* the object you've chosen. Imagine you *are* that object. What would your view be of the world? What would your thoughts be?'

She sneaked a quick look at the teacup.

'Because sometimes this ploy can be useful in poetry.'

Then she read out a haiku she'd written herself, all about *being* a lemon.

I am a lemon
Sitting in a bowl,
If you cut me I may sting!

There was a moment's silence.

'Traditionally, of course, a haiku would be written about a landscape or a season,' Fleur added, a little pink in the face now. 'Or something like the moon, or the snow, or . . .'

And suddenly there were tears in my eyes – there were tears! – and my nose was running.

'Ooh,' whispered Brenda, putting her hand on my arm. 'Are you OK?'

But the whole room was wobbling now behind a watery screen. It was like the water running down the inside of a fishmonger's window. There seemed no way it was going to stop.

'Ah, bless,' Brenda said, scrunching my arm quite hard with her fingers. 'Is it to do with that little accident you were in last year, poppet? That you told us about the other week?'

Because for some reason I'd told the group all about the accident at Streatham Ice Rink. I couldn't even remember why.

'No, it's not to do with that,' I said.

'Ah . . .' Brenda hesitated, glancing up at my skating injury. 'Is it just that you're going through *a bit of a time*?' she suggested, cautiously withdrawing her hand.

'Well, that snow's going to put paid to the trains this evening!' someone announced after a moment.

And we all looked out through the high little window, and saw that there was indeed snow again, falling fast and silent.

'Yes, and there are already so many hold-ups on the Northern Line,' said someone else. 'I think it's quicker getting the bus.'

Yes, everyone agreed: the snow and the works on the Northern Line were making life pretty difficult. Then Fleur said, 'Well,

snow's actually quite *apt* when thinking about haikus, isn't it!'
And without further preamble she proceeded to read out a poem
by Emily Dickinson while we all sat and listened:

> My friend must be a bird,
> Because it flies!
> Mortal my friend must be,
> Because it dies!
> Barbs has it, like a bee.
> Ah, curious friend,
> Thou puzzlest me.

'BARBS,' I wrote, in my notebook.

Then we broke for coffee.

'So how are you doing, Sybil?' asked a woman, coming over
to speak to me after a while, as I sat there with my coffee. 'Are
you feeling a bit more ... on top of things now? After
that ... *difficult time* you mentioned?'

I looked at her. The woman had a kind face, but I could no
longer remember her name. Also, I couldn't remember what I'd
told the group about the difficult time. I felt suddenly a little
horrified. It seemed there was something wrong with me. It
seemed I was going around sharing my sorrows with people I
hardly knew, and forgetting I'd even *done* so.

' ... because sometimes,' the woman was saying, sitting down
on the chair beside me, 'it's a question of *giving* it time, isn't it?
Time's a great healer ...'

'Do you think so?'

'I know so.'

'Do you mean in the sense that time numbs us?' I asked. I was
genuinely interested. 'I mean, maybe it's more correct to say,
Time is a great anaesthetist. Like that patient in the poem we
were reading the other week: you know, maybe Time etherises
you and stretches you out across the sky.'

'Sorry?' The woman looked slightly appalled now, and I felt a wave of contrition. *I'm sorry, sometimes I just say all the wrong things*, I wanted to confess. *I say all the wrong things these days, at completely the wrong time.* But it was too late to backtrack, and so we both ground to a conversational halt and looked down at the floor. My head thudded. There were some handouts lying at the foot of our chairs: pale green sheets stapled together, with poems on them. They looked a bit like the worksheets I'd been cobbling together for Professor Muir. I reached down, picked mine up and read the title of the first one. 'The Definition of Love', by Marvell.

> My love is of a birth as rare as tis
> For object strange and high;
> It was begotten by despair
> Upon impossibility . . .

'I'm sorry, but I'm not sure what half of this is supposed to mean . . .' said the woman, reading her own sheet. She sounded quite irked about poetry too now, after my etherised patient comment. '"Where feeble Hope could ne'er have flown",' she read. '"But vainly flapp'd its tinsel wing".' She looked up. 'I mean, did they even *have* tinsel in the seventeenth century?'

'Well, I think probably not as in "Christmas tree" . . .' I said. *Also, the only Hope I know is not the slightest bit feeble*, I wanted to add. *She could break your arm in two.*

'So . . . just to get you up to speed, Sybil, with what we were doing last week . . .' Fleur whispered, coming over to my chair after a moment and crouching down beside the two of us.

'Right. Yes . . .' Momentarily I put my hand up to my right ear because the high-pitched buzzing sound was there in my head again.

'Are you OK?'

'Yes. I'm fine, thanks.'

'So. What we were doing last week – weren't we, Sheila?'

'Yes,' agreed the woman.

'. . . is we were talking about our found objects. And this week, after the break, we're going to be thinking about how we can use these objects for our longer pieces. For instance, for our odes.'

'OK.'

From outside the window, beyond the buzzing, came the sound of a reversing lorry and a dog barking. It was 6.55. Somebody in the corridor was saying '. . . so if you *could* do that for me, Bill, I would be eternally grateful . . .' 'Yeah . . .' Bill was saying, and whoever he was, I had the sense he was probably feeling quite put upon.

'O-K!' Fleur concluded, and she rose to her feet and headed back across the room, to the whiteboard. She took the lid off a marker pen she was holding, and started to write something up, beneath the Shakespeare sonnet. Everyone stopped talking, and raised their heads to look.

Inspiration, she was writing, just managing to cram the final *n* on to the edge of the board. Then underneath this, she wrote: *The Poetic Impulse: Creative Strategies for Freeing Your Mind.*

'So,' she said, replacing the cap on the pen. 'Round Two! And just so everyone's singing from the same hymn sheet – Sybil – can I ask you to describe the found object you've brought in this week? As you weren't here last week?'

'Oh . . .' My heart leapt: I had not expected this. 'Well, I've brought in this little . . .' I hesitated. 'Teacup I found.'

'A teacup?'

'Yes. I mean, it *is* genuinely a found object. I did *find* it; it's not just something from my kitchen cupboard. I came across it last weekend when I was walking home from a party. I just saw it sitting there on this wall and I – I picked it up. I don't know why, really. I suppose it just spoke to me.'

I stopped talking. There was a moment's pause. Then Fleur said, 'And what did it say, Sybil?'

'Sorry?'

'What did it say?'

'Well, I don't know,' I said.

'You don't know?'

'No. Not entirely.' *This was* your *idea, Fleur,* I wanted to point out; *you did* ask *us to do this.*

Fleur's gaze flittered up to the scar on my head, and away again.

'I was hoping,' I added, 'that inspiration might, y'know . . . strike this evening.'

There was another short, contemplative silence.

'Well,' Fleur said, 'it's certainly . . . a nice little object to work with, Sybil. Quite . . . evocative. About all sorts of things. Cups of tea. Family teas. Tea leaves. Tea ceremonies . . .'

'Thank you,' I said, my heart a kind of stone in my chest. 'That's what I thought. I thought maybe I could write about tea clippers or something.'

'So has anyone else brought anything new in, this week?' Fleur moved on, looking hopefully around the group. 'Any advances on Sybil's little teacup?'

I waited, my smile hanging on. I curled my right hand around the cup, feeling the smooth ceramic edges of it and the sharp section where it was chipped, and wished I had never brought it in with me, or even picked it up in the first place. I wished it would spirit me away somewhere, anywhere – like Aladdin's lamp, or Dorothy's ruby shoes. The silence continued for a moment longer, then Brenda said:

'So, what I've brought in this evening, Fleur, is a leaf.'

She twirled a small, damp-looking maple leaf between her thumb and forefinger.

'Great!' Fleur said. 'Smashing. And how about you, Morag – what have you . . . ?'

'Well, I've brought in a leaf as well, Fleur!'

'Me, too. How funny!' said Sheila.

'Great. So. Three leaves and a teacup!' said Fleur, her voice strangely tight.

And everyone glanced at me again, sitting there with my strange little find.

'So . . .' Fleur continued, 'has anyone brought in any other—' but suddenly, from the far end of the room, there was a peculiar kind of commotion: an eruptive kind of sighing, a breathing-out and rustle of paper, and a woman sitting at the end of the row, who'd introduced herself in Week One as Olivia Barnes Graeme, said, 'Well, I haven't brought in any more found objects, Fleur, but I *do* have a lot of poems here. I've been feeling inspired this week for some reason.'

'Excellent!' Fleur said, a look of panic appearing on her face.

'So, OK to read out?' Olivia went on. 'Is that what we're doing now?'

'Well, we certainly . . .'

'Great. Only there's quite a few of them, I have to warn you!' She reached down and took a piece of crumpled-looking paper out of her bag. 'I was thinking about what you said last week, about using household objects as metaphors.'

'Oh, yes?'

'And so here's my first one . . .'

'OK!'

Then she just launched into it.

'Corkscrew!' she began abruptly. 'Helix of *despair*! Spiralling the twists and turns of your *affair*!'

'Ah!' I heard Fleur whisper, tipping her head a little to one side. Two points of high colour had appeared in her cheeks, now, bright pink circles, like the cheeks of a woman drawn by a child.

'I see the glint of your destruction in that twist of steel . . .' Olivia muttered, while we all sat very still, startled into sudden obedience, heads bowed, as if we were being told off, or listening to a sermon in church.

'. . . *turn on, turn on, until the cork is riven, separated, split . . .*'
Olivia spat. Then there was a pause. 'The end,' she confirmed.

A few people clapped.

'Yes. I—' Fleur began. 'Well, that was—' But actually Olivia wasn't *quite* finished: she had concluded *Corkscrew* and now she was continuing with another poem, about a crumpet. It was called *Crumpet*:

> *Crumpet!* (she read, as the clapping died away)
> Will you *burn*
> my fingers
> or *warm* my heart?
> catch *light* or fall
> *butter-side*
> *down . . . ?*

'Next, a poem about a rolling pin, though to be frank I got a bit stuck with this one, Fleur. I think I was running out of steam by this point, I couldn't think of much to say about the —'

And suddenly I found that I was speaking, that words were emerging from my mouth; I was saying, 'Well, maybe you should just have bashed the bastard over the head with it!' my emotions appearing raw and strange, like some terrible secret bursting forth at a Quaker meeting. 'I mean . . .' I added, blushing, alarmed at my own candour, 'maybe . . .', but it was too late now. A kind of shock wave had already begun rippling around the room and all the members of the group had turned in their seats to regard me – this outspoken young woman who was normally so demure, this crazy girl with the scarred head and the broken teacup. Then, with great forbearance, and without further comment, Olivia looked down and resumed her reading. She finished her rolling-pin poem, which lasted several more stanzas – 'Roll on, roll out, and form new shape . . . make, bake, awake . . . !' and everyone clapped again, more briefly this time, then someone read quite a risqué limerick about a hot water bottle, and Olivia shot me a look.

'OK!' Fleur said after a moment. She pushed her hands beneath the backs of her legging-clad thighs, and briefly closed her eyes. Then she opened them again.

'So. What I want us all to do now,' she said, 'for the next part of the session, is to write down as many similes as we can think of, to describe Poetry itself.'

Silence.

'Poetry itself?' said Brenda.

'That's right!'

'Similes to describe Poetry?'

'Absolutely! I'm going to give you ten minutes!'

'Wow!' someone observed. Then, because there seemed no other option, we all picked up our pens, and for a short time the room became almost silent again, apart from vague sounds of scratching biro tips and ambient noise. I wrote nothing, though. No words would come, after my strange little outburst. I felt quite depleted. For the first time in my life, I felt I might have crossed some sort of threshold into oddness. *Poetry* . . . I wrote. But poetry was no use to me. Poetry, as my grandfather might have said, was no better than a poke in the eye with a sharp stick.

'Five more minutes!' Fleur announced after a while, flicking her silk scarf more resolutely around her neck. And I thought of another afternoon I'd spent with Simon once, that January, about a month after the ice-skating debacle and a few days before Helen had phoned to tell me he was hers. He had suggested we go to the Tate Gallery together to have a look around, and while he was peering at a sculpture called *Woman with Her Heart Broken*, I'd sneaked down the spiral staircase and gone into the shop, which was all glittering with remaindered Christmas decorations, and I'd bought the notebook for him, because he liked Magritte. Then I'd gone back upstairs with the notebook in my bag and we'd looked at some other pictures for a while: we'd walked hand in hand through the galleries and looked at paintings by Degas and Corot and the pre-Raphaelites – and in particular we'd stood considering a painting, on loan from St Petersburg, of some ancient bearded bloke called Ded Moroz, who was a Slavic version of Father Christmas. 'Sounds like *Dead Morose . . .*' I said, and I started laughing, because Dead Morose was not the kind of Santa you'd want coming down your chimney on Christmas Eve—

('Three more minutes,' Fleur said, from behind her desk.)

—and I remembered that I'd laughed and laughed while Simon had looked on, his expression blank, *dead morose*, in fact—

('Two more minutes.')

—until one of the wardens had come hurrying over and asked us to leave because we were *disturbing the peace for the other gallery-goers.* That trip to the Tate was probably (I suspected, later) the afternoon that Simon had been trying to break it to me about Helen, this woman who was clearly so much more the right woman for him; it had probably been the beginning of the end. Because it was less than a week later that Helen had called and told me, herself. And so in the end I'd kept the notebook, because I'd run out of days to give it to him.

'One more minute!' Fleur called, as if this was how long the oxygen was going to hold out in the room, and I put down my pen, closed the notebook, and sat there, like a refusenik.

'Lost in thought, Sybil?' Fleur murmured, above everyone's heads. She stood up and walked quietly across the room. 'Lost in thought?' she said again, crouching down beside me.

'Well, I just don't feel very poetic this evening,' I whispered.

Fleur sighed lightly. 'The words will come to you.'

'Will they?'

'Yes, they will.'

We both regarded the little teacup, sitting there on the flip-out arm of my chair, as if a tea-lady from the 1950s was about to come round suggesting a top-up. 'May I have a look?' Fleur asked, and she picked it up and turned it round, very carefully and gently, as if it might be a thing of some value. 'The cup that cheers,' she read out. She smiled a little sadly, her gaze flicking up to my scar again. 'We don't give ourselves enough breaks, do we, really?' she said. 'Tea breaks or otherwise.' Then she rose, padded quietly back across the room and reinstated herself behind her desk.

'Time's up!' she yelled, and I practically leapt out of my skin.

'OK, who's going to go first? Any volunteers?'

She looked around the class.

The class looked back at Fleur.

It was late-night opening upstairs in the lending library, and I had twenty minutes after the session ended, to wait for the bus home. So after everyone else had gone I went up there, with my collection of things, to hang around for a while behind the shelves. Also, it occurred to me, I should probably borrow some book or other; I should at least try and borrow the book Fleur had recommended that night, even if I never set foot in the place again.

'Good evening,' said a woman in a high-necked blouse as I pushed the doors open. She was wheeling by with a trolley full of books. 'The library's closing in ten minutes.'

'It's OK,' I said, 'I'm not going to be here for long.'

'The lending desk closes in five,' she said. And she wheeled on towards a door with a poster on it saying *Enter a World Of Adventure*, and disappeared through it.

For a while I couldn't locate the Poetry shelves at all. I walked past Pottery and Ceramics, past Parenting Skills, Personal Development, Philosophy, Psychology and Pet Care, but there was no Poetry. I walked past an old man sitting beside a shelf that said *Withdrawn Fiction: 10p*, and a big woman in Scholl sandals and beige socks, reading a book called *Bring Me My*

Arrows of Desire. I walked past a carousel displaying off-the-peg reading glasses – *See Clearly Again for only £3.99!* said a sign – a claim which seemed improbable to me, like one of Jesus's miracles. Pinned to a cork noticeboard beside the carousel was another poster I hadn't noticed the last time I'd gone there. It said:

THE WORLD ENDS TOMORROW!

(according to Nostradamus)

So please make sure you return your overdue books

Which felt oddly reassuring, somehow, as if there might at least be someone working within a four-mile radius who hadn't completely lost their sense of humour. I headed towards the Information Zone, a space full of computer terminals and moulded, low-level furniture. There was a library assistant sitting there behind a lending desk, reading a book.

'Excuse me,' I said, approaching him. He didn't look up.

'Hello,' I said, and this time he looked up.

'Yep.'

'I'm looking,' I continued, disconcerted, 'for *The Poetic Impulse: Creative Strategies for Freeing Your Mind*?'

'Hah! Aren't we all!'

He peered at me. I peered back. *I know you*, I thought. *I've seen you before.* But I couldn't think where.

'Or have you got any books on haikus?' I asked. 'Any Bashō, maybe?'

'Bashō . . .' he replied, looking up at the ceiling, as if Bashō might be up there, swinging from the light fittings. There was a metal badge pinned to his shirt which said **Ask Me! I'm A Librarian!** and his skin was librarian-pale, admittedly, almost translucent, as if he spent most of his time residing in some nineteenth-century opium den. More likely though, I suspected, he played computer games late into the night; probably he played computer games and ordered pizza in. And I realised, with a jolt of surprise, why he was familiar to me: he was the man I'd spoken to at the conference dinner the previous week – the man who'd made the origami frogs.

'So I think I *might* know where we keep Bashō,' he said.

'Great.'

He put his book down on its opened pages (*Zen and the Art of Motorcycle Maintenance*, I noticed), and slid down from the high swivelling chair he was sitting on. It was identical to the chair I sat on at the Institute. *I've got a chair like that*! I almost burst out, because sometimes, at odd moments, things like that still mattered.

'Yeah, I'm *pretty sure* I know where Poetry is,' he said, 'assuming Margery hasn't wheeled it all away . . . Come with me.'

He headed off, fast, across the carpet tiles. I hesitated. Then I hurried after him.

'Bashō's a funny name, isn't it?' he said over his shoulder as we proceeded. 'Quite violent for a poet.'

'Violent?'

'Though I suppose you *can* get violent poets . . . the beatniks were off their heads half the time. And performance poets! I was at a gig the other night, and one of them started head-butting the mic.'

I couldn't think what to say.

'The thing I hate about poets,' he added, 'is the way they stretch out the words at the ends of the lines. Have you ever noticed that? As if they're the most significant words. Instead of just being the ones at the end of the line.'

'I know what you mean,' I said. Because, actually, I did.

'Cool things though, haikus.' He stopped abruptly at a shelf marked *Oriental Culture*. 'I used to write them, myself. Bits and pieces. Load of crap mainly.'

'Oh.'

'I used to write cinquains too.'

'Cinquains?'

'Five-line poems.'

'Right.' I wondered how many secret poets there might be in the world. Maybe there were thousands; God – maybe there were *millions*! It was a curiously worrying thought.

'Here you go.' He pulled a book down off the shelf. It had a picture on the cover of an ancient man sitting under a tree. It was called *A Zen Wave*.

'Great,' I said.

'Funny – I'm reading *Zen and the Art of Motorcycle Maintenance* at the moment.'

'Yes, I saw.'

'Really? Have you read it?'

'No.'

'Why not?'

'*Why not*?' I asked. This seemed a bizarre question. 'I don't know. It's just a book I haven't read.'

'Blackbird,' he said, apropos of nothing.

'Singing in the dead of night,' I replied. Something rattled and resonated in my brain. I couldn't think why. It was hard to tell if he even recognised me from the week before, but now I was aware of a slow heat flickering upwards in my face, like a burner on low flame. I cast around for somewhere else to look, someone else, something to distract me. There was a group of four elderly people sitting around a table, half-hidden behind a screen. They were eating biscuits and drinking tea. It looked a peaceful scene – zen, even. It made me think of my grandparents, having tea in their flat in Blackheath. 'Oh, look – they've even provided us with side-plates!' I heard one of the old women say to her friend. It seemed such a small thing to be pleased about that I suddenly felt quite ashamed of myself.

'So, I don't know if this one's any use to you,' the librarian said, handing me *A Zen Wave*, 'but it looks like all the others are out on loan.'

'Yes, well, I expect the other—'

'Sorry?'

I paused. 'I expect the other people in my poetry class,' I began again, 'have taken them out.'

He hesitated. 'So are you going to the poetry classes?'

'Yes,' I replied. ' "Poetry for the Terrified". In the basement.'

'Wow, that *does* sound fucking terrifying!'

I wanted to laugh, and I also felt aggrieved. I felt I should be upholding some principle to do with knowledge and self-improvement and kindness, but I didn't know what those were any more, or whether I'd ever known. Looking at him again I noticed that his eyes were an uncommon greyish-blue. They were like a Siamese cat's eyes, steady and unblinking. Truthful, even. Although his **Ask Me! I'm A Librarian!** badge seemed basically to be some kind of lie. And at least *I* don't have to hang around at work with a label pinned to my front, I thought. Even if I do have to wear a lanyard. And at least I have my own room at work, where I can hide, and not disconcert people with observations about violent poets.

'To be honest,' he said, 'I don't think you need poetry classes to be a poet, do you? It's one of those things you're either good at or not, isn't it? Like woodwork.'

Woodwork? 'Well, that's what I'm trying to find out,' I said.

'I mean, I went to a woodwork class once and I never wanted to set eyes on a fucking magazine rack again.'

'I see.' I was not a prude but I was not convinced you should talk about fucking magazine racks in a public library, a place where there might be old people and small children around. A place where there *were* old people and small children. I thought

158

of the day when Jane Beauchamp had suggested I try poetry as a way of helping me cope with Helen's catastrophic reappearance in my life, of how I'd seen a sign printed on lilac paper and pinned up on the library's noticeboard, like some message specifically aimed at me – *Poetry for the Terrified: Ever wondered if you could pen a haiku or an ode?* – and how, like an idiot, I'd signed up, how I'd paid £85 up-front, and gone along almost every Friday night for the past seven weeks, like someone confessing to drinking too much or owning far too many shoes. And it didn't seem to be helping; I appeared to have been feeling sadder and more troubled as the days continued, so much so my head throbbed and my eyesight was a blur and I could hardly even see straight half the time. I could hardly even *read*.

'Yeah, I spent ages on that magazine rack,' the librarian said. 'Doing all the measuring and dovetail joints. Then I just gave it to Oxfam.'

'Maybe it's just that you don't like magazine racks.'

'You may have a point. Because I don't like magazine racks. I think they're redundant.'

'So how about magazines? Do you think they're redundant?'

'Pretty much. Most of them.'

I could feel the frown increasing on my face. I'd imagined when I'd first spoken to him – at the conference dinner and even, for a moment, that evening – that he might be quite a nice person; he'd certainly seemed unusually frank. But now I was beginning to wonder how he'd ever got a job in a library in the first place. He seemed to have some sort of problem with the general reading public, and even with the contents of the library's own Journals and Periodicals shelves. Now I felt like taking him down a peg or two; berating him for his lack of respect towards magazines and magazine racks and evening classes and book lovers. *Don't you know that vulnerable people go to libraries?* I wanted to snap. *Don't you know some people visit places like this for comfort and support, and not stupid conversations about woodwork classes?*

Then someone called out, across the library floor. It was the woman in the high-necked blouse.

'Bill, we have to close the doors now,' she called, from some invisible location beyond the Information Zone. 'Can you go and sort them out, please?'

Oh, I thought: so *you're* Bill.

'OK, Marge,' said the librarian. Bill. 'With you in a sec. I'm just helping this . . .' He glanced at me. 'Library user.'

He didn't move, though. Neither did I. We just stood and looked at each other. I wondered whether he would eventually recognise me: whether he might say, 'Hey, weren't you at that dinner the other night . . . ?' But he didn't. I peered out, across the expanse of carpet in the Children's Reading Zone. It looked like a calm green ocean. Like Greenwich Park at lunchtimes. I remembered sitting on a library carpet like that once when I was small, a very long time ago, reading books about volcanoes and hamsters and outer space.

'Cinquain comes from the Italian for five, by the way,' Bill said. 'As in "cinquecento". Which happens to be the kind of car I drive.'

Now he was showing off about his car! *Men are all the same*, I thought. From Raglan with that awful old Rover he drives, to Simon with that bloody Alfa Romeo his boss used to lend him – a car so low that the first time he'd ever driven me anywhere in it, I'd opened the passenger door and just rolled straight out onto the pavement.

'And the thing that's cool about cinquaines—' Bill was saying.

'You see, that's what some people find really annoying,' I interrupted. 'The way you can't just say "this is a five-line poem". The way you have to give it some stupid name. That's what really annoys me about poetry!'

He looked startled. 'So don't go to poetry classes, then.'

'Yes, well, I'm booked onto them now!'

'So un-book them.'

'Hah! And waste £85?'

'It depends how much you think your time is worth. Maybe one of your evenings is worth more than £85.'

I stared at him.

'Sorry,' he said, 'that came out wrong. Sometimes I say stuff and it comes out wrong.'

'Anyway,' I snapped. 'Thanks for the book.'

And I strode over to the lending desk, took out *A Zen Wave* with my Wandsworth Borough Libraries reader's card, and headed out.

I took the 196 bus home, catching it just before it pulled away from the stop.

'Chancing your luck,' remarked the driver.

'Yes,' I said, hurtling up the stairs to the back seats, my heart thudding, the middle distance a fog in front of me, the near distance also a kind of fog. I sat, staring down at the street, my notebook and the ridiculous teacup and the book of poems in the bag on my lap.

'Then sometimes we get these *windows* where we don't have to do anything at all!' I heard a man observe to his friend in the seat behind mine.

'And did you know that pigeons can detect *metal*, and they don't even need *eyes*?' someone else remarked across the aisle. I thought: that's quite interesting: that pigeons can navigate without the advantage of sight, and I felt sad, that there was no one in the whole world I could have a conversation like that with any more. Maybe even Simon had not been the kind of person I could have spoken with, about eyeless pigeons.

As the bus neared Stockwell Road, I got my library book out and read some poems.

Puny frog,
Don't give up
Issa's here!

But who's Issa? I wondered. What makes Issa so special? I turned the page.

Lo! The cherry-blossoms have forced
A daimio to dismount

(But what's a daimio?) Feeling slightly sick, I put the book
away again.

It was gone ten when I got back to the flat. I let myself in through
the iron security gate, then the main door, then the front door.
'Hello?' I called out tentatively, but Esther wasn't there: it was
Friday night, after all, and she would be out having a social life.
She would be out at some club or restaurant with Paul. There
was a note from her, though: she'd scribbled it on a piece of
paper torn from a Hello Kitty notebook and propped it up
beside the fruit bowl in the kitchen.

Sybil – that book I mentioned is 'Overcoming
Heartbreak' by Elaine Pritchard.
PS. Your nemesis rang.

I picked the note up. 'Nemesis,' I said out loud, my voice hollow
and peculiar-sounding in the quiet flat. I couldn't imagine what
Helen could possibly want from me, or how she could have the
nerve to phone me at my flat. If it was to say that Simon was no
longer hers it was all too late anyway: she'd already destroyed
what we'd once had. Or if it was to break some other news to
me – well, I didn't want to know about that either.

Pinning the note to the cork board beside the clock, I went
back into the hall and picked up the post that had been lying on
the doormat since mid-morning. There was a postcard from my
mother (*Darling Sybil, arrived yesterday. Weather and food
amazing, Dad and I sitting here having glass of Madeira on
balcony*), a bank statement, a flyer depicting stuffed crust pizzas
and a leaflet from an organisation called The Trinitarian Bible
Society. This bore a photo of a youngish couple wearing

identical yellow T-shirts and sitting in a rowing boat. They were rowing inexorably towards an enormous waterfall. Beneath this was a quote from the Bible:

> And they said, Believe on the Lord Jesus Christ, and thou shalt be saved, and thy house.
> Acts 16.31

They looked like Helen and Simon, I thought, the way I imagined they might look in a few years' time, if they sat together in a rowing boat, heading towards a massive waterfall.

For supper that night I ate two packets of Hula Hoops and one kiwi fruit with the skin still on. I wondered what Simon might have made that day in The Olive Branch. Perhaps something magnificent involving buckwheat and faro. Perhaps Helen would have come round to eat it with him, telling him how amazing he was, not only in bed but also in the kitchen. Taking some milk out from the fridge door I let the bottle slip from my grasp, and the explosion, and mess of smashed glass and liquid, was quite spectacular. I mopped up the milk and swept up the shards, then I went to my room and got into bed. I lay on my back and tried not to think of Simon and Helen in bed together themselves, probably at that very moment. The sexy older woman with the gullible young lover. It was too much to think about. I looked up at the ceiling which seemed a long distance above my head for some reason – very high and far away, like looking up and up at the sky on a summer's day. I heard the phone ringing in the kitchen – three times, within half an hour – but I ignored it each time. *I forgot to reply to Clive-the-detectorist*, I thought, as I lay there. *And to look for that information for Dr Appalsawmy.* I was forgetting a lot – and yet at the same time, I was remembering too much. A faint, rabbit-like shape in the ceiling plaster reminded me of a line in

Madeline, a book my grandfather had used to read to me when I was small: I'd sit on his lap in my grandparents' kitchen in Blackheath, and he'd recount to me all Madeline's trials and tribulations, in his lovely old Bermondsey voice.

I slept eventually, and at some point I dreamt of Peter Edwards. It seemed I knew him well in this dream, it seemed to me he was some sort of long-lost friend. For some reason he'd sent me a postcard: a black-and-white photo of a big park – Greenwich Park, in fact – I knew this, even though it looked nothing like Greenwich Park and was covered in a thick layer of snow. It looked more like the Tundra, some kind of permafrost. On the back of the card he had written:

snow
has
fallen
snow
on
snow

He'd written it like a line of poetry. And in the dream I wanted to write back, because there was something important I wanted to tell him, about snow and the way it fell: some crucial bit of information about the way it covered things up. So I went into a newsagent that had suddenly materialised in the middle of the park, and I bought a postcard – one of those old-fashioned blank ones that says *Do not write beneath this line*. Then I looked in my coat pocket, pulled out a pen, and wrote:

I am writing beneath the line

As if that was the answer to everything.
Then I sent it.

7

Thames Embankment
Man dressed as wizard,
I can tell
You're not floating;
You're just hiding
The seat you're sitting on
With a suspiciously
Long
Cloak

Riverboat journey
Twenty minutes late this morning
What is the Oxo building?
What does the Oxo building do?

on the tube
I drop my book:
words fall like leaves

I spent quite a while the next morning typing out a timetable to pin up on the staff noticeboard. The formatting would not behave itself at all: it kept slipping around itself, whatever I tried to do with the line breaks and the font sizes:

Tuesday   9am
staff meeting Maud Forrester Room Monday: Visit from
        NYC researcchers,

Lecture Hall C
Wednesday: microfosssilssymposium
Thursday: TED talk staff update
Friday: 1pm Lunchtime talk: The
Circadian
Clock: Howtime flies

NB. The days are in the wrong order; this was unavoidable, I
wrote eventually in biro at the bottom of the page. Then I pinned
it up and returned to the indexing. There seemed no further
way to avoid it now other than open my window and jump out.

'Today's edition of *Sesame Street* is brought to you by the
letter f and the number 482,' I observed to Jane as she walked
through the office.

She paused.

'Sorry, Sybil?'

'Nothing.'

I was losing my mind.

Shortly before midday, on my way back from the kitchenette, I
stopped outside Professor Muir's door. The enquiry I'd received,
days ago now from Dr Appalsawmy, was not something I could
ignore much longer, and it occurred to me that Professor Muir
might know where the Institute kept its information on Peter
Edwards. Although as soon as I'd knocked on the door, it
became clear that this was probably not the moment to ask. He
was evidently having a rather tense meeting in there. There was
the sound of low, serious voices and a distracted clearing of
throats.

'. . . absolutely essential that we don't throw the baby out with
the bathwater . . .' I could hear Professor Muir uttering, and
someone else saying, 'Yes, but with respect, Jeremy . . .' and then
a third voice said, 'Oh, wasn't that a knock on the door?' so I
knocked again; it seemed too late to retreat now. There was a

small pause. Then Professor Muir barked, 'Yes?' and I braced myself, and pushed the door open.

'Hi,' I said, peering round. 'Hi,' I added to the small group of people assembled disconsolately in front of Professor Muir's bookcase. They reminded me of people slumped in an airport departure lounge. One of the people, I saw to my dismay, was Helen. Most of the rest, I didn't know at all. 'Sorry to interrupt,' I continued, 'but I was wondering if you might happen to know . . .'

'Yes? Know what, Sybil?'

'Sorry. I was just wondering if you might know where we keep documents relating to . . . Peter Edwards' recent work,' I concluded. I glanced swiftly at Helen, and away again.

Professor Muir looked oddly taken aback for a moment. He puffed out his cheeks and exhaled. 'Peter's recent work . . .' he said, his voice suddenly tinged with sadness.

'Yes.' My heart flipped. 'I'm sorry, maybe I—'

'No, it's fine, Sybil.' He paused, and seemed to consider my query quite carefully. 'So, I'd have thought all Peter's work would be under E for Edwards in the general archives,' he said, as everyone in the meeting adopted expressions of quiet respect. 'Though I believe the more recent stuff – all the more recent correspondence and so on, is actually on the Pending shelves. Beside the Special Collections Room. Because I don't think anyone's quite been able to . . . . I mean, it seemed rather too . . . soon, after . . .'

'Ah,' I said, embarrassed. 'Right. Yes, I hadn't thought to look on the Pending shelves.'

For the briefest second I glanced at Helen again. She was sitting stony-faced, beside a blue-suited man I didn't recognise: probably some colleague from LMIC. No doubt I had interrupted some very important point they'd all been discussing about TED talk trailers and teasers and press releases.

'OK, thanks, then,' I said to Professor Muir. 'I'll look there, then. Thanks . . .'

And I backed out of the room and ran upstairs. Although now I actually had some useful information, I couldn't quite bring myself to carry straight on to Archives. Only a few weeks earlier I'd managed, briefly, to get myself locked into the Special Collections Room up there, and I'd been quite wary of setting foot inside ever since. I'd gone up to look for some files on early Irish *ogham* script for one of the Celtic specialists, meaning to nip in for just a moment or two, and as I'd stood at the back of the room between the window and the high shelving unit, I'd heard the door close gently shut – a door which, *for security reasons, could only be opened from the outside, unless you had your lanyard with you.* 'Oh – hello?' I'd shouted, running over to the door, panic assailing me – because, of course, I didn't have my lanyard with me, I never had my lanyard with me. Stupidly, I always left it hanging over the back of my chair. Also, it had suddenly occurred to me, I didn't have my *phone* with me, either – and it was late in the day on a Friday afternoon! What if no one knew I was in there? What if I had to stay there all week-end, freezing cold, hungry, dehydrated, surrounded by box files full of vellum documents? I'd been about to start hammering on the door with the flat of my palm, to shout, 'Hey – can anyone hear me!' when Helen had appeared on the other side of the thick glass pane, an expression of shocked puzzlement on her face.

'Sybil!' she had mouthed, her words a little muffled. 'What on earth are you doing in there!' She pushed down the handle, and I stepped out. 'You shouldn't ever go into the Special Collections Room without your lanyard!' she continued, her voice suddenly loud now it was not behind glass. 'Rule Number One! I'd have thought you'd know that!' I hadn't replied; I could not bear to speak to her, or even thank her for liberating me. I simply moved on and past, a small part of me even wondering if it was Helen who'd pushed the door shut in the first place.

I remained in my room for the rest of that morning. I sat at my desk till gone midday, checking paragraphs in Raglan's book, as the snow outside the window turned to sleet. I read about the anaerobic preservation of wooden boat hulls; I read about Ancient Egyptian winnowing methods; I read about mules; I read something Apicius the cook wrote in the first century AD about spelt pottage, and which Helen had decided to quote from, in her Winchelsea musings.

It's certainly amusing to consider, she chuckled, *how we, in the twenty-first century, might relate to the serving of artisanal spelt pottage in chunky Beakerware™ bowls!*

I hated the way, every time she mentioned Beakerware, she added that little ™ sign. It just did not sit at all well with the rest of Raglan's book, which was rigorously academic in tone, full of footnotes and appendices and learned references. Helen's little tacked-on chapter looked even more dubious in comparison. I turned to my notebook.

Odi et amo, I scribbled. I paused, my pen hovering.

> I hate and I love
> Like Catullus
> But mainly these days
> I just hate you, Helen

I wondered if I should tear the page out and stick it between the bricks of a wall somewhere, as embittered Roman slaves had used to, to put a curse on their masters.

'Sybil! Got time for a quick catch-up?' Raglan asked, suddenly appearing in my doorway just as I had finished the *n* of *Helen*. 'Yo! Sure! Great!' I yelled, leaping up, and banging my knee against my desk. Raglan stood and waited as I bent to give it a rub.

'OK there?'

'Yep, all fine! Just – you know – banged my knee . . .'

'Well, OK . . .' said Raglan, and we left the room and headed awkwardly forth, along the corridor. As we progressed I felt suddenly very aware of my junior status within the Institute, like an A level student summoned to explain some missing homework. Professor Muir's meeting had broken up, I noticed, as we walked past his door. His room was completely empty, everyone having apparently headed on to further, important segments of their days. I found myself envying the man in the blue suit, who was probably, at that very moment, legging it back across the park to the comparative warmth and sanity of his own office.

'This weather!' I observed as we passed one of the long windows on the landing.

'Ah, yes, indeed . . .' Raglan looked briefly out at it. 'Yes, you'd have thought we'd seen the last of the snow . . .' We waded on, the plasterwork ferns frozen in the ceiling cornicework above our heads, the strip lighting a dim white blur.

'For God's sake! Now the bloody *photocopier's* playing up!' Hope Pollard's voice boomed out as we headed past one of the administration offices. Then she started rattling the paper-feed trays. We both pretended we had not heard this.

'So how was Crete last weekend? How did your Knossos lecture go?' I asked as we arrived at the top of the stairs and began to head down the first flight.

Raglan put his hand out to the handrail. 'Well, of course, I hardly did the subject justice, Sybil,' he said. 'Peter would have said it so much better than I did.'

'Yes, of course,' I agreed, attempting to sound quietly respectful of Peter Edwards' expertise – before realising I'd simply appeared to condemn Raglan's own.

'Yes, he'd been doing a lot of research into those amazing little terracotta goddesses last year. He'd have given a brilliant lecture on them.'

'Yes, I'm sure . . .' I whispered. 'In fact, I saw some of his Minoan finds when I was in the British Museum the other day.'

'Ah, yes, indeed . . .' Raglan replied, nodding seriously, and we plodded on, each step glittering with chips of mica, each landing an awkward turn in our conversation. 'In fact, on the subject of Peter Edwards,' I continued, 'I was meaning to—' but he interrupted.

'So, how's life for *you* at the moment, Sybil?' he said. 'How are things going now, after that . . . little contretemps at the start of the year?'

Why? Hasn't Helen told you? I wanted to retort. *Didn't she ever tell you the reason for the contretemps*?

'Yes, things are going fine now, thanks,' I replied. We arrived at ground level and turned left into the café.

'Good. All OK then? Everything OK?'

'Yes, everything's fine, thanks,' I said. I felt a little confounded. 'So how are things going *for you* in general, Raglan?' I asked, as we headed over to a table and sat down.

'Yes, well, things are going OK.' He nodded. 'Better than they've gone for a while. In particular, it's a huge relief to be getting the money in, now.'

'The money?'

'From LMIC. As part of their sponsorship deal. Specifically the Beakerware deal.'

'Oh. Right. The Beakerware.'

'It opens a lot of doors. The revenue we'll be getting in, after Helen's findings, and all the ensuing publicity. It means we can make plans.'

'What kind of plans?'

'In terms of getting *A History of Trade* published, for a start. And expanding the shop. And being able to hang onto newer staff members like you, Sybil. To be brutally frank!'

'Ah.' I looked down at my hands, then up again. There was a strange taste in my mouth. It alarmed me to think that my job might have been quite so precarious. That, as *last in* at RIPS I would presumably have been *first out*, if LMIC hadn't turned up to rescue us all. At the same time, it upset me to think how soon the shop was going to be expanded and everything shifted and upheaved: how, in a few weeks' time, a lot of new display shelves were going to take up a large proportion of the gallery, causing at least a fifth of the exhibits to be packed up and shipped off to Barnet.

'So, there was something I was meaning to—' I began, but before I could embark on the subject of Peter Edwards again and where exactly I might locate his Knossos files in Special Collections, Ailsa Crawford, the rather gloomy woman who worked in the café, approached with an order-pad.

'What would youse like?' she asked.

'Ah, yes, well now . . .' Raglan replied as if this was an intriguing question, and we both ordered cappuccinos as if our lives depended on them. Ailsa could sometimes have that effect. She came back with them a couple of minutes later, both contained within Beakerware cups, and plonked them unceremoniously on the table.

'Ah! So they're in the café *already*!' Raglan proclaimed as she left again with the empty tray. 'Helen told me they'd be here soon, but I didn't realise quite *how* soon!'

'No.' I reached out, put my hands around my beaker and took a sip. It felt like drinking from a poisoned chalice. I thought of the teacup I'd found: its modest little message.

'Yes. Rather impressive,' Raglan observed, carefully tilting his beaker around and peering at it. 'Not entirely unlike the real thing.'

'No. Not entirely.'

Raglan took a sip. Then he frowned and peered out through the café window, at some crows bouncing around the grass in the distance. I waited for him to say something else, but it was as if his train of thought had been deflected at the last moment, as if he'd actually been wanting to talk about something of far greater importance – to say, for instance, that in the Middle

Ages, people had believed ammonites were curled-up snakes that had been turned to stone by God; or that a long time before that, even before the age of mankind, there'd been the Proto-erozoic era, when the world was full of blind, drifting jellyfish.

'So . . .' I began. I cleared my throat. 'I know John's all lined up for the print run next week, but there was just one thing I wanted to ask beforehand, about Helen's—'

But before I could continue, before I could say 'Helen's dodgy findings' or 'weird behaviour', Raglan said, 'So, the proofs are at a fairly advanced stage then, I'm presuming?', and my courage abandoned me.

'Because time is somewhat of the essence now,' he added.

He looked at me, as if trying to divine something. Then he looked again at the beaker in his hands. 'Of course, in an *ideal* world, Sybil,' he said, 'we wouldn't have to be doing any of this. We wouldn't have to bother with selling tourist tat. Or scrambling to get our publications to print.'

'No,' I agreed.

'We'd be properly funded by the government.'

'Yes.'

'We'd be recognised as an academic institution. We wouldn't have to rely on giftware revenues and—' He made a sign of quote marks with his fingers '—commercial tie-ins.'

I put down my beaker, my heart flailing like a line of washing in the wind. I couldn't work out what he was trying to tell me, just as I didn't know how to tell him all my own doubts. I thought of a Sunday supplement feature I'd read recently – a *day-in-the-life* featuring Raglan, *the celebrated archaeologist recently hailed as the saviour of London's Royal Institute of Prehistoric Studies*. I didn't know what to say to someone like that.

'So . . .' I began.

The rim of the beaker was wonky. It was wonky and thick and it had a price-tag of £19.99, and a label saying *Carefully made in Kent by The Spinning Plates Collective*. It had as much to do with the Beaker People as a bottle of Fanta. I was amazed that Helen could ever have been so disrespectful to her own field of expertise.

Raglan smiled. 'Ah, well,' he said. 'I suppose even RIPS has to move with the times. Even Peter would have acknowledged that. Pure research sometimes has to make room for commerce . . .' And when I looked across at him I saw that his brown eyes were quite translucent in the slanting spring light, and contained the most melancholy expression I'd ever seen.

'And of course, it's entirely up to you if you'd rather not discuss any personal concerns you may have, Sybil,' he said, 'but I will say this: *keep yourself busy*. Work is a great antidote to stress. In its various guises. Work can fill the void, in a very positive way.'

'Right,' I said, alarmed. I wondered how much he actually knew, about my *personal concerns*: what stories Helen might have spun, during their arm-in-arm walks. *And once someone's started lying*, I thought, *what's to stop them? Where does it end?*

'I'm not wishing to pry in any way, of course. It's just that your work on *A History* isn't going at quite the . . . *pace* we'd hoped for. Given the rather imminent deadline. It's not as if we don't already have the green light from various academic quarters.'

'No.'

'And Helen's been getting a little anxious. What with all the publicity tie-ins.'

He glanced at me. Then he swigged the last of his coffee and set the repellent beaker down again on the table. He looked at it for one last moment, like a parent looking at a startlingly bad piece of artwork produced by their only child. 'An item that must be rather close to your own heart, too, of course,' he smiled, pushing his chair back. 'The humble beaker. The topic behind your own dissertation triumph a few years ago!'

'Yes,' I said. And I almost told him then, about Helen. But I decided not to. Because it was possible he might start to doubt my sanity, then. Which was probably just what Helen wanted.

'Anyway. Nice evening lined up?' he enquired, as we both pushed our chairs back and stood up to leave. 'Getting up to anything nice?'

I thought of my flat, of its four walls. I thought of Esther, and how tricky it was turning out to be, these days, sharing a flat with her. 'Well,' I said, 'I thought I might go for a swim.'

'A swim? Excellent plan! Where do you go?'

'Sorry?'

'Which pool do you use?'

'Oh . . .' I tried to think of one. 'Tooting Lido.'

'Really? Aren't the lidos a bit cold at the moment?'

'Hmm . . . Yes, maybe you're right . . . it might be a bit . . .'

'Unless you're planning to break the ice!'

'Yes . . . And I already did that last year, at Streatham Ice Rink!'

I stopped talking. Raglan was peering at me. At the scar on my forehead. Then, apropos of nothing, he said, 'Do you know the wonder of the world?'

I hesitated. 'The wonder of the world?' I asked, as we began heading towards the door. For a moment I thought he might be referring to Waterworld, a swim centre in Bromley I'd used to go to with Bethany Cowley when we were teenagers. Or maybe he'd had some peculiar religious vision.

'It's just a little poem that came to me,' he said. 'After our conversation about poetry the other night. It's rather beautiful, in its own way, and I – well, I *wondered* – if you knew it. It goes like this: "The wonder of the world",' he continued, launching into it, '"the beauty and the power . . ."'

'Right . . .' I said.

'". . . the shapes of things, their colours, lights, and shades . . ."'

175

'Hmm, I . . .'

'". . . these I saw. Look ye also",' he added, ' "while life lasts".'

He stopped. I waited, in case there was more, but there didn't seem to be.

'Well, that's lovely . . .' I said – because it was, really – and for a terrible moment I thought that he might cry, as we stood together in the café doorway, or even that *I* might, because the world *was* sometimes wonderful, that was undeniable, and life was short, and death was sad, however you looked at it. And the working week was full of pitfalls and people trying to catch you out. But then I pulled myself together because crying was no good to anyone, it was not going to achieve anything, so I said, 'Actually, I think I *have* read it somewhere, that poem. Isn't it the one in the front of all those Everyman books?'

'No, that's: "Everyman: I will go with thee, and be thy guide".'

'Ah . . .'

I had no desire to schlep all the way back to the fifth floor with him after that, so I pretended there was some research I needed to do in the Comparative Zoology Gallery, and we said goodbye at the foot of the stairs.

'Did you know, climbing all five flights every day for a year is the same as scaling Mount Kilimanjaro?' Raglan observed as he began his ascent. 'According to Helen.'

'Really? I didn't know Helen had been to Mount Kilimanjaro as well,' I said, and I turned and headed into the gallery. There *could*, after all, have been some research I needed to do in there – some fact-finding for Dr Appalsawmy, for a start.

'Hi,' I said to Danny as Raglan disappeared around the half-landing.

'Hello, darling.' The low, world-weary pitch of Danny's voice always suggested he might have recently emerged from some kind of trauma – fled an armed bank robbery, perhaps, or been hauled from the wreckage of an overturned coach. He was the calmest, most collected person I knew. He was sitting, as usual, on a small wooden chair just inside the doorway, one of those funny balloon-backed chairs with inexplicable, symmetrically drilled holes in the seat. I'd sat on that chair myself once, during a strange *episode* I'd had one evening at the start of February: RIPS had hosted a *Friends and Trustees* event to celebrate the new ties with LMIC, and I'd suddenly come over faint during Helen's presentation and had to sit down, my head bowed, a paper plate of crisps in my hands. 'I'll call you a cab, sweetheart,' Danny had whispered, leaning down to me as she'd droned on, and I'd wanted to reach out and put my arms around him. 'Hold me, Danny,' I'd wanted to say, and I'd wanted to press my tired, sorry head against his middle-aged midriff and ask him to take me home himself.

'Penned any good poems lately?' he asked now.

'None at all. Not a single one.'

'So, you're not a poet and you don't even know it?'

'Nope.'

'Thought you'd come and look around for inspiration, though?'

'I thought I might.'

'Not skiving off work or anything, then? Or coming to get an eyeful of my manly physique?'

'No, nothing like that, Danny. Heaven forbid.'

I whizzed on, through the archway into Room 1. A corner of the room had already been cordoned off, for development into the improved shop, but for the moment it retained an elegant expanse. Something about the stillness of the exhibits and the way the light shone into the room was still quite beautiful. I stood and looked for a while at the Institute's star attraction: Terence, a huge, taxidermied tortoise standing in a case. He was a creature I sometimes talked about when school groups came to look around. 'Terence has been here for nearly half a century,' I would tell the children standing there with their clipboards and their worksheets, 'and before that he was alive for well over a hundred years.' There was a sign on the case that said *Charles Darwin encountered this tortoise on the Galapagos Islands in March 1835. It survived until 1964. Imagine outliving both Charles Darwin and John F Kennedy!* it said beneath this, on one of Helen's new kid-friendly panels. She'd felt it was important, in her role as *interpretations consultant*, to make the signs more *relatable to kids*. Even though – as I'd pointed out during a staff meeting – a lot of visiting schoolchildren might not actually know who John F Kennedy *was*. 'Surely you have to be old enough to know that,' I'd said. 'I mean, if you asked them where they were when Kennedy was assassinated, they'd have said "*waiting forty years to be born*".' And she had shot me a look across the table suggesting she hated me almost as much as I hated her.

Terence's future was safe, of course. Helen had plans for post-cards and jigsaw puzzles and plush toy versions of him. A lot of the smaller, uglier exhibits, though, had already been ear-marked for storage. The fossilised eels and the small, un-lovely trilobites and the bits of dark, brackish Viking boat. I headed over to the display cases and looked at a piece of mammoth-hide in there. I observed its doormat texture. Then I looked at some fossilised dinosaur eggs lying in the case beside it. Five of them, in a fossilised nest. There was something potent about those eggs, as if the baby dinosaurs were still in there, biding their time. *Dinosaur babies*, I wrote, in my notebook. Then I headed across the shiny herring-bone-patterned floor into Room 2, to look at the alligator, smiling gently in its mahogany case.

The Great Survivor:
The alligator was here
when the dinosaurs were roaming the

The word 'earth' was missing. This was my fault: the formatting had gone wrong when I'd typed it a few weeks earlier. I'd stuck the panel up anyway.

A burst of sunshine breaking in through the window suddenly lit up all the exhibits on the far side of the room. Next door, Danny began to whistle a tune. He was so upbeat, despite having to sit at Primordial Swamp level all day. I spent a couple more minutes peering at things in cases:

Skulls (seal, pig, dog, ostrich, juvenile elephant)

Swan stomach

Kiwi skin

Axolotl

Then I went into the Gems Room to look at *The Language of Stones* – a display of gemstones some Victorian antiquarian had once assembled, for no reason other than the compulsion to collect things and put them in a case. I'd shown them to Simon once, when he'd come to see me after a shift at The Olive Branch. He stood looking into the case for such a long time I wondered if he might be thinking about engagement rings. Hanging alongside it was a chart linking various gemstones to different emotional states; there were quite a few dire ones in there, relating to perfectly innocent-looking pebbles. Despair was there, beside Dissembling and Desolation. Fear was there too, and Sorrow and Regret. 'Wow,' he'd said, 'they were a laugh, those Victorians,' and I'd smiled, and put my hand in his. 'There are *some* positive emotions,' I'd pointed out. 'Look: ruby means Love, and tiger's eye means Courage, and Hope's a garnet.'

'But wasn't that woman we met in the corridor called Hope?' he'd said. And I'd started to laugh.

A tear welled into my right eye now, tipped over and rolled down my cheek. They arrived out of the blue sometimes, my tears, like nosebleeds. I wiped my face with the back of my hand and looked at my watch. It was too early for any more tea-breaks. Too early for anything except going back upstairs to carry on with Raglan's book. I emerged from behind the pillar and returned to Room 1.

'Helen's in, by the way,' Danny said, as I headed through the doorway. 'Just to warn you. She came charging in here about twenty minutes ago.'

Because I'd told him once that I was not the biggest fan of Helen, even though I'd never told him why.

'Was she looking for me, by any chance?' I asked.

'She was, as a matter of fact.'

'So did she look a bit . . .'

'She wasn't looking too happy. She had quite a face on her.'

'Really? Not like one that launched a thousand ships?'

He smiled. 'Can't hide down here forever anyway, can you? You'd better get a move on, while the coast is clear.'

'OK,' I said, my heart suddenly racing. 'Thanks for letting me know.'

'No problem.' He looked up as a palaeontologist proceeded sombrely past into Room 1, holding aloft a small dinosaur skull. 'Alas, poor Yorick,' he added.

I moved fast after that – swiftly, stealthily, up the back staircase; quickly, quickly, like a cat burglar, up all the flights. Because Danny was right: you couldn't hide in the basement forever, despite some people being clearly out to get you. No, despite that, I thought as I leapt up the steps, you sometimes had to go ahead and risk it. You had to take your chances.

And just before I reached the safety of my office and its four, enclosing walls I met her, as he had warned me I might. There she was, standing in the semi-darkness by the foot of the Archives stairs; she was waiting for me like the bearer of bad news. Or just the bad news.

'Oh!' I said, a peculiar fear setting up in my chest, a kind of airlessness.

'Been on another little break?' she enquired. I did not reply. Glancing to my left, I could see all the things in my room, just out of reach. I could see my desk and chair and bag and coat; I could see the little teacup balanced on my list of keywords; I could see my computer, the screen still flickering at the Winchelsea Hoard pages.

'So I gather you've been wanting to see me?' I said, as she began to head along the corridor.

'Well, I'm not entirely sure where you've been getting that idea from,' she said, drawing level with me.

'Probably because everyone's been telling me, Helen. They've been saying you've been trying to reach me. Also, you rang my flat,' I said, this fact just occurring to me. 'Because my flatmate left me a note saying you had.'

Helen seemed to consider this for a moment. Then she carried on. 'Leaving that aside,' she said, 'it would be interesting to know why you're turning the indexing into such a perform-ance, Sybil! I mean, what's the hold-up here? What page have you reached, for goodness' sake?'

My brain rattled. I couldn't think which page I'd reached; I could hardly recall, suddenly, the order of the alphabet or the days of the week. Something seemed to have gone wrong with the normal functioning of my brain.

'Why does it bother you so much, what page I've reached?' I asked. 'Why is it so important?'

'Because it just is!'

'But why?'

Helen stared at me. Her eyes really were very pretty, it occurred to me, very pretty and round, all the whites showing around the irises.

'The thing is,' I said, 'indexing doesn't work like that anyway, does it? It's not a question of which "page" you're on. I mean, it's more like a zigzag, isn't it. Or a cat's cradle. Or a pin-ball machine.'

Helen went on staring. 'Indexing is like a *pin-ball machine*?'

I breathed in. 'I mean, sometimes I might be on V for votive figures,' I explained, 'and sometimes I might be on C for . . .' I peered over at the alarm clock sitting on the windowsill in my room '. . . carbon dating.'

'*Carbon dating*?'

'For instance,' I replied, warily. 'Sometimes I'm way *beyond* C. Like, V for Viking, or W for Winchelsea, or Z for . . . Anyway, it's coming along perfectly fine,' I said. 'Thanks for asking.' I breathed out again.

Helen made a strange sighing noise through her nose.

'What's taking you all this time, though, Sybil?' she burst out. 'I mean, are you deliberately stalling or something? I couldn't get any sense out of Raglan either, when I spoke to him just now. He's on a different bloody planet half the time, anyway – no wonder this place is falling apart! And you do *know* I'm meant to be doing the final read-through, don't you? So if you're going to be faffing about till the middle of next week you'll leave me no time whatsoever!'

I looked at her. 'Well, I'm sorry you're worried about the timings, Helen,' I said. 'But if the schedule's gone pear-shaped I think we know who to blame for that, don't we?'

For a second Helen appeared not to know what to say. Then, in a low, almost strangulated voice, she said, 'You need to get a grip, Sybil. That's all I'm saying. Because we're running out of time now.'

'Time for what, though?'

'For it to be with the *printer*!'

'That's a circular argument, Helen! It doesn't mean anything! It's like saying "because I said so"!'

'I *do* say so!' she said, marching on.

After she had gone, I went into my room, sat down and looked at the page I'd left open on the screen: *The wheat husks discovered during the dig match a variety only previously known to have been grown in Southern Italy. The team found no cereal-plant pollen or agricultural evidence to suggest the wheat was*

*grown in Britain, leading to the compelling theory that trade with
that part of the Mediterranean was almost certainly a factor in
the lives of the Sussex Beaker People—* until all the words began
to float in and out of focus again, all the little black dots descend-
ing like dark snowflakes; disintegrating, then rising upwards
every time I blinked.

8

Mist haiku 4

Leaves in bud
Leaves of absence
And the pathways
Misty grey

A text arrived on my phone as I was heading across the park that evening. I pulled it from my pocket. It said: *CU@8 EX*. It took me several seconds to work out what this meant – then I remembered the film I'd agreed to see with Esther. Time had turned and spun, clanked and shuffled round to *that* day, my own social arrangements carrying on almost despite me. *Looking forward to it*! I texted back.

Which was not true. But social niceties had to prevail – even though (it occurred to me as I headed out of the park onto Burney Street), I'd actually booked a hair appointment that evening. I'd completely forgotten about the appointment – it had gone right to the back of my mind somehow – and now it had come back.

For a moment I wondered if I should call and cancel my evening with Esther. Maybe I should just give up on the entire evening and go home to bed. But then I reflected that the salon, being in Brixton, was only a few minutes' walk down the road from the Ritzy cinema, where we were supposed to be seeing the film. My appointment, at six thirty, didn't actively *clash* with the time of the film. Besides, turning down another night out with Esther was almost certainly more than our friendship could bear. So I decided to continue with both arrangements, and carried on to the station.

The hairdresser's I'd booked to go to was called *A Cut Above*. I'd once used to go to the same hairdressing salon as Simon: a theatrically lit, retro place in Camden called *Mop*. There'd been a poster above a basin advertising haircuts from the fifties – *the crew, the flattop, the forward-combed boogie, the flattop boogie* – but nobody had ever emerged with one of those cuts. Simon had always favoured a longer style, anyway. It was almost the same length as Helen's. Although his hair was a beautiful chestnut brown while hers was quite a brassy blonde, as far as I was concerned.

The main thing about *A Cut Above*, anyway, was that it was not *Mop*. It was not *Mop*, with its memories. That much was clear, as soon as I walked in. The cylindrical hairdryers ranged around the walls suggested that, and the smell of setting lotion, and the wonky posters advertising cheap cuts from trainee stylists. The walls were a murky green, and there was a mural of mad-looking fish. The whole place was fish-themed, for reasons I couldn't work out.

'Hi, I've got an appointment at six thirty,' I said to a girl sitting at a desk behind a bowl of hard white mints. She was wearing an asymmetrical tunic, a bit like a dental hygienist's, and she had a correspondingly asymmetrical hairstyle.

'Cool. She won't be long,' the girl replied. 'She'll definitely be with you by quarter to. We're running a bit late.'

'Right.' I looked at my watch. It almost *was* quarter to. I thought of Esther, already waiting in under an hour's time outside the cinema, of the expression on her face when I arrived late. 'It's just that I . . .'

'Should be six forty-five, at the latest. She's pretty quick once she gets going.'

'OK.' This information did not fill me with confidence. I went across to a short line of plastic chairs beside the window, and sat down.

'Would you like a coffee?' the girl called over.

'No, I'll be fine, thanks.'

'Or a cup of tea?'

'I'm fine, thanks.'

There was a pile of old *Hello!* magazines on the window ledge. I leant forward and picked one up.

The Queen Smiles Bravely After a Difficult Week
Princess Anne Visits Sick Children
I'm So Happy with David, Rebecca confides.

But why did the Queen have a difficult week? And why is Princess Anne visiting sick children? And who are David and Rebecca? I no longer seemed to know these things. Fleetingly, I wondered if I should just stand up again and leave; I'd begun to lose faith in the whole idea of 'transformation as a healing power' – as Jane had quoted to me recently from a magazine she'd been reading at work. A transformative haircut seemed as unlikely now as the idea of poetry being therapeutic. Glancing down at the windowsill, I noticed there was a little fortune-telling fish lying there on top of its red and white plastic packet. I picked it up and looked at the list of emotions written on the back of the packet.

Moving head = jealous
Moving tail = independent
Moving head and tail = in love
Curls up entirely = passionate
Motionless = dead

Only when I placed the little cellophane shape on my palm, it did everything at once: it moved in all directions then fell off completely. Which meant that I was jealous and independent and in love and passionate and dead, all at the same time. There was a radio on somewhere, playing a song I didn't know. There was a smell of warm sulphur and hairspray. I listened to the song and looked at the mural on the wall and tried to work out what all the fish were for; the reason for their existence. They seemed to have no bearing on the name 'A Cut Above', unless you counted fish cutlets. Even the clock had a small, plastic goldfish attached to one of its hands: the fish bounced upwards every second and when it got past twelve it spent the next thirty seconds bouncing back upside down.

'Hi! In for a tidy up?' boomed a large woman, emerging through a door between two basins.

'Yes, I—'

'I'll take your jacket.'

She took my crumpled coat from my lap and hung it up on a coat-rack on the wall.

'Ooh – have you got your phone in here?' she asked, patting the pocket. 'Do you want to hang onto that?'

'No, it's OK, thanks.'

'Sure?'

Now she unpegged a grey smock – reminiscent, I couldn't help thinking, of the deathly woollen ponchos Hope Pollard wore at work – draped it around my shoulders and did up the Velcro beneath my chin.

'So what can I do for you today?' she asked, leading me to a chair facing a mirror at the back of the salon.

'I'd just like it a bit shorter, please,' I said, sitting down. 'Nothing too drastic, but I think it's time for—'

'—a little change?'

'Yes.'

'Are you sure you want it short, though?' She pulled doubtfully at a strand of hair near my right ear.

'Well, not *too* short. I'd just like a kind of—' I began, but I didn't know what to call it any more, this style I was after, this transformative look: what name did it have?

The woman picked up a comb. 'How about if I cut it reasonably short at the back and sides . . . and leave it longer on top . . . ? A bit Pixie-ish? Like Katie Holmes has her hair? That would suit you.'

I didn't know how Katie Holmes had her hair. I didn't know who Katie Holmes was. I felt I might have known, once, but now I didn't.

'Still quite long at the top, though,' the woman went on, 'and sweeping a bit to one side.' She gathered up my hair between both hands and pushed it around my head. In the mirror, I saw her catching sight of my skating scar, and frowning. 'That sound like the kind of thing? Shall we go for something like that?'

Then she let my hair fall back, picked up something that looked like a plant-sprayer – probably it *is* a plant-sprayer, I thought – and squirted a fine mist of water over my head. Next she picked up a comb and combed my hair, rather unceremoniously, straight over the front of my face. 'Nice weekend ahead of you?' she asked. 'What do you do during the week?'

I bent my head forward, like someone praying. 'I work,' I said, my voice rising guttural and strange from behind the curtain of my own hair, 'in an institute.'

'Come again?'

'In an archaeological institute.'

'Really?' She picked up some scissors and began to cut. 'Do you mean the one down in Greenwich?

'Yes!' I said, startled. It always surprised me when people had heard of RIPS. Everyone had heard of the Maritime Museum, and the Observatory, but RIPS was such a place apart – a place full of oddballs worrying about bits of pottery and rock – that it was amazing to me that anyone knew of its existence.

'I saw a thing on telly a few weeks ago,' she continued. 'One of those *Weird Wonders* programmes.'

'Ah, yes . . .'

'Why is it called "Weird Wonders"?'

'I don't know,' I said. Looking down I saw, with some concern, that there were already quite lengthy curls of my hair landing on my lap – they were falling fast, like something inevitable – like leaves or tears.

'It's always interesting, though, isn't it?' the woman said, continuing to cut. 'Finding out about the past.'

'Yes, the past is always interesting.'

'It's a way of finding out about yourself sometimes, isn't it? Like in those family history programmes.'

'Yes, it is.'

She sighed. 'All those artefacts, telling you bits and bobs about people,' she said. Then, placing her left hand onto my shoulder, she leant forward and plugged something into the wall. A hairdryer? I wondered, peering up, a hairdryer already? But no, it was not a hairdryer, it was a pair of *clippers*. 'Actually, I didn't—' I began, alarmed, but she had already switched the clippers on, and the noise was already too loud: the metal teeth had already been placed against the nape of my neck. 'Actually, I don't—' I shouted above the whirring, but it was too late – she had already shaved a strip up the back of my neck. I could feel it: the blunt, vertical line of it. 'Oops, sorry: did I catch you?' she said, because she'd nicked my skin now, just a little – there was a definite pain there. 'Ooh, sorry, darling!' Then she switched off the clippers, turned abruptly to the shelf and picked up something that looked like a make-up remover pad.

'And there was me being so careful to avoid your little . . . scar, there . . .' she said cautiously, dabbing at my neck. 'Just hold that there for a moment, love. Just to stop the flow.'

'The thing is—' I began, accepting the make-up remover pad and pressing it against my skin.

'I'm going to cut the front now,' she continued. 'Just with the scissors.'

'The thing is . . .' I said.

'What, love?'

'I didn't want it this short. I just wanted a trim.'

She hesitated. 'Well, that's not what I understood you to mean,' she said, a little huffily. She turned, a clouded look of regret on her face as if clippers probably *had* been a bad idea, picked up the scissors again and recommenced snipping. 'It's only half-done at the moment: when it's finished you'll get the whole look properly,' she said. 'It's going to be on trend. It's going to be *on fleek*. I'll tell you what, though: your fringe has got a mind of its own.'

But I didn't even *want* a fringe! I thought. My hair is not that kind of hair. Suddenly I couldn't bear it any longer. 'You know, this really wasn't the look I wanted at all,' I said, more robustly.

She stopped.

'So what did you want?'

'Not this! I didn't want this!'

'You know, you're just thinking it's too short because it's new. When you get used to it you're going to love it.'

Then she brushed the cut ends of my hair from my shoulders – all the long hair Simon had loved – or so he'd used to tell me – the wavy, mid-length hair he had run his fingers through, and caused to become tangled sometimes, in moments of passion.

'Do you want to see the back with the mirror?'

'No, it's OK, thanks,' I said.

And, after she'd dried it some more, and swept something through it that she called *conditioning serum*, I slid down from the chair, pulled the tunic off from around my neck and went up to the till. I paid £48 to the girl with the asymmetrical hair – £8 more than I'd used to pay at *Mop* – took a mint from the bowl, and emerged *transformed*, into the evening.

'Samson was transformed, of course, when *his* hair was cut . . .' I recalled Jane reading out to me from her magazine the previous week. 'You mean Samson, as in Samson and Delilah?' I'd replied, 'because it didn't end very well for him, did it? He ended up having his eyes gouged out and having to grind corn for the Philistines.' She'd looked at me. 'It worked out OK for Delilah, though, didn't it?' she said.

It was five to eight. Now I had to run to get to the Ritzy, I had to pound along the pavements, to see a film I didn't want to see with Esther, who would almost certainly still be angry with me, and would be even angrier now I was late.

But when I eventually arrived in the foyer entrance, she did not appear to be there at all. I scanned the crowd, but she was not amongst the groups of people hanging around the ticket desk, or with the larger group on the pavement outside. I took my phone out of my pocket. She had left a text.

Sybil – got held up. Won't make film tonight. Soz. E X.

Unexpectedly, my heart lifted; strangely it soared, at the prospect of being left alone, and surplus to Esther's requirements. It was sometimes beautifully simple, being stood up. Also, these days, it was usually for the best. And I was on the point of setting off again – heading thankfully back home with my terrible haircut and my guilt and the loneliness I was somehow, increasingly, learning to embrace, when I became aware of some other presence – someone regarding me – and I looked up, and there was Bill, from the library – there was *Brixton Bill*, leaning against the ticket kiosk with a couple of friends.

I put my right hand up to my face and felt my cheek growing warm. There was nothing to hide behind, though – not even my own hair any more – and now I couldn't even *escape* without drawing attention to myself, a whole crowd of people having suddenly materialised around me; having somehow risen up from the pavement to prevent me from getting away. Bill was leaning very still and watchful and wearing a pale green T-shirt with a lot of writing on it. I couldn't see what the writing said, but maybe it was some new opinion about Nostradamus and the end of the world. He turned to his friends, and I could see that he was smiling about something. I remained un-moving within the moving crowd, my face hot, my heart hammering, and prayed that he wouldn't speak to me; that he would ignore me, that he would simply—

'Hi,' he said.

'Hi,' I replied.

Now his friends turned to look, and a gap opened up through which I could read the writing on his T-shirt. It said:

> I can only please one person a day
> Today is not your day
> Tomorrow does not look good either

'You've had your hair cut,' he said.

'I know.'

He turned and began speaking to his friends again. I thought of the conversation we'd had a few nights earlier – the ridiculous exchange about magazine racks and five-line poems. *It's that girl who goes to Poetry for the Terrified*! Maybe he was telling them that. *It's that girl who writes haikus in the basement.*

I looked away but I could sense him still watching me.

'So are you waiting for someone?' he asked after a moment, across the crowd, 'or are you here on your own?'

'Yes, I'm here on my own,' I replied, abruptly. 'I quite often go to the cinema on my own, actually. I've never seen what the big deal is, sitting on your own in the dark.'

'Right.' He hesitated. 'I think it's the sitting on your own in the dark that bothers some people.'

'It's quite liberating,' I said. 'You should try it.'

'Yeah, you should, Bill!' one of his friends said, and began to laugh.

'You can sit with us, if you like,' Bill said to me. 'This is Max and this is John.'

I felt myself clenching my fists, as if about to punch them.

'Hi,' I said.

'Hi,' said Max and John.

'And your name is?'

'Sorry?' I said. 'Oh. It's Sybil.'

'Sybil?'

'Yes.'

He considered this for a second. 'So we're practically twins.'

'What?'

The queue began to move forward again, and Max, John and Bill moved too, till they were swallowed up into the dark, popcorn-smelling embrace of the auditorium.

I turned left, plodded along a lower row of seats and sat down, a great expanse of empty moquette all around me. I loved the Ritzy – I'd been there so many times over the years, most recently with Simon – but it did not feel romantic any more. The upholstery smelt of greasy hair and popcorn and old smoke, and *Get Over It* was clearly not the kind of film I should ever have agreed to see with anyone, not even Esther, not even in an ironic way – as Bill and his friends were obviously doing. I sat through all the adverts and trailers, several rows in front of them, and sensed them looking at the back of my head. From time to time I thought I heard the low drone of their voices. The male repartee. I thought I heard Bill whisper, '*Yeah, Bashō!*'

In the dim light I leant forward, unzipped my bag and took out my notebook.

Popcorn, I scribbled in the darkness.

Flip-back seats

Smell of sweat

And I realised that I had to go. I had to. I stood up. Half-stooped in the semi-darkness, I edged my way back along the row of seats to the illuminated Exit. I didn't look round as I went. I didn't need to, to know that Bill and his friends were all still sitting there in a row, like the three wise monkeys.

'You OK, love?' asked the woman standing behind the sweets counter in the foyer. She was a big woman and she was eating a big packet of M&Ms, all to herself.

'I'm fine, thanks,' I said.

'Film not your cup of tea?'

'Not really.'

'They're not for everyone, these films.' She tipped in another handful and glanced around as if my date might be just round the corner. 'You have to be in the right mood.'

'Yes.'

'I mean, if you're not in the mood sometimes for these rom-coms...'

'Yes.' *Stop talking, please stop talking.*

'Mind you, Leonardo DiCaprio's pretty easy on the eye!'

'Yes.' I felt suddenly light-headed again. 'He's quite... I mean, he's pretty nice-looking, but, actually,' I concluded, 'I think you might be thinking of another film.'

The woman looked at me. 'You all right, honey? You look...'

'Yes,' I said, and I turned and fled. It seemed imperative to get away now, as far and as fast as possible. I ran down Electric Lane, past the rows of shops and the little cafés, past the entrance to the market and on to Rushcroft Road. Then on, again. I crossed the road at the pedestrian lights and on, to Coldharbour Lane. On Windrush Square, glancing up at an empty shop window, I noticed a small poster stuck to the glass. It said: *Bill Posters Will Be Prosecuted*, and I thought of Bill again, and I also remembered a sign that had said exactly the same thing, on a brick wall which Simon and I had used to walk past on our way to the tube station in the mornings. It had turned up there a week or so after the RIPS Christmas party, and the first time we'd noticed it, I'd observed that it was *very self-referential*: 'It's very self-referential,' I'd said, 'sticking a poster on a wall that says "*Don't stick posters on this wall*"!' And Simon, who'd appeared to be deep in thought about something – amaranth grains, perhaps, or the gym membership he'd decided to take out, or possibly some decision more far-reaching and complicated than that – had looked vacantly at me.

'What?' he'd said, letting go of my hand.

Maybe I should have said something different, I thought now. Maybe I should have said, 'Poor Bill Posters! What did *he* do that was so wrong?'

But I think we were already past playing word games.

> Rising early
> Mascara-smudged
> The moon disappearing
> And I still miss you

I woke in the early hours the next morning and went into the kitchen to make myself a cup of tea. The back of my neck felt cold. It had a strange new directional quality, like the nap on a piece of fabric. It was like a boy's hair. I sat, peering out through the window, and thought of all the ways in which my life had lately unravelled. I didn't know what conclusions to reach any more, about anything; I had learned nothing. When I looked out through the window all I could see against the darkness was the upsetting outline of my newly shorn head.

My mother rang early that afternoon, while I was going through all the old receipts in my purse. They'd been accumulating for months: the café receipts, the bus tickets, the grocery bills from the Co-op. Even the Streatham Ice Rink receipt was still in there.

'We've been swimming in some volcanic pools,' my mother said, after we'd been chatting for a while.

'Cool.'

'Actually they were quite warm,' I heard my father quip in the background: my mother must have put me on speakerphone.

'I was thinking of going swimming myself, actually. At Tooting Lido,' I said. 'But then someone said it's probably still closed for the season.'

'Sorry?'

'It's probably closed.'

'What is?'

'Tooting Lido.'

'Oh . . .'

'So,' I continued, twisting the phone cord around my little finger, a strange lump in my throat, 'were they lovely and warm? The volcanic pools? Were they like those ones those monkeys sit in, in the Himalayas?'

There was a little silence. Then my mother said, 'In fact, they weren't all that warm . . .' She sounded doubtful: as if, in some troubling way, I was a source of great regret to her. Probably I was. Probably we *both* were, me and my father. 'They're not like hot *springs*,' she said. 'The volcano erupted a long time ago, darling. Thousands of years ago.'

'Millions,' my father said in the background. 'She ought to know that!' he added. 'Considering where she works.'

I reached out, pulled a little piece of bread off a granary loaf that Esther had left on the table, and put it in my mouth.

'Talking of volcanoes,' I said, 'I've been checking references about volcanoes recently. About volcanic eruptions causing crop failures and ultimately bringing about the fall of Ancient Egypt.'

'Really?'

'Yes. Raglan Beveridge writes about it, in his book.'

'Well. Goodness me. And what else have you been up to recently?' she asked. As if I was also, perhaps, contemplating the destruction of some ancient empire.

'Well, as I said, I was thinking of going swimming yesterday,' I said. 'But in the end I didn't. And I was also planning to go to the cinema. But I didn't do that, either. I mean, I went, but then I changed my mind.'

There was another small pause at the end of the line. 'Are you all right?' my mother said. 'You sound a bit . . .'

'A bit what?'

'Distant.'

'Well, I'm eating some bread,' I said. 'I've got some bread in my mouth. Maybe that's why. Also, I had a really bad haircut yesterday,' I confessed, reaching up to stroke the depressing shortness of it. 'Which has got me down a bit.'

'A bad haircut?'

'Yes. It's really, it's just . . . awful, Mum. On top of everything else.'

'Tell her – your hair *is* on top of everything else!' my father said.

My mother ignored this.

'It'll grow, love,' she said, after a moment. 'Hair grows. That's one thing you can say about it.'

'I know,' I said. 'I know hair grows.'

'Sorry?'

'It doesn't matter.'

I swallowed the bread, and felt it lodge halfway down my throat, like a fish too big for a seabird's gullet. I tried to picture the place my parents were in, but it was not a scene I could conjure. The previous day, the screensaver on my computer had displayed a picture of a craggy seaside grotto. 'Journey to this far-flung isle,' a sentence beneath had suggested, 'and you'll be standing on what was once considered *the end of the world*!' Maybe it was somewhere like that.

'The thing is,' I said, 'I'm just finding things quite stressful at work at the moment. Raglan's being quite weird about things – quite jumpy and odd – and I've got this copy-date coming up really soon for the reprographics department, and Helen—'

'Hah! That woman!'

'Yes. She's being odd, too. She keeps wanting to see me about work stuff, and then not wanting to see me. I bumped into her yesterday, and she was just being horrible about it.'

'Well, she *is* horrible, darling, as we know!'

'Yes, but she was being . . . hostile. I don't know, but I'm sure she's up to something . . .'

'Up to something? Even more than she's already been up to?'

'Yes. I just think – I mean, I've even been wondering if she and Raglan are having some sort of—'

But before I could say it – before I could say 'affair', I heard my father's voice again.

'Food!' he proclaimed, and my mother interrupted.

'Darling, can I call back in a bit? It's just, our food's arrived.'

'Sure.' I could still feel the impression of the bread against the pink inside of my throat. *I'm scared, Mum*, I wanted to say. *I'm scared, and I'm sad and I don't know what to do.* 'What is it?' I asked.

'What's what?'

'The food?'

There was a pause. 'Mine seems so involve some sort of squid . . .'

'Closest living relative to the ammonite,' I said.

'Sorry?'

'The squid is the closest living relative to the ammonite. One of the palaeontologists told me that recently.'

'But surely an ammonite's much less squidgy than a squid . . .' my mother said; I pictured her prodding a fork doubtfully at the meal in front of her.

'That's because it's fossilised,' I said. 'In life it was a soft creature, with a hard outer shell. Like a crab. But then it turned into stone. Like the lava pools you and Dad were in: they were boiling hot lava once, but now they're just kind of petrified bathtubs.'

And we said goodbye.

Returning the phone to its cradle, I glanced up at the notice-board. It still bore the little message Esther had written:

That book I mentioned is 'Overcoming Heartbreak' by Elaine Pritchard. PS. Your nemesis rang.

I spent the next hour lying in our own small plastic bathtub, in bubbles designed to transport me away *on a cloud of vetiver, lime and ylang ylang, restoring a sense of tranquillity.* I switched on Esther's little old transistor radio that sat at the side of the bath and listened to three love songs, back to back (as the presenter said). The songs suggested that I was all out of love, that I wanted to know where love was, that love hurt. I lay there, listening. Then rising up out of the water, like Poseidon rising from the depths, I stepped out, dried myself, put on my dressing gown and went back into the living room. I switched on the television and watched *Who Wants to be a Millionaire?*, lying on my stomach on the wine-stained carpet.

Question: Who first deciphered Linear A pottery fragments at the ancient archaeological site of Knossos? Was it:

a) Sir Arthur Evans   b) Sir Arthur Conan Doyle
c) Heinrich Schliemann   d) Dr Henry Heimlich

'I'm sorry I didn't make it to the Ritzy last night,' Esther said when we bumped into each other in the kitchen later, around six o'clock. 'To be honest, Paul and I got carried away in bed; we just got caught up in the heat of the moment. We were having this afternoon of passion. And then it was too late to catch the film.'

'Right.' I looked across at the kitchen cabinets. 'Well, that's . . .'

'We've been having just the most fantastic sex, me and Paul, to be honest. Best sex of my life. I mean, completely no comparison with Lucas.'

I resisted the urge to put both my hands over my ears and shout *I'm not listening, I'm not listening*! I had never met Lucas.

But I couldn't help thinking he might have been more interesting than the impressive but monosyllabic Paul.

'Cracking haircut, by the way,' Esther added, pulling open the fridge door and getting out a small pot of yogurt.

'What do you mean, "cracking"?' I asked.

'I mean it's . . . *definite*. Bold. Where did you get it done?'

'Brixton,' I said. 'In a fish-themed hairdresser's.'

'A fish-themed hairdresser's?' Esther turned to look at me. She frowned slightly. 'You're wearing your dressing gown,' she said.

'I know I'm wearing my dressing gown.'

'So are you getting ready to go out or something?'

'No. I'm just wearing my dressing gown.'

'Right . . .' She hesitated. 'Well, it's fab,' she said, after a moment. 'Your hair. Really definite.'

Which I suppose was her way of apologising. I was still not sure, though, what she meant by *cracking*. And shortly before seven she went out again in any case, with Paul, to see *Les Misérables*. 'Bye, Sybs!' she called happily, as I sat, chewing muesli like a camel in the kitchen. 'Bye,' I croaked back. It always intrigued me, that people who booked tickets to see *Les Misérables* always seemed so cheerful about it.

9

Anglepoise
This black-hooded woman
Is watching me work.
Sometimes I hear her ribs ring

Looking down from the bus on Monday morning I thought I saw Bill again, inspecting a crate of oranges outside the Fruit-ilicious greengrocer. It was something to do with his stance, and height, and the colour of his hair. Also, it seemed to be the sort of thing he might do. Then, when I looked more closely, I saw that it wasn't him, only someone who looked like him. It was funny, I thought, as the bus trundled on, because the people you might want to see – the people you might perhaps want to strike up some sort of conversation with – are never the people you actually *do* see. You could spend your whole life not seeing the people you might actually *want* to see. Yet you could bump into your enemy almost every day of the week.

In the Institute's little car park I noticed somebody had scrawled a new line of graffiti on the short stretch of brick wall outside the car park. It said:

This wall belongs to Lionel Richie

Which made me smile, despite myself – and also reminded me of the song that had been playing the night Simon and I crashed into the side of Streatham Ice Rink.

I worked on the words *threshing, chaff* and *treasure trove* that morning – the word *trove*, I learned, coming from the French verb *trouver*. Which was, I supposed, just another way of saying *found objects*.

Shortly before eleven I received another email from clive-the-detectorist@aol.com. *Just wondering if you ever received my email concerning Roman ballisters on 1st April*? he'd written, peevishly. There was a new email, too, from a mudlarker called Denis Sivcek who had found a stash of clay pipes beside the Thames at Vauxhall. He was quite excited about it. There was one pipe, he said, that was completely intact, and had a really detailed love-heart engraved on it.

Dear Denis, I wrote. *It's actually quite common to find clay pipes in the mud around the Thames – even quite elaborate ones – because of all the dockers who worked there in Victorian times.*

But then I deleted this, because it sounded quite mean – like the joyless kind of put-downs Helen would have made in the margins of my old essays. And all the time, as I sat there, I tried to work out what she was up to. It was obvious she was up to something, with her urgent little copy-date enquiries. I just could not fathom what it was.

I am in the dark, I informed my notebook.

But my notebook wasn't giving me any answers.

Greenwich Mean Time, I added.

Time is a great healer

Time and relative dimension in space

Time and tide wait for no man

Time will say nothing but I told you—

'Coffee, Sybil?' Jane suggested, putting her head round the door, and I practically rocketed out of my chair.

'Sorry,' she said. 'Did I startle you?'

I worked on the index for the rest of the morning. Helen's Winchelsea chapter was like the magic porridge pot, constantly producing more porridge. Yet somehow it also had to be finished in the next two days. 'You OK, love?' someone asked me when I went outside for a breath of air late that morning, and I looked up, a little blurry-visioned again. It was the woman I'd seen a few times before in the park – the one with the buggy and the small boy and all the bags. She was peering at me with a look of motherly concern.

'You was looking as white as a sheet just then,' she said. 'When you was going over to the bin. Like you was going to pass out.'

'Was I?' I said, squinting up at her against the bright, rain-filled daylight. I wondered what I looked like these days; how I came across to the world. 'Maybe it's because of my job,' I said. 'I work in the Royal Institute over there. It's enough to make anyone pass out.' Which was meant to be a friendly display of banter. Of work-related humour. But the woman was looking at me now as if regretting speaking to me in the first place. She stooped for a moment to pick up a toy her child had lobbed onto the pathway. 'You don't look too well, anyway, pet,' she said. 'You should look after yourself.'

On my way back across the grass I picked up a copy of the *Metro* that someone had stuck between two rails in a fence, and turned to the horoscopes page.

Mars is moving through the part of the sky that governs hard work and commitment, Pisces! Watch out for surprises mid-week because Mars will turn retrograde and Jupiter is going backwards

I thought: is there a part of the sky that governs hard work and commitment? I wasn't convinced about that – or about Jupiter going backwards. I wasn't even sure I believed in surprises mid-week.

Back indoors I slid a new sentence into place on the fridge door.

love something important, I wrote.

Which was really just a grouping of available words. Then I printed out a memo I'd typed up the previous Friday, and pinned it to the noticeboard.

Late in the afternoon there was a small party in the boardroom on the 3rd floor, to celebrate the launch of Helen's Beakerware range.

It was also, coincidentally, the Mary Anning event.

This fact had managed to edge its way in, too, on the reverse of the press release. The Institute had been planning the Mary Anning event for months, to mark the two hundred years since she had discovered the ichthyosaur, in 1811. This had always been quite an important bicentenary, in palaeontological terms. But it seemed to have become a bit of a side-show now.

I abandoned my work shortly before four, went down to Floor 3 and slipped in through the door of the Maud Forrester Room. I did not pick up a Beakerware flyer as I went in; I couldn't bring myself to look at the photo of Simon that I felt sure would be on it. I was the last to arrive, in any case: the rest of the staff and all the Trustees were already there, beakers in hand, hanging around the Institute's portrait of Mary Anning. The room was very crowded and there were several people there I'd never seen before: I presumed they were Helen's LMIC colleagues, or TED talk directors, or possibly representatives from the Spinning Plates Collective. They were all wearing quite smart, celebratory clothes, but they seemed, on the whole, to have quite a serious, un-celebratory look.

'Hi, Sybil,' Jane mouthed wanly to me across the room as I stood in the doorway, and I gave her a little wave.

I was there just in time for the end of Professor Muir's opening speech about the *new, dynamic relationship between RIPS and the London Museums Interpretation Centre*. 'And from beakers to Beveridges, let's hear from Professor Beveridge himself about the main reason for this exciting event,' he was saying in a depressed voice, his words rolling on with a kind of weary inevitability. And then it was Raglan's turn to talk, mainly about Helen, it seemed – 'who is well-known to all, of course, as the director of the London Museums Interpretation Centre, but is also here wearing her academic – indeed, her academic *celebrity* hat this afternoon, as Beaker People expert and discoverer of the Winchelsea Hoard!' At this, Helen flashed a beautiful and nauseating smile, and everyone made strange murmuring noises of approval and held their beakers aloft. It was like a Druidic ceremony, some weird ritual at Avebury or Stonehenge. I wondered what on earth had happened to everyone. 'And as well as recently unearthing these new, quite ground-breaking developments within the study of early trade routes,' Raglan continued – then he paused for a second and looked down, into the depths of his beaker, 'Dr Hansen's presence has also introduced a new direction,' he mumbled, almost apologetically, 'for our commercial work here at RIPS.'

A few of the staff and Spinning Plates people clapped. A few of the Trustees moved position and looked suddenly rather upset.

'And of course, what better occasion to celebrate Dr Hansen's success, than in the bicentenary year of Mary Anning's *own* great discovery!' he concluded sadly.

Yes, everyone agreed, nodding, it was a very apt year. Then we all topped up our drinks and said Cheers, and after a couple of minutes people began to move cautiously around, to strike out like wandering tribes and join up with other straying little groups.

I thought of the Christmas party that had taken place just over four months earlier. I thought of the G&T and the IPA and the whisky mac. There were some ichthyosaur-shaped cheese straws on plates. They were doing the rounds. They'd been baked by Hope, Jane whispered to me as she moved through the crowd with them on a tray, and they were as dry as sticks, she added – dry as old ichthyosaur bones. So I gave them a miss.

'What are we doing here, Jane?' I asked her.

'I honestly couldn't tell you,' she replied. 'I really have no idea why we're all raising our glasses to Helen Hansen.' She looked at me with an expression of sweet concern. 'She's hardly the next Mary Anning, is she?'

'No,' I said. 'But then, who is?'

'I found your sandwich box again, by the way,' she went on. 'You left it out by the General Wolfe statue this time. It was just sitting there on the steps!'

'Really? Was it? God . . .'

'Anyway, I've brought it in. I'll nip down in a bit and pop it back in your tote bag, when I've a moment. And so you don't forget to take it home.'

'Thanks, Jane,' I replied. I couldn't bring myself to tell her that I had never taken my tote bag home, not once, since I'd been given it.

'Fabby haircut,' she added, politely. 'Where did you get that done?'

'Brixton.'

'Well, it's very . . .'

She moved on.

I picked up a beaker from one of the trestle tables ranged around the sides of the room, and took a sip. The rim of it was just as thick and annoyingly awkward as the one I'd drunk my coffee from in the café with Raglan. The fruit punch also tasted horribly of artificial guava, but I felt that the alcoholic version was best avoided. I stood for five minutes, ten minutes, talking to no one. I thought of Jane heading down to the Reception cupboard with my lunch box and wished I'd asked her just to stay with me, to not bother, but she'd left the room now so it was too late. I could hear Helen's voice without even turning round to look at her. I knew she was standing at the far end of the room near the fire extinguisher, impressing a Bronze Age jewellery specialist, but I could not bear to go over there, I could not even bear to dissemble. I had begun to feel increasingly worn out these days, by the sheer fact of her presence around the place. By the fact that she had *won*. She had won the game. I looked around, but there was no one else I could contemplate talking to, Raglan being surrounded now by a group of oddly hostile-looking Trustees, and Jane presumably still hunting for my bag down in Reception. Danny wasn't even *there*; having dutifully wheeled the picture of Mary Anning up in the lift, he'd headed back to the safety of the gallery. And Peter Edwards – a man I imagined I might well have liked if I'd ever met him – was sadly and unavoidably detained in Camberwell Cemetery.

I reached out, poured the remains of my fruit punch into a nearby pot plant, and put the beaker down on the table. Then, aware that Helen was trying to catch my eye, I went to stand further away from her, near the long window, beside the portrait of Mary Anning. The room was emptier there – and besides, I liked Mary Anning, this woman who'd discovered a dinosaur before people had even known what dinosaurs *were*, before they'd comprehended what it was they'd been trampling underfoot. There she stood, on the beach at Lyme Regis, with nothing except a pickaxe and her bare hands to help her dig; there she was, with only a wicker basket and her little dog Tray at her feet. She looked a bit like Jane, I always thought; she had the same quiet stance and steady gaze. In the picture she also looked on the verge of discovering something, or maybe she'd already discovered it. 'Hi, Mary,' I whispered, and I reached out and touched the painting's frame.

'Sybil – communing with the great Mary Anning?' Raglan asked, roaming towards me with an opened wine bottle. His hair was uncharacteristically messy-looking, I couldn't help thinking, and his eyes were rather bloodshot. He almost looked as if he'd been in a fight.

'Hi, Raglan . . .' I said, disconcerted. I looked back at the portrait, at Mary Anning's calm face and her neat hair tucked demurely beneath her bonnet.

Mary Anning, 1799–1847, said the sign hanging beside the picture.

Anning's childhood discoveries included the first correctly
identified ichthyosaur, in 1811, and some important fish
fossils. As an adult she was fairly well-known in geological
circles, though sadly never truly recognised in her lifetime.
In 1817, her finds came to the attention of Thomas Birch, a
British fossil collector, who purchased several specimens.
He later auctioned off his collection, donating the proceeds
to the Anning family during a period of particular
financial hardship.

'I mean, sometimes it's just easier at parties, isn't it?' I said.
'What is?'
'Talking to inanimate objects.'
'Well, I've never done that . . .'
'You should try it.'
'Hah! Perhaps!' Raglan agreed. There was a short silence.
Then he said, 'Oh, Sybil!'
'What?' I asked, my heart leaping.
But he seemed to lose his nerve, to conclude that whatever it
was he'd planned to say should probably remain unsaid. 'Can I
tempt you to a little wine?' he said, instead. 'I gather these
wondrous goblets hold a whole 250 mils.'
'Well,' I said. 'That's very impressive.'
I frowned and looked down again, slightly blurrily, at a newer
information panel hanging beside the official one. The
kid-friendly one. Helen had written it.

FUNNY FISH FINDS!
Next time you're at the beach, why not go rock-pooling and
see what you can find? Maybe you'll find a starfish or a
crab! You might even find an ichthyosaur!

Yeah, in your dreams, Helen! I felt like scrawling beneath.

Raglan cleared his throat. 'Or perhaps some more fruit punch?'

'Well, that's a tempting offer.' I peered around at the people gathered there, and the big blue display boards and the bits of broken old china, and the party food. Helen's Beakerware was arranged in ugly-looking pyramids on one of the tables. One of the TED talk people was discussing lighting cables. Someone from the Spinning Plates Collective was talking about win-win situations and export markets and low-hanging fruit. And my head ached, and my heart ached, and I felt eroded. I felt like the badlands.

'I've got to go now, Raglan,' I said.

'Go where?'

'Just out for a bit. For some fresh air.'

'Really?' He looked quite startled, as if fresh air was a novel concept. 'Are you sure I can't tempt you to some more fruit punch on your way out? It's got all sorts of health-giving properties, I believe. Wheatgrass and all sorts, I gather.'

'I'm sure, thanks,' I said, and I turned to leave.

'Sybil!' Helen called as I began making my way across the room. I froze and glanced over. She was still standing beside the trilobite cabinet with the Bronze Age specialist. She was also wearing her grey dress, it occurred to me – she must have changed somewhere since I'd first spotted her earlier that day. It was the same dress with the blue flowers that she'd worn at the Christmas party. That she'd first seduced Simon in.

'Where are you going?' she called.

'Out,' I replied.

'But why?' she said. 'It's pouring with rain!'

I hesitated. I looked through the window. It was pouring with rain.

Before she could continue, I hurried to the door, turned left and headed towards the lift. The park was calling me – the park was my friend: beautiful, beautiful Greenwich Park, with its cherry blossom and its crows and its rubbish bins and its invisible benches and its eternally hopeful sundial. If I was in love with anything any more, it was the park: it was where I needed to be, amongst the corvus corvus and the rainclouds and the bins.

I pressed the Call Lift button, stepped in through the opening doors and pressed again for the ground floor.

Then at the last minute, on impulse – a Blind Sybil kind of hunch – I pressed Button Five and rose upwards instead, to the Prints and Archives Room.

10

Spring trends this season:
Statement-making textured bobs
Cool colour combos
(with thanks to Hair magazine)

Study some ecclesiastical designs;
use sweet wrappers
for the stained glass windows
and sequins
for the glitter
of haloes
(with thanks to Constance Johnstone)

Usually when I went up to Archives there was no one else around, but that afternoon Mr Won was there. Mr Won was the Institute's sole surviving volunteer, ever since a purge of interested amateurs had seen off all the others a couple of months earlier. I liked Mr Won. He was a matter-of-fact man. You'd never have caught *him* at a boardroom party. He was sitting at a high table near the window that afternoon, looking at prints of geodes: little halves of lumpy, hollowed-out space-rock. As a child, I'd found one of those rocks myself in our back garden and had kept it on my bedroom windowsill, along with various other peculiar treasures. 'That fell out of the sky,' my father told me, when I'd shown it to him. I'd used to imagine it was a hatched alien's egg from Mars.

'Hi, Mr Won,' I said.

'Good afternoon, Miss Wiseman,' he replied, glancing up, then looking back down at the prints.

I looked around the room, soothed by the calmness of it, the absence of effortful partying. There was something gently consoling about the Prints and Archives Room, even when you couldn't find what you were looking for: it had that in common with the gallery in the basement. They were the beginning and the end of the Institute, the Alpha and Omega. They were like little chapels for people who didn't believe in God. *I could come and hide up here sometimes*, it occurred to me now. *I could hide from all the parties and all the lying and all the people I don't want to see.*

'So what's going on, downstairs?' Mr Won asked. 'What's everyone celebrating?'

'Mary Anning,' I replied. 'And also, the London Museums Interpretations Centre. We're having a party because it's sponsoring the Institute.'

'Is it? What's the Institute done to deserve that?'

'I don't know.' I hesitated. 'Been desperate, maybe.'

'*The desperate institute,*' Mr Won said. He seemed amused by this idea.

'Anyway,' I said. 'I thought I ought to get back to work, because I've been asked to find some information, about Peter Edwards. Someone's looking for information on the last Minoan artefacts he found. And Professor Muir suggested I should look on the Pending shelves.'

'Ah. Dear old Peter.' Mr Won smiled.

'Yes,' I said, and silence fell. I didn't really know what else to say. It seemed that a moment of solemn reflection might be in order. I thought briefly of the volunteers who'd worked alongside Mr Won when I'd first joined the Institute – two fifteen-year-old schoolgirls called Lauren and Heidi, doing work experience on Wednesday afternoons, and three retirees – Joan, Pam and Joan ('the Pam sandwich', as Raglan had referred to them). I'd liked Lauren and Heidi and Pam and the Joans; they'd sometimes helped me laminate the information panels, or file negatives of the microfossils, or staple worksheets together. Then we'd always gone down to the café afterwards, and ordered afternoon tea from grumpy Ailsa Crawford. They'd left several weeks ago, though, Lauren and Heidi and Pam and the Joans – as if Helen's Weed-Out Wednesdays had included them.

Fortunately, Mr Won was proving harder to shift.

'So what are *you* doing up here this afternoon?' I asked him. 'If you don't mind me asking?'

'Well, I'm just sitting here considering these pieces of rock,' he said. 'These particular rocks, of course, having arrived from a completely different planet.'

'I know how they feel,' I said.

Mr Won regarded me. He was one of those people who looked long and hard at you, as if he was either short-sighted or thinking something profound.

'So,' I continued, moving further into the room, 'I don't suppose you'd know where I'd find Pending?'

'No idea. None whatsoever, I'm afraid. Try looking behind things,' he suggested, after a moment, beginning to pack up his things from the desk as I headed across the room. 'My wife's always complaining that I never look *behind* things. She's always saying, "Not everything can be right in front of you. You should know that",' she says, '"being interested in archaeology!"'

'Well, I'll certainly bear that in mind.'

Mr Won clipped his briefcase shut, slipped down from his chair, and headed towards the door.

'Things become layered,' he added, pausing in the doorway. 'Or sometimes, of course, one thing can lead to another. Paper trails. Tracks and trails. It's like detective work. For instance: how can you tell there's an elephant in the fridge?'

My heart leapt.

'Footprints in the butter!' he said, without waiting to hear my answer.

I began to look around as soon as he'd gone. Behind things and in front of things. But now I felt strangely daunted. Even when I eventually located the Pending shelves, right at the back of the room, I realised they held hundreds of files, so finding anything immediately useful about Peter Edwards seemed unlikely. I pulled out some old marbled box files labelled 'RIPS Photographs' and started looking through them. The first box just contained pictures of the building over the decades – the Institute standing foursquare and unchanging through the seasons – and the box beneath it contained prints of various Victorian palaeontologists in frock coats and top hats, solemnly hanging onto bits of dinosaur bone. I carried on looking. There were several files containing single images of RIPS' exhibits – all the aged zoological curios in the Comparative Gallery and some of the bigger skeletons, as well as pictures of the megalodon thigh-bone that resided in the lift. In a few pictures it was even propped companionably between two palaeontologists, like a bizarre colleague. And there, too, was Terence the tortoise, who'd outlived Darwin and John F Kennedy; and there was the baby mammoth unearthed from the Siberian permafrost in 1908, and the perfectly preserved grasshopper in the piece of amber. Then, searching beneath the pictures of Terence, I came across some smaller Polaroid prints, most of them bundled together into groups with elastic bands. I pulled the elastic band off the top bundle and took it over to the window. And there he was, finally: there, at last, was Peter Edwards. I recognised him from the framed print that hung outside his room – even though in these photographs he was not wearing an Arran jumper, and was significantly younger. Late twenties, at most. My kind of age. And appearing with him, in some of the prints, was

Raglan – *Raglan B and Peter E*, someone had confirmed on the backs of the pictures – and Raglan looked correspondingly young too. Young men in the 1980s. I could tell, because they were both sporting long, dark grey woollen coats and quite comical New Romantic hairstyles. In one picture they were standing on the steps of the Institute, the sun shining, broad smiles on their faces and their arms around each other's shoulders, and in another they were standing in a forest, pointing and laughing at a heap of rocks. *Fossilised Wood Pile*, announced a sign hammered into the ground beside the rocks, as if some extremely ancient lumberjack had once stacked them there.

I felt I was snooping, looking at these. Witnessing this old friendship. It felt like rifling through someone's private chest of drawers. But at least, I thought, I've found something: I've located *something*, perhaps, for Dr Appalsawmy. And I headed over to one of the tall wooden ladders beside the window, wheeled it along to the K shelves and began to look for evidence of Peter Edwards' last Minoan project.

'Oh, Sybil, you're here – you're up *here*!' someone said, just as I was on the point of pulling out a file I'd seen labelled *Knossos (excavations)*; and I looked down, and there, somewhat surprisingly, was Jane. She was standing in the doorway, a worried look on her face, and holding a crumpled piece of paper. 'I've been looking all over for you in the park!' she said. 'I thought you'd gone outside! What are you doing up here?'

I wondered how to reply in a way that would not be stating the bleeding obvious.

'Well, I'm just looking for something,' I said. 'For the information that bloke in Cambridge asked me for the other day.'

Jane hesitated, the piece of paper clutched tight in her hands. I recalled something an old teacher of mine had said to me once when he'd caught me wandering around school carrying a single sheet of paper. 'Oldest trick in the book, you know, Sybil!' he'd said. 'Makes you look as if you're on a mission. They do that in the army, you know!'

'I've . . .' I began now – but there was a sound of movement in the corridor outside. I looked up. Something slipping, or shifting on a shelf, perhaps.

'Anyway, I've just brought this for you . . .' Jane said hurriedly, heading fast across to the table where Mr Won had been sitting earlier, putting the piece of paper down and smoothing it out flat. She glanced around, as if trying to locate the source of the noise. 'I just . . . found it, when I went to put your lunchbox away in your bag. It's just . . . *a few more keywords . . .*' she added, raising her voice.

'Are you OK?' I asked.

'Fine, thanks. Professor Muir mentioned them to me, you see,' she went on, her voice still oddly loud. 'He thought – I mean, he said that . . . he just wondered if you could possibly check to see whether—' But now she jumped, and turned, as if trying to work out who it might be, outside in the corridor, or whether it *had* only been the sound of papers disturbed in a sudden draft. 'The thing is, apparently he *had* been going to mention them earlier—' She glanced up at me again, still perched there at the top of the ladder. '. . . and then,' she said urgently, lowering her voice to a mutter, 'I came across this, Sybil, in the coat cupboard. When I was dropping off your lunchbox.' She nodded her head towards the piece of paper. 'And I do think they're probably quite important,' she said. 'These . . . *keywords.*'

I looked out through the window. For a moment it seemed to me, from that high position, that it really might be possible to swing straight through it and go sailing out above Greenwich Park – above the whole of London, even – and never be seen again. Despite what I'd written in fridge magnets, about never flying through windows. Jane had always been my mainstay at the Institute, my confidante, my friend, but now even she seemed to be presenting me with arbitrary and baffling additions to my workload. *I really should have gone down to the park* . . . I thought, and the room seemed to spin a little, to tilt and slip in the spring sunlight.

I shifted my position on the ladder.

'Anyway, it shouldn't take you too long,' Jane said resolutely. She smoothed out the paper again. 'It's only a short . . . list, Sybil. If you wanted to come down and have a quick look?'

I knew I should; I knew I should, but I felt suddenly very tired. In the corner of my eye an aeroplane was sailing, tiny and silver and full of precious lives, half a mile above London. Jane was wearing a very pretty Liberty-print top that afternoon, it occurred to me, but its swirling mauves and pinks suddenly clashed with the greenness of Greenwich Park. The whole room clashed.

'So, if I could just leave it here with you, then?'

'Right,' I said.

'OK. Super. So I'll leave it here, then . . .'

And she left the room.

Of course, I did not resume my search, after that: I did not spend any more time looking in the Knossos files, seeing as all the information I might need suddenly seemed to be on the bit of paper Jane had just brought in. I descended the ladder and headed straight over to it. When I picked it up I saw that it was not a list of keywords at all – or even anything to do with Professor Muir. It was a crumpled, somewhat faded sheet of fax paper, upon which Jane had hastily scrawled,

Sybil: FYI!!

Gingerly, I picked it up. The fax was dated 28th October the previous autumn. At the top it said:

Sender: Peter Edwards
Recipient: Helen Hansen

And beneath this it read:

Helen –

Sorry about the fax: the internet's almost permanently down, here. In fact, there's still a modem somewhere in the building . . . Anyway, thanks for hanging around this evening to pick this up.

I'm getting in touch because I've been worrying about your Winchelsea Hoard findings, in particular I've been having doubts about the dating results. Then last night I was speaking to a colleague here about some Minoan finds she made last year. Carbon dating initially suggested these were around 2700 BC (i.e. virtually Cycladic and thus extremely exciting!!) but a subsequent recalibration corrected this to only 1800 BC (i.e. slap-bang in the middle of the Minoan Golden Age, and 900 years younger) – fluctuations in carbon-14 being the usual suspect. I'll fax over the graph readings separately: they make interesting – though somewhat disconcerting – reading.

I suppose what I am saying (though I'm no expert in this area) is: are you quite sure your Winchelsea grains are the *turanicum monococcum* variety, and not just bog standard *triticum monococcum*, found in boring old Sussex? I can't help wondering about this, Helen. Many apologies for pouring a certain amount of cold water on your theories – I just wanted to mention these concerns so you have a chance to thoroughly review the dates/varieties before the PR machine goes into full swing!

Peter

PS. I haven't been able to get hold of Raglan – I gather he's currently down some ditch in Andalucia. Please remind him he owes me at least four pints now, the old fossil – tell him I'll see him in The Swan next week – I'm keeping a tally after last time!

I stopped reading and looked again at the date on the top of the sheet. I thought: *but you never did see Raglan in The Swan the following week. You never even made it back to London.* And I thought how unhelpful to the whole Winchelsea Hoard theory this fax was. How unsupportive of the Beakerware project. How much better if it didn't exist at all. Then I thought of those canvas tote bags hanging in the cupboard in Reception, one mine, one Helen's, but otherwise identical. It would be easy to confuse them, an easy mistake for someone to make. Maybe, for a moment, when Jane had slipped my lunchbox in there and seen the fax, she'd even imagined she was rescuing one of my crumpled-up poems.

I ran back down the stairs to my room, the fax in my hand, and grabbed my coat from the back of my chair. Then I picked up my little teacup from where it was perched on top of the type-script – I held it for a moment, clutched it against my jumpered heart – then I dropped it into my bag along with the fax, and headed towards the door. And as I was edging past my desk – sidling my way past all the clutter and confusion and piles of airbrushed history that I'd been ploughing through for months now, nearly three months – the door opened and there she was: there was Helen, in the flesh.

'Oh – off home now, Sybil?' she said. 'I thought you were upstairs in the Archives.'

I froze.

'Why did you think that?' I said.

'Because Jane told me. I just collared her outside.'

'Oh God,' I said. 'Is she OK?'

'Of course she's OK!' Helen snapped. 'What on earth do you mean?'

I didn't reply. I thought of the day when Helen had briefly locked me into the Special Collections Room – no doubt to get me out of the way while she'd pulled out the incriminating fax she'd so carelessly allowed to end up in the Archives. My mind raced, but it was also, somehow, operating very slowly – it was a slowly racing mind.

'Anyway,' I said cautiously, 'I *was* up there. In the Archives. But then I came back down. To pick up a few bits and pieces. That I'd forgotten. I mean, if you were looking for me up there,' I added, 'you wouldn't have found me . . .'

Helen stood, breathing rather hard, as if she'd been running. Presumably she *had* been – just as I supposed Jane must have been, earlier: both of them running around the building in pursuit of some kind of truth, or some kind of lie. She looked pretty dishevelled, anyway. Her lipstick was smudged and her thick, neck-extending necklace appeared askew, and she was still, for some reason, clutching one of the beakers from the party – one of the big ones. I stood and contemplated her, aware of my bag with its incriminating contents, hanging like a sling from my shoulder. *This is my David moment,* I thought: because if it was ever going to happen – the *mature confrontation* my mother had suggested – it was now.

'So the reason I'm in a hurry, Helen,' I began, 'is because I've just —'

But before I could carry on – or even blurt out something foolish – she broke in with an observation I had not expected at all: a *curveball*, as my father would say.

'Yes, so, just for the record, Sybil,' she said, cutting a swathe right through the middle of my sentence. 'I feel I should tell you that Simon and I are – officially – a thing of the past.'

I blinked.

'We have been for quite some time, in fact,' she said. 'I ended things quite a while ago – I realised it was all rather . . . a dead end. Not the best idea. We weren't quite as right for each other as we'd initially thought. Majoring on the "ancient grains" thing turned out not to be so promising either, in terms of the Beakerware campaign . . .'

I stood, stone-like.

'A *dead end*?' I said, and now I felt a great sorrow beginning to well up from somewhere, a hollowness, deep as a mine, sharp as rock-salt. I thought of the texts Simon had sent me – those little *How are you*? messages he'd sent in February and March before they'd all finally petered out in April. I thought of the ways we had often been happy, even when we had not understood each other. *I should have told you*! I thought. *I should have told you how I was.*

'So do you like destroying things?' I asked, my voice emerging croaky and strange from my throat. 'Because it seems to me that you do.'

Helen looked surprised. 'On the contrary!' she said. 'I like creating things!'

'Like the facts?'

'What,' she said, 'are you talking about?'

'Because the thing is, that's what real academics do! They admit it when they've got it wrong!' I said. 'Which is what you should have done, Helen. Even if you *were* a long way down the line with your Winchelsea Hoard theories and your TED talk and your stupid Tupperware.'

Helen's complexion had grown rather pale, it seemed to me. Marble-ish. Alabaster-like. She looked even more blanched and shocked than Jane had, earlier. Glancing at her, I wondered if she might even have started to find what I was saying funny – it *was* quite funny, in a way – the idea of covering something up that already *had* been covered up for millennia. The expression on her face was certainly suggesting *some* kind of emotion. I really thought she might start to laugh – ha ha ha ha ha ha ha! – and maybe we could even call it quits one day, one happy, sunny day of forgiveness. Maybe we could, in time, let bygones be bygones and *move on*, as Esther kept recommending.

But then, it appeared that she had not found it particularly amusing, and something quite peculiar happened. She gave a sudden little cry. 'How *dare* you suggest I'm not a real academic!' she spat— 'and go rummaging through my personal affairs! And how *dare* you call it Tupperware!' and, raising the hand in which she was still holding her large *beaker (turquoise, £19.99)*, she flung it hard across the room towards me. Hurled it. 'Oh!' I said, looking upwards, my left hand already raised to protect my head, and I considered it for a second as it came spinning fast towards me. It turned 90, 180, 360 degrees, spilling dregs of fruit punch as it went, allowing gravity to pull it almost graciously downwards before making quite a startling, earthenware-and-bone-sounding impact against the side of my head and continuing on, onwards and downwards, and breaking into small fragments against the bookshelf behind me.

I put my hand up to my face, and brought it down. There was blood. There was blood on my hand. It seemed Helen had got there first, with her own David moment.

'Oh,' she said. 'I didn't mean to do that. Sorry.'

I swayed. I felt a momentary blankness, a kind of nothing. 'So what did you mean to do?' I heard myself say. But it appeared I was speaking from some other part of the room – from some other dimension, from Time and Relative Dimension in Space. And now I really did start to move, before Helen decided to perhaps pick up a dinosaur leg-bone off a shelf and finish the job properly. I turned without further comment, moved shakily out into the corridor, my hand up to my head, a lot of blood beneath my palm now, walked to the lift and pressed the Call Lift button.

'Sybil!' Helen called behind me, then the lift arrived – *thank God, thank God* – I rushed in before she could reach me, and pressed the button for the ground floor. 'I didn't mean to do that, Sybil! I didn't mean to hurt you!' I heard her wail as the doors closed, and my pulse was racing now, and the blood was continuing to run down the side of my face, and, putting my hand up again to where the beaker had hit, I realised this was happening because it had struck my old Streatham ice-skating scar.

Finding an old paper hanky in my coat pocket, I held it against the bleeding as the lift continued to descend. And for a moment, while I stood absolutely still in that moving box, I felt almost calm: quite peacefully suspended. I was between things: between floors, between outcomes, between ignorance and understanding, between worlds, like my namesake Sybil on her way down to the Underworld. Then the lift stopped. '*Ground* floor!' said the automated voice in its usual tone of mild indignation, and as soon as the doors had parted wide enough I got out and ran as fast as I had ever run in my life: I ran across the marbled floor of Reception, past the bust of Schliemann and the bust of Evans, past the bones and the stones, past Jane already sitting there again behind the desk, wise and inscrutable as the Keeper at the Gates of the Year – 'Oh Sybil! Are you OK?' she called out – but I didn't stop, didn't speak, just ran past all of it, like a greyhound let loose from a trap, aware of the sound in my head again – the singing, the high-pitched electrical buzzing, like tinnitus, or the noise of interference on a radio.

I ran down the front steps and raced across Greenwich Park. I could not see straight, and the blood was running, running, running down my cheek, across my knuckles and into the paper hanky. I didn't have a clue where I was going. But it seemed I was going there.

11

> three crows
> sat upon a wall
> and their names were
> Amo
> Amas
> Amaranth

When I arrived at London Bridge a lot of the Northern Line seemed to have ground to a halt. Half the trains on the Northern Line appeared to have stopped operating. A handwritten sign on the platform read:

Smile! One day, normal service will resume!

I peered at this as I headed bloodily past. It made me think of Fleur Baird at the poetry classes, with her whiteboard and her Emily Dickinson quotes. It was not helpful, as departure board information went.

'You OK, love?' a woman asked as I squashed myself into the next available train.

'Yes, I'm fine, thanks,' I said as the train moved on.

'You don't look fine.' She peered at the blood.

'I just had an accident at work. It opened up an old injury. But it's not as bad as it looks.'

'It looks bad, though. You ought to get that seen to. Some of it's dripped onto your coat collar, look.'

'Has it?' I said, peering down.

'That's going to be hard to get out. You ought to sit down.

Honestly, that blood's going to take some shifting. You'll need to get your coat dry-cleaned. You should go to A&E.'

'Do you think so?'

'Guys' is round here somewhere . . .' she said vaguely, looking up, as if it might be right above us, on the upper side of the tunnel ceiling. Maybe it was. 'Here – I've got some hankies.' She pulled a packet out of her bag and offered it to me. 'Take one. Take the whole packet. I'm getting out here.'

'Thanks,' I said, taking the packet from her as she moved on towards the door.

'Find a seat, love.'

'Yes . . .' I looked around. There were no seats. There was hardly even available floor. As the train began to move again people looked at me then away, as if the woman who'd given me the hankies had been my last remaining link with normality. *Is this a bad injury?* I wondered. *Maybe this is one of those bad injuries you read about . . .*

'I got a injury like that when someone hit me with a cricket bat,' observed an elderly Rasta man.

'Oh dear,' I said. I wanted to cry. I thought: *I should have asked Jane for help, but I didn't, I just ran straight past her.* The flow of blood was lessening, but not stopping. There was still a singing noise. I put the blooded hanky into my pocket and held up a new one as the train rambled on. *This train is about to depart. Please mind the doors,* a rather beautiful voice advised as we finally pulled into Stockwell, and I got out, my bag suddenly as heavy as a boulder, the hanky pressed to the side of my head, and joined the crowd moving along the platform. I turned left through the archway and headed back up the stairs for the Victoria Line.

On Brixton Road I went into the Ladies of the Beehive pub. It was mercifully empty. One of the taps was running slightly, making a peaceful noise against the porcelain, like some tiny ornamental fountain. I stood beside the basin and mopped at the blood as well as I could with a damp hand towel. I did not want to look into the mirror and consider the injury beneath the blood. I did not want to think about the way I had been hurt. I threw the paper towel in the bin and emerged again, heading past the bar and the hanging beer tankards and the peanuts arranged over the pictures of half-naked-woman and on up the road to the library.

The woman called Margery was there when I arrived. She was standing on the other side of the doors, in the middle of Blu-Tacking a note to the double glazing. It said:

CLOSING AT 6pm TONIGHT
OPEN TOMORROW 9.30am

I looked at my watch. It was quarter to. It seemed Margery had decided to lock up early. She gave me a bird-ish look as I approached the doors and halted on the other side of the glass. She did a double-take when she registered the drying blood, but she did not quite meet my eye. I stood and watched the blobs of Blu-Tack spread greyly against the glass as she pressed the sign down with her thumbs. She continued for several seconds, the expression on her face unchanging. Then, when I did not go away, she turned a key that was hanging in the lock and pulled the door open a chink.

'We're closed,' she said.

'But it's only quarter to.'

'I'm locking the doors.'

'But locking the doors doesn't make it six o'clock.'

'Nevertheless, we're not allowing anyone else in.'

'Why not?'

Margery didn't reply. She glanced at the side of my head. *I'm going to call the police*, she looked as if she was thinking.

'There are still people in there,' I pointed out. Because there *were*: there were over half a dozen people in there – including a woman peacefully clearing up scissors and balls of wool at the Creative Community Table, a couple of old men reading newspapers and some children in the Children's Zone, playing with Lego bricks. 'I just want to make a few photocopies,' I said, through the tiny gap between the door and the doorframe. Because a thought had formed itself as I'd made my way there: I'd pictured myself going around the corridors at work the next day, Easter Bunnyish, sticking copies of the incriminating fax to various surfaces: revenge at last. 'I just need to get a photocopy of something to a friend of mine,' I said. 'It's important that he sees it, this . . . document . . . It's just that he's away on leave at the moment,' I continued, ad-libbing wildly, 'and the photocopier where I work has broken, and—'

'That's not my fault,' Margery said. She glanced again at the blood on my face. 'It's not my fault your friend's on leave and your photocopier's broken.'

'I know, but—'

'Our photocopier's been switched off.'

'But it would only take half a minute—'

'As I say, the copier's been switched off.'

'Yes, but . . .'

'I'm sorry.'

No you're not, you're not bloody sorry.

I looked around the side of her head, at a poster that said, in huge, red letters: THE ONLY THING YOU NEED TO KNOW IS THE LOCATION OF THE LIBRARY *(Albert Einstein)*. Einstein was often right, of course, but that opinion at that particular moment seemed to be a kind of lie.

Then, from somewhere else, some unknown hinterland of shelves and books and machinery, someone else was speaking. 'Actually Marge, it hasn't been switched off,' they were saying – and I peered around the edge of Margery's outraged face, and there was Bill. He was heading fast towards us across the foyer. He was carrying, for some reason, a papier mâché palm tree. He

227

seemed, at that moment, to be the only friend I had left in the world.

'I was about to switch the copier off,' he told Margery, putting the palm tree down on a desk and walking over to the door, 'but I got diverted.' He glanced, then stared, at my face. 'So I can do it for you, if you like,' he said after a moment, talking to me through the glass.

Margery sighed a long sigh, as if everything about her work at North Brixton Library was a huge burden to her.

'We should not be doing this, Bill,' she said. 'We're supposed to be firm with people who turn up after closing time.'

'But it's not closing time yet! It's not even ten to closing time. You've jumped the gun, Margery. Also, this . . . customer appears to be injured in some way.'

'Well, to be quite honest, Bill, the place she should actually be is A&E, isn't it?'

I stood on the pavement and watched them arguing about me, my vision sliding in and out of focus. I thought: *I am a person who turns up after closing time. I am a person who is no longer welcome inside public buildings.* I felt like someone who has finally slipped through a kind of net.

'Just let her in, Margery, for God's sake,' Bill was saying now. 'The library's not going to self-destruct! Come in for a sec,' he said to me, urgently, pulling the door open and speaking quickly through the gap. I felt a momentary desire to laugh.

Margery glared at the two of us. 'Well, I'm not staying behind to set the alarm, that's all I'm saying!' she snapped. 'The First Aid box is in the cupboard if you need it. Which you will. Top right. Bandage and dressing tape,' she added, in a magnanimous kind of afterthought. Then she strode off towards the other end of the library, and through the door marked *Staff Only: Enter a World of Adventure.*

'Thanks,' I said to Bill, walking in. I pushed the bloody hanky into my pocket, and wondered how bad I looked. 'Thanks . . . Margery . . .' I called out across the carpet tiles.

'Yes,' Bill said, 'I think that ship has already sailed.'

I looked at him. I stood by the poster that said *The World Ends Tomorrow (According to Nostradamus)* and the rack displaying off-the-peg reading glasses and I felt revealed, exposed – my injuries there for all to see.

'So what happened to your head?' he asked.

'Someone threw a mug at me at work.'

'Nice.'

'Not really.'

'My ex-girlfriend threw a mug at me once,' he said. 'But it didn't actually draw blood.'

He picked up the papier mâché tree and put it down again.

'So what do you want to photocopy?'

'It's a bit complicated,' I said. Even though it wasn't really: the only complicated thing, it seemed to me, was what this whole expedition across town might suggest about my mind – the internal workings of it – what it might reveal about the person I'd become. I wasn't the person I'd once been, that was for sure. I wasn't the girl who'd travelled alone to her grandad's funeral the previous September, or even the girl Simon had gone ice-skating with in December. I wasn't sure he would even recognise *that* girl any more. And if he was in the process of moving on without me, launching off into the rest of his life, well, good luck to him; maybe Helen had done us all a favour.

I looked around. People were leaving now, for real. Margery was clanging a bell from behind the shelves, like some doomy town crier.

I cleared my throat.

'So. It's for a friend of mine. The photocopy.'

'OK.'

We headed wordlessly to the copier on the other side of the Information Zone.

'So do you want it A4 or A3?'

'A4 will be fine because it's, you know, it's A4 already . . .'

I shifted my bag into my right, blooded hand and began to rummage inside it with my un-blooded one.

'And after this you should probably go and clean up a bit . . .'

'Yes, I probably should,' I agreed. Because it was far too late to pretend I looked anything except slightly freakish. I took out my notebook and the little cup, which were both lying on top of the fax in my bag, and I put them down on the set of wheeled shelves beside the copier.

'You have a teacup in your bag,' Bill observed. 'Do you often carry teacups around?'

'Yes,' I said, my heart sinking.

He didn't speak for a moment. Then he said, 'Do you want me to photocopy that too?'

'No, it's all right, thanks.'

'Because even photocopying a paperback is a threat to Margery's peace of mind.'

I looked around, in case Margery suddenly materialised again from behind a pillar, full of vengeance, like one of the Furies. *I don't know what I'm doing here actually, Bill*, I wanted to say. *I'm just trying to help someone at work who's been a bit lost recently – quite badly lost, in fact – and then I found this bit of paper at work today, this bit of writing that was like a letter from somewhere else, some other time and place, some sort of message—*

But I didn't say any of this. I said, 'Actually, it's fine. I can do it next week, when our copier's fixed. Because I'd hate to, you know, keep you and Margery back.'

Bill considered this. 'Nah, it's not a problem,' he said. 'It's always fun winding Margery up.'

I hesitated for a moment, because it seemed to me that he was actually finding the whole thing quite funny, and besides, my reason for being there did suddenly seem ridiculous, it seemed to highlight how far along the path of oddness I had travelled; and the strange singing noise had really established itself in my head, now, the singing, sighing sound. 'The thing is,' I heard myself saying, beneath the noise, 'when I came across it today, this bit of paper, a lot of things seemed to . . .' but nothing was in focus now, either '. . . a lot of things . . .'

Bill was peering at me. 'You OK?'

'Yes.'

'Sure? Because that's really quite a nasty . . . I mean, you look . . .'

'I'll be fine.'

'OK, then.'

I watched him as he took the fax from me, turned and lifted the lid of the photocopier. There was still a sheet of paper sitting on the screen – it *had* been sitting there anyway, beneath the lid – only now it caught in the vacuum of air as the lid went up and slipped towards me, brushing past my face in a little updraught, then drifting in a slow zigzag to the floor.

'People are always leaving bits of paper in there,' he said.

'Yes . . .' Oh, but the singing was very loud in my head now; it was like the sirens singing from the rocks! – it was like the Furies closing in on me— 'People always do that,' I heard Bill saying, placing the fax down on the screen. 'They leave behind all kinds of crap you'd think were quite . . .'

I was aware of myself bending to pick up the fallen sheet of paper, and I was not quite in the same room any more, or even in the same part of time, but as I lifted it towards me I saw that the text printed on it was arranged in poetic form, that it was, actually, a poem. And it was a poem I *knew*, because I'd laughed about it once, years earlier, at school – it was the poem *Mrs Beeslack* had asked me to read out and give my considered opinion on.

I was angry with my friend
I told my wrath, my wrath did end

I was angry with my foe
I told it not, my wrath did grow

It was as if all the words had started lifting themselves off the page and begun crashing their way, like strange blackbirds, straight into my head—

And I watered it with fears

Night and morning with my tears

And I sunned it with smiles

And with soft deceitful wiles

And something odd had started happening to the library, now: it was growing dim

and wavy-edged around me, and the books

were slipping and sliding along the shelves, and Bill's voice in my ears was loud and quiet at the same time

'And it grew both day and night.

Till it bore an apple bright.

And my foe beheld it shine,

And he knew that it was mine.'

'. . . you *sure* you're OK?' – he was saying, and now a door was

opening

somewhere in a wall, and a woman

in a peculiar ruffle-fronted blouse was emerging through it like

Elizabeth 1st,

and on the edges of

my comprehension,

I wondered

if this person was perhaps a Girl Guide leader or maybe Brown
Owl,

or

one of the Pams from the institute,

or even

Mrs Beeslack, returned from over a decade ago to

reprimand me for my cynical attitude towards poetry –

'And into my garden stole,

When the night had veild the pole;

In the morning glad I see—

'Bill!' the woman was calling out, across the library's expanse,
'Bill—'

and as I was falling,

a part of me knew

it was pure coincidence,

coming across that old poem one afternoon in North Brixton
Library; it was

not exactly an unknown piece of verse, after all. And Margery
was yelling now –

'BILL! You're going to have to HOLD HER!' she was
bellowing – and

I knew that none of this was anything to get excited about.

But at the same time a part of me—

the part that had always believed

in telepathy and

hunches

and kindness prevailing,

in some strange and complicated way—

that part—

knew

it

was

a sign

THE NORTHERN LINE

1

In the wind
A black crow
Flying backwards

Light on in
A night-time room:
The moon captive

Time is a great healer, of course. As Jane had once said. As Esther told me, and my mother, and Brenda at the poetry classes.

Yes, Time is a great healer and it is on our side, and it flies, and it weighs heavy, and it will say nothing but I told you so. And I didn't mind people telling me this, not really, even though I was pretty sure time did nothing much except exist, and people, and the choices they made, were finite.

I remember that I'd gone into churches quite a lot the previous winter, a few weeks after my grandfather died, and before I'd even split up with Simon. I went there on my own. It was nothing to do with religion. I just liked the quietness in there, and the embroidered hassocks and the stained glass and the dusty postcards and the funny old velvet curtains hiding hallowed things. Also, I liked those tea-lights that you could light in the entrance. I'd even done that once or twice, at a church not far from my flat: I'd put 50p in the slot and lit a candle. But I'd always liked candles anyway: the dinner party kind, and the little twisting ones on birthday cakes, and those lopsided ones that came in looped pairs from strange shops that smelt of joss sticks, where you could also buy dream-catchers and Guatemalan worry dolls in tiny hessian sacks. I also liked a vanilla candle that my mother had given me for my twenty-sixth birthday, and another one in the shape of an apple that Simon had bought me one weekend, and which was so realistic I'd almost bitten into when I returned home late from work one night, only to discover that he still wasn't home, himself. He was out somewhere. Who knew where? Not there, anyway. So I'd lit it while I was having supper, and realised that it's possible to see the shadow of a flame's heat even though you can't see heat itself. There was just this shimmer of shadow, cast by nothing. There was something interesting about that, I'd thought. There was a metaphor there somewhere.

Around Day Four in hospital (or perhaps it was Day Five or Seven or Nine), a nurse gave me some bits of paper. Another pile of photocopied sheets. 'See how you get on with these, love,' she said, so I looked at them from my slightly raised position in a peculiar, elevated metal bed. The words on the paper were printed in a large font size – 16 point, maybe 18 point, the lines double-spaced, the paper a kind, non-bureaucratic ivory.

'I got it off the internet,' the nurse said. She was standing at the side of the bed, perfectly three-dimensional but also, at the same time, shimmering ethereally in and out of focus.

'Rather than me waffling on and tiring you out, I thought you might want to have a read in your own time.'

Which appeared to be something I had, now: time.

I also appeared to be a patient – this dawned on me as the days went by. I was lying in a ward beneath an exceptionally white cotton sheet and the type of blue nylon blanket I'd once used to place over my dolls in their cots. For a while, before someone brought me my old pyjamas from somewhere, I wore a peculiar cotton gown that had *For NHS Use Only* printed all over it in small letters and four different coloured blocks – green, red, blue and black, like the colours in those four-way biros. Also, for quite a long time, my head seemed to be wrapped in some kind of bandage. I seemed to have a plastic tube going up my nose and down the back of my throat, and some other terrible plastic tube coming from somewhere between my legs, and a needle going quite painfully into the back of my hand and another one going into a vein in my arm. I didn't know what those tubes and needles were for. I didn't like to think about them too much. There was a view through a window of ventilation shafts and a roof and an occasional, alighting pigeon and a greyish sky. Sometimes people would come and ask me strange questions. They would ask me to take one number away from another, or they would tell me to look at pictures in a book and tell them what they were. A ball, an apple, a cat. Sometimes I didn't remember the pictures if they took the book away from me, and sometimes I did. It was hard to know why.

After the nurse had gone that afternoon I read the pages she had given me. I read them slowly, because of all the tubes and needles and because it seemed to be taking a while for words to fall into place, and for me to know what on earth I was doing there. *You blacked out, Sybil,* people kept saying, *when you were in the library last week. And someone called an ambulance and the surgeons put you under for a bit – a few days – they gave you these drugs that put you under, and now you've come round and they're making you better.*

BACKGROUND:
Previous mild head injury (MHI) leading to delayed neurological deterioration (DND). Little is known about the characteristics of DND after an MHI
CASE STUDY:
An accountant falls from a ladder while at work, breaking several ribs. He is dazed from the fall, but quickly regains

consciousness. Because of his injuries, he must stay off work for two weeks. During that time, the only problem he notices is the pain from his broken ribs. However, when he returns to work, he discovers that parts of his job which used to be easy have become difficult. Mistakes he would not have made before his fall are now common occurrences. It is likely that the fall didn't just injure his ribs but also resulted in an injury to an area of the brain that controls the complex skills he needs at work. He does not make the connection between the injury and these new cognitive difficulties, which delays the diagnosis of MHI by several weeks.

'I thought it was the easiest way to explain a DND,' the nurse said, shimmering back in to see me. She looked down at a chart and ticked a box. 'Which is what you had, Sybil. After your accident. It's just lucky you were in a public place when you collapsed, and not alone at home.'

'A DND?' I said. An image of a CD came into my head, circular and shining.

'It's short for "delayed neurological deterioration", as it says in the notes. What you have at the moment is neurological amnesia. To be honest, it was lucky you *had* that second crack on the head. Because if you hadn't, you wouldn't have come into A&E. And we wouldn't have known about the DND.'

She stopped talking. I tried to imagine how I had arrived at the hospital. Whether the woman with the ruffle-fronted blouse had sat in an ambulance with me. Or the other librarian, the one I'd liked who'd worn a T-shirt. I'd talked to him once or twice: something about Einstein, something about magazine racks. I thought: I hope I didn't look too bad; I hope I wasn't an unsightly mess. Then I remembered that his name was Bill. And then other things began to fall into place. Over the hours, over the days. I thought about Helen Hansen, and how strange it was that she had practically killed me – she'd

240

almost killed me *twice*, in fact – but she had also, in a peculiar way, saved my life.

The nurse told me one morning that someone was going to remove the tube from my nose and that it might feel a bit weird – there might be a bit of *tugging*, and I might feel a bit sick. And as for the tube between my legs, they were going to give me a sedative and then they would take that away too. Probably also, in a couple of days – although the bandages would stay on for a bit – they would remove the needle from the back of my hand.

'And then you'll be back in the land of the living.'

She gave me another piece of paper. This one was a lunch menu.

> *Beef Casserole or Ploughman's Lunch.*
> *Egg mayonnaise sandwich.*
> *Peaches in Custard or Tapioca Pudding.*

But who eats tapioca? I thought. What even *is* tapioca? It was something my grandparents used to eat during the War. And who eats *Ploughman's Lunch*, unless it's 1982 and they're sitting in some beer garden in Sevenoaks or somewhere? I thought for some reason of the Wedderburns in Colliers Wood with their melting cheeseboard and their games of Kan-U-Go, and of my mother sitting there on one of their wicker garden seats, and I felt a sudden burst of longing for all the people in my life I no longer saw, not on a regular basis, not even sometimes; I certainly didn't go to the cinema or the pub with them. It just seemed to me there were a lot of people I'd lost touch with.

'I don't know what I want,' I said to the nurse.

'I'd go for the peaches in custard,' she replied, heading out of the room. 'They'll come round with lunch about 11.45,' she added. 'So if you could get that box ticked . . .'

I lay back against my pillows, I lay back in Time and Relative Space and closed my eyes. I felt I might have travelled some distance to get there. Maybe it *was* 1982, or 1863, or 2021. Maybe I was not even born yet. The ceiling tiles had a recurring pattern that looked like Ancient Greek actors' masks: happy-sad, happy-sad, recurring. This seemed significant, for some reason. I recalled something I'd learned once about the prophet Sybil taking Aeneas down to the Underworld, and how she'd warned him that the journey back was not going to be easy.

All night long, all day, the doors of Hades stand open.
But to retrace the path, to come up to the sweet air of heaven,
That is labour indeed.

Across the ward, the bed opposite mine had a curtain pulled around it, and the curtain had a print of halved lemons and cucumbers on it. The lemon and cucumber halves seemed important, but I couldn't think why. *Perhaps I'm on drugs*, I thought, then I realised that I *was*: I *was* on drugs, and also someone had shaved my hair from the right side of my head and put stitches in. When I put my fingertips up beneath the bandage, I could feel them.

Most afternoons while I was there someone would switch on a television that sat on a high, swing-out ledge to the right of my bed, and I would watch TV: *Bargain Hunt*, *Antiques Roadshow*, *Brainbox Challenge* (*that* was a good one), *Countdown*. *Consonant, please, Rachel, and then another consonant . . .* Then early one evening, as I was attempting to piece together all the jumbled-up letters on the screen, I thought: *I wonder what happened to Raglan's book. I wonder if it ever made it to John in the ice house.*

Which was when I knew that I must still be myself, more or less: that I was still Sybil Wiseman, aged twenty-six, who'd once worked in some strange kind of institute somewhere on the other side of London.

The needle was taken out of my hand the next morning, and

the chrome IV stand was wheeled away. A new nurse came along every few hours after that and gave me some pills. I didn't know what the pills were, but I presumed they were painkillers, because whenever I turned my head to the left it still hurt. So I tried to lie as still as I could, like some injured animal lying in long grass. At the side of my bed there was a white Formica surface bearing objects that seemed to belong to me in some way. There was a jug of diluted orange squash and a cardboard box of hankies. There was a bell like the kind you see on hotel reception desks, and a Bible, just in case. The little teacup I'd found was not amongst the things, and neither was Peter Edwards' fax: I didn't know what had happened to them. I supposed they had got lost. Lost and found, and lost again. I felt quite sad about the cup.

I discovered later that my parents had cut short their holiday and come to see me the day after I'd gone in. They'd arrived straight off the plane from Madeira – with a Madeira cake. I wasn't awake the first time they'd come in, though, so they'd taken it away again. Then they'd returned with it the next day, and the next, and the next. They'd sat at my bedside for four days in a row, hanging onto that Madeira cake and waiting for me to wake up.

'You've been out for the count for nearly a week,' my mother said eventually, sitting beside me on Day Five, after I'd finally come round; and her brown eyes clouded with tears. 'Like Lazarus,' my father added. 'They put you in a sort of coma to help with the healing.'

'They didn't put Lazarus into a coma, Tony,' my mother said.

'But she was still out for the count.'

'Is that useful information right now?'

'I was just pointing it out. Because I've always thought Lazarus was probably just concussed. A lot of these so-called miracles have basis in medical fact.'

'I'm sorry,' I said. 'I'm sorry.'

'Don't be sorry, it wasn't your fault,' my mother said, turning back to me and smiling, the way she had always used to when I was a child and something had gone wrong at school. Because it never was my fault – even when sometimes, of course, it was.

Esther came in a couple of days later, with Paul. They sat side by side, hand in hand, like babes in the wood, as if everything about the hospital slightly terrified them. I remembered something Esther had told me once, about holding hands with Paul: 'Sometimes we hold hands in the car while Paul's driving,' she'd said, 'and I always feel sad when he has to let go to change gear.' And if that wasn't love or something close to it I didn't know what was.

'So I feel really guilty now,' she said, 'because if I look back, there was obviously something wrong with you, Sybil.' She sighed. 'I should probably never have dragged you off to that restaurant. Or stood you up, that time.' She slipped her hand out from Paul's for a sad, loveless second, to unzip the bag on her lap. 'Anyway. Loads of people have been asking about you, and saying nice things.'

'Really?' I said. I wasn't sure I deserved nice things said about me.

'Someone even came round from your poetry group a couple of nights ago, and brought you this.' From the bag she pulled out a card in an envelope, and handed it to me.

'Thanks,' I said, reaching out my left arm, which felt stiff and heavy as a block of wood but seemed to still function, pretty much, as an arm. I opened the envelope. The card inside bore a picture of a cartoon man in a hospital gown, his bare backside on show.

Heard you went to theatre in a revealing gown

And everyone at Poetry for the Terrified had signed it.
Get well soon, Sybil! Fleur had written.
Come back soon to are little group! Olivia had scrawled.
Hope flutters its tinsel wing! Brenda had added.

One afternoon, I got up. My legs, thin as bird legs, bore me along a short corridor, through a grey door and into a room the size of a large cupboard. It contained a shower cubicle and a *Dudley Duoflush* toilet and a basin and a sign saying *Now Wash Your Hands*. I sat down on the lid of the toilet, amazed to be alive and to be happy that I was, and that people actually put signs up on walls to remind you of the rules of good hygiene. It was as if there was an answer for everything; there was kindness and good advice. I could almost have written it all down in my notebook. I didn't, though, because I didn't know where my notebook was any more. I supposed I had lost that, too. After I'd gone back to my room I poured myself some orange squash from the plastic jug, and I thought: *I will never have to write another poem again if I don't want to, not for as long as I live*. The orange juice tasted like the squash Simon and I used to buy when we went to the Ritzy cinema. There had been these thin-walled plastic cups of squash when we'd first gone there – you pushed a short white straw straight through the foil lid, and it seemed like the most significant thing, for some reason – sitting beside your new lover in a dark cinema, drinking orange squash from a plastic, foil-lidded cup. It had been one of those namelessly beautiful things.

'I'm surprised no one picked up on your post-traumatic responses before, to be honest,' a consultant surgeon said, on my last day in hospital. He was wearing a very clean green surgeon's tunic, I noticed, but when I looked down at the floor I could see splatters of dark blood all over the tops of his white clogs.

'Temporal injuries can do all sorts of peculiar things,' he added. 'Blurred vision, for instance.'

'Yes.' I felt a bit sickened by the dark splatters.

He sighed, reached out and rearranged the white gauze at the side of my face. 'Oversights happen, though, I'm afraid . . .'

'Yes, I know,' I said.

'So. If remembering things is giving you headaches at the moment, you might find it helpful writing yourself a few notes. Little to-do lists, or aide-memoires.' He turned, lifted a pad of writing paper off a small swing-out desk and offered it to me.

'I don't think I *will* find it helpful, to be honest,' I said. 'Note-taking's never really been my thing.'

He looked at me.

'But I thought you worked in some sort of . . . editorial capacity? Isn't note-taking what you're supposed to do?'

'Only sometimes,' I said. 'Sometimes I just sit and look through the window.'

He glanced down at his clogs. I noticed a look of alarm cross his face, as if he'd only just registered the blood splatters. 'OK,' he said. Then he stood up and walked away.

2

Helen had checked over *A History of Trade* in my absence: Jane told me this when I went back to work the following week. She'd also arranged an extension of the deadline with Repro John because of *circumstances*, and had got the proofs to him just before the final cut-off point.

'Yes, she pulled an all-nighter last week, apparently,' Jane added ruefully, 'then she literally ran over to the ice house with it first thing the next morning.'

I tried to picture Helen and John standing in the ice house that morning, arguing the toss over print runs. It was quite a terrifying image, like one of the illustrations on Jeremy Muir's *warring dinosaurs* worksheets.

'Anyway, at least we tried, didn't we, Sybil? We tried our best,' Jane said, looking suddenly very sad. She sighed. 'And at least you won't have to bother yourself with it any more. Because it's all done and dusted now, isn't it? All in the past.' She paused. 'Plus, on a brighter note,' she added, more cheerfully, 'she's at least left the Trustees now.'

I looked at her.

'What?' I said.

'Didn't you know? Raglan's book was basically the last thing she did here. Apart from the TED talk, of course.'

'Really?' I said, feeling my heart tighten. 'I *didn't* know that, actually,' I said, 'I mean, I'd assumed she'd be here forever.'

'Pressure of work, apparently. Is what she said.'

247

'I see.' I hesitated. I didn't know what to think. I suppose I should have felt pleased at this information, but instead I felt oddly cheated. It was as if something rightfully mine had just been taken away at the last minute. Like my little cup. Or that fax.

'Yes, I think she slipped away pretty quietly,' Jane said. 'No questions asked. Not at LMIC either, apparently. But maybe there were too many skeletons in the closet for her to feel entirely . . . at ease.'

'Yes, or tote bags,' I said.

I went down to the park that first lunchtime I was back. I sat on the second step of the General Wolfe statue and ate the sandwich I'd made for myself. Then I ate an orange, one of those big bright oranges that peels in one go. The peel looked a bit like an elephant's face, I thought: it had a trunk and two wide ears. But I didn't write this down. I ate all the segments, neatly, one after the other, then I did the crossword in the *Metro*, because it seemed I did still need to be doing *something* with pen and paper, despite what I'd told the hospital consultant – even if it was just glorified doodling.

> 5 across: winter weather (4)
> 7 down: 'how are the mighty . . .'? (6)
> 5 down: part of the verb 'to have' (3)

It was too easy though, the *Metro* crossword: I'd always been able to do it in two minutes flat.

I got up from the step, threw the paper and the orange peel in the bin and made my way back down the path towards the Institute. There was no one else in sight. And looking up at the sky for a moment I thought: *it's summer*. Because it was – it was suddenly summer, all across London, and for the first time in months it seemed too hot to be wearing my Doctor Martens boots and the coat I'd bought at the People's Dispensary for Sick Animals. So I took off my boots and I carried them, and I took off my coat and I put it in my bag. Underneath the coat I was wearing a dress I'd bought a few months earlier – it was pale blue and 100% cotton and it had no sleeves, and my arms looked unbelievably white in it as I continued across the grass and into the cool gloom of Reception – they looked as white as tinned hearts of palm, or the limbs of the preserved axolotl in the gallery. I don't care, though, I thought. I don't care what I look like.

I stood by the window after I'd gone back upstairs and looked down at the park where I'd just been sitting: at the sundial and the statue, and the path between the cherry trees. Then I went into the kitchenette, to make a cup of tea. Hope Pollard had brought in a box of biscuits that morning and left it on the windowsill. The box said *Coffee Break* on the front, and there was a painted-on purple ribbon. I took two biscuits from the crinkly plastic case: a yellow one and a pink one, the tops of them crunchy and sweet and shiny as gems. Then I went back into my office and sat down on my swivelling chair. I thought about Bill, and what he'd said once about performance poets and Bashō and photocopiers and Margery's attitude to Closing Time. I also thought, for some reason, about the boots he wore – which were the same as my boots, only bigger and a dark pink ox-blood. I thought about the strange colour of his eyes – that greyish-blue – and about the shortness of his hair, which I imagined would feel soft, like suede, if you put your hand up to it and touched it; stroked it, like a cat. I thought about the paleness of his skin and the slightness of his frame and the lightness of his voice and his opinion that Margery could be a bit of an arse, and I remembered those origami frogs he'd made out of the place-cards at that terrible dinner.

Around four I phoned John in the ice house to ask about the progress of *A History of Trade*.

'Ah – we're actually only just setting up the rollers now, in fact,' he told me, sounding quite sheepish for once. 'After that final delay at your end you missed your printing window and then we had a delay at *this* end, I'm afraid. But we'll start the run first thing tomorrow and we'll still have the finished copies in the shop on the date we first agreed.'

I sat very still. 'So it's not actually been printed yet?' I said.

'Not yet.'

'So,' I said, my heart thumping. 'So would there be any chance I could squeeze in a couple of teeny-tiny amendments? At this stage? Would that be at all possible?'

For a moment there was a silence at the other end of the line: a computational kind of nothing. Then, in a flat voice, John said, 'How many words?'

'Not many. Fifty at most. Just near the end. A tiny little oversight. I need to add it to Biographies.'

'Not Biographies again? It was that final mess-about with Biographies that made you miss your window. For goodness' sake! Get it to me in the next two hours,' he said, his Old Testament voice of doom returning.

'Thanks, John,' I said.

And quickly, before he could change his mind, I put the phone down. I closed my eyes, and breathed in. Then I opened my eyes again, put out my right hand and reached over for the printed copy of the final proofs, which Jane had placed so sadly on my desk earlier that day ('*So here it is, Sybil, in all its glory . . .*' she'd whispered). And in the Biographies section at the end, between *Eames (Elizabeth)* and *Evans (Arthur)* I looked for the entry for Peter Edwards. I saw that it was much shorter than the version I'd worked on before, on my computer. It now read:

Edwards, Professor Peter (1956–2010)
Author of *The Minoan Civilisation: Their Life and Their Legacy* (amongst other publications: see Bibliogaphy).

Professor Edwards worked at the Royal Institute of Pre-historical Studies, London, and was well-known for his work on Minoan civilisation.

It had been significantly edited. Cut. The final *mess-about*.

So I switched on my computer and opened up the file called 'History of Trade SW/HH final sign-off'. Then I re-instated Raglan's earlier version:

Edwards, Professor Peter (1956–2010)
Professor Edwards was a world authority on Minoan civil-isation and a key figure at the Royal Institute of Prehistorical Studies, London, where he worked from 1984 to 2010. He came to the world's attention as a leading expert on Minoan civilisation when he excavated an extraordinary treasure trove of artefacts during his world-famous Knossos exca-vation in 1988. He wrote numerous books on the Minoans, most notably *The Minoan Civilisation: Their Life and Their Legacy* which remains the definitive work on the subject, and is essential to an understanding of those Early Peoples.

And at the end, after 'peoples', I added:

His findings were not welcomed in all quarters, casting doubt, as they do, on the danger of relying on Carbon dating in the absence of other corroborating data, especially with regard to some recent much-hyped 'discoveries' – yes, I am talking about you and your 'Winchelsea Hoard', Helen Hansen! – but nevertheless his research now looks to be incontrovertible.

Then I opened up an email to John, attached the file, and wrote: Thanks for waiting, John: please see text REINSTATED on p. 484 (in Biographies) and please note NEW SENTENCE ADDED which begins 'His findings'. Now all good to go.

Then I pressed Send. 'Two wrongs don't make a right!' I remembered Mrs Beeslack saying once during an English lesson – but perhaps, very occasionally, they did. It was like two minuses sometimes making a plus. I was so relieved that I hardly knew what to do with myself any more. *I don't even need to be here*, I thought, as I sat looking out through my window at the high blue sky. I could have been anywhere that day, done anything at all.

3

Mudlark
Skylark
Lark ascending
In the park

It's funny, though, how you don't always escape from a place immediately. You don't go careering off as quickly as you might think. So I stayed for the rest of that day, hanging around the gallery and the café and the cataloguing room. I filed some papers to do with limestone and water erosion and the shale byngs of Broxburn, catalogued three small trilobites and a fossilised bird called Jinguofortis perplexus, wrote to Dr Appalsawmy, apologising for the delay, and answered a new email enquiry from Clive-the-detectorist, who pointed out that I had not replied to his email for nigh-on three months now.

Dear Clive, I began, I'm so sorry I . . .

Then I stood up and went into the kitchenette to make myself a coffee.

It was quite late on Friday afternoon now. There was a meeting going on upstairs, a smell of stewed filter coffee and a view of the old Millennium Dome through the window. There was a vase of dried-out flowers and a tea-stained flyer about megalithic structures. My attempts at poetry had gone from the fridge door, I noticed – whisked away by some unknown hand. Just a single sheet of paper was stuck there, now – attached at each corner by four magnets I'd never seen before, in the shape of dinosaurs. I went over to take a closer look. It appeared to be a list of flower names:

campanula
sea pink
dog rose
grape hyacinth
hollyhock
flax
cornflower

'Ah! Looking at Raglan's list of flowers!' Hope Pollard said, crashing into the room as I was trying to fathom the significance of this.

'His list of flowers?'

'Yes, he jotted that down a while ago, actually, when he was over in Crete. Apparently he didn't find a single artefact he was looking for, but he *did* see all the wildflowers on that list. He said the sight of them was really rather . . . He said it made him think we should all be looking *around*, more often. At the world. While it's still – look-at-able . . .'

I thought of the Neolithic grave Raglan had written about in his book: the one that had been scattered with hollyhocks, cornflowers, grape hyacinths, wild roses.

'The wonder of the world,' I said.

'The Seven Wonders?'

'No, just the one,' I said. 'The singular wonder.'

Late that afternoon, I carried out a few more tasks that had been waiting for me to finish. I moved some dinosaur knucklebones into a newly labelled drawer, and replaced a bulb in the old overhead projector. I laminated some information sheets and wrote accession codes on some fossilised razor-shells. I informed and labelled and organised. I did all the things I should have done months earlier. *This might actually have been quite a good job for me*, I thought. *I just arrived at the wrong time.* Then I stood at my desk, and I cried – more than I'd cried about anything in all the years I'd been alive. I cried for Simon, and I cried for my grandfather and I cried for Raglan, who'd also lost a man he loved, a man he was in love with, before he'd ever had the chance to say goodbye. Then I dried my eyes, picked up my things and went downstairs in the lift, to the gallery.

Danny was sitting there on the wooden chair, where he always sat.

'You've caught the sun,' he said, as I walked in. 'Been out sunbathing?'

'Nope. I've just been out in the sun.'

I blinked, and waited for my eyes to adjust to the primordial gloom.

'You're not looking so pale now, anyway,' Danny said. 'You look almost healthy these days.'

'Well, thanks, Danny!'

'No offence.'

'None taken.'

'Funny that expression, isn't it?' he added. ' "*Catching the sun*". As if the sun's a big tennis ball or something.'

'You're a poet,' I said. 'And you don't even know it.'

'I *do* know it, thank you very much! I live for metaphor!'

I smiled. 'What are you like?' I said.

And I shifted my gaze away, to peer around the great cavern of the Institute. My vision was still not what it should have been. I did not think it ever would be. Focus! somebody had said to me at the hospital: find a point and focus on it, the way a ballet dancer does; the way a dancer turns and turns but somehow manages to stay upright. So I looked at the pillars of the building, and focused on those. Then I looked at the display cases extending along the corridors, and at the lift and the alcoves, and up at the little carved monkeys peeping out from the carved ferns. I looked at the potted date palm and the tortoise that had outlived both Charles Darwin and John F Kennedy, and I thought of the portrait upstairs of Mary Anning, who'd been *fairly well-known in geological circles, but sadly never truly recognised during her lifetime.*

If you let the walls close in on you in a place like this, I thought, they will. They'll close in and squash you flat. And floating into my head came a dream of the way Simon and I might have been, in a different existence, a different set of circumstances: I thought of the people we might have become, and the conversations we might have had, if only life, in the form of Helen Hansen, had not intervened.

'You OK?' Danny said. 'Not planning another blackout?'

'No,' I said, looking down. A stack of worksheets was sitting on the information desk, waiting to be picked up by visiting schoolchildren before being discarded as they squashed themselves back onto the coach. There was the information I'd cobbled together about the shale industry, and the worksheet I'd compiled for Professor Muir; and there was the quiz I'd thrown together when I hadn't had a clue what I was doing, what on earth I was going to do with my mind.

Dinosaur Alphabet! Did you know there's a dinosaur for every letter of the alphabet! Why not look out for them in our Dinosaur Room? We've given you some letters for the first one as a clue.

A---l------a-------s
B
C
D
E
F
G

256

And how did you manage it, Raglan? I thought. How did you get through those days of whiteout? Because I'd once heard someone say that people are happy in similar ways – but when it comes to sorrow, when it comes to grief, you're always on your own.

'Oh, I was meaning to say,' Danny said, leaning down and pulling open a drawer in his desk – it was one of those desks with drawers that are never totally visible to the visiting public – and he took something from it. A small parcel. He handed it to me. 'Someone came looking for you with this, a few days ago,' he said, 'so I told him I'd hang onto it for you. I could have put it in your in-tray, but things go walkabout round here some-times, don't they?'

He smiled. 'He seemed quite sorry to miss you. The bloke that brought it round. He said he went to the hospital to find you, but you'd already left.'

'Right . . .' I said, and I looked down at the thing Danny had given me. It was an envelope, more than a parcel – one of those padded Mailmiser envelopes with huge staples at the top – the kind that can draw blood (I knew from experience) if you opened it without enough caution. And I could tell straight away what was inside it, before I'd even ripped the seal; I knew, from the size, and the shape it made against the envelope, that it was the notebook, it was my book of bad, sad poems.

I pulled it out and looked at the cover – at that poor man still standing there in his bowler hat with the apple covering his face – then I looked inside, at all the words I'd written, and all the gaps between the words, and I saw that tucked inside the middle pages, beneath the slim red ribbon, were two pieces of paper:

Peter's fax to Helen, folded neatly in half; and a receipt of some kind – a ticket to somewhere, a return from somewhere. I pulled the receipt out. On the printed side it said:

and on the other side was a sentence: a single line, written in green biro. It said: *Well, it could be worse, you could be going round with an apple stuck to your face.*

'What's funny?' asked Danny.

'Nothing. Just something.'

'Nothing or something?'

'Both.'

I put the notebook into the big square pocket of my dress, and walked over to call the lift.

'Oh, and the guy said if you ever feel like meeting up some time for a cuppa . . .' Danny called after me.

I turned.

'A cuppa?'

'That's what he said.'

I pressed the lift button.

'OK,' I said. 'Well, thanks . . .'

And maybe I will go round to see you later, I thought as I stood there waiting. Because of all the people I know in the world, the ones I like best always have the strangest ways of telling you things you might need to know. And not everything happens for a reason, I thought, but sometimes there's a reason for what happens next. I didn't laugh and I didn't cry, I felt absolutely together. The choice of floors was engraved into the little steel plate beside the lift. Floors, or *strata*, as some of the older Trustees called them.

Floor 0	Gallery
Floor 1	Reception
Floor 2	Offices
Floor 3	Offices

| Floor 4 | Offices |
| Floor 5 | Archives |

It looked more like a poem to me, though, the way it was laid out. A cinquain. And I was heading up to my office on the 5th floor: I was going to get out at line 5 and hang around up there until the end of the day. But it's funny how you can sometimes be in a place – how you can even be in between places – but in your head you're not there at all any more.

You're already gone, you've already flown.

Acknowledgements

A lot of people helped me while I was writing this book, and I'd like to acknowledge their support and encouragement. For her patience, humour and brilliant eye for detail I would especially like to thank my agent Georgia Garrett at Rogers, Coleridge and White, and my editor Moira Forsyth, for her precision and clear-sighted comments. The Royal Literary Fund has been a fantastic financial and professional support, particularly in enabling me to set up an RLF Reading Round project while I worked on the novel. Huge thanks also to Creative Scotland, The Scottish Book Trust and the Arvon Foundation for funding and freelance employment, respectively, which helped keep things afloat.

For their friendship and keen-eyed writerly comments I owe many thanks to Elizabeth Ezra, Rose France, Janice Galloway, Lesley Glaister, Reif Larsen, Margaret Ries, Cherise Saywell, Kate Tregaskis and Alan Warner. I'd also like to thank Nick Booth and Dr Wendy Kirk in UCL's Earth Sciences Department, and staff at UCL's Grant Museum, for showing me around their amazing collection.

Various books and articles have inspired my fictional references to ancient grains and artefacts:

'Ancient DNA reveals how wheat came to prehistoric Britain' (Quintin Schiermeier, *Nature*, 26/2/2015)

'Errors are Feared in Carbon Dating' (Malcolm Browne, *New York Times*, 31/5/1990)

'Feeding Italy for Millennia: the history of ancient grains'

(Dr Maurizio Polizzi, University of Palermo; article published in *L'Italo-America* 2018)

The Roman Cookery Book – Apicius (ed. Elisabeth Rosenbaum, George G. Harrap & Co Ltd. 1958)

Museums and How to Use Them (Eugenie Alexander, BT Batsford Ltd. 1974)

Hunting the Past (LB Halstead, Hamish Hamilton 1982)

A description of Lieut. Col. Thomas Birch's 1817 purchase of Mary Anning's fossil collection can be found in, amongst other places, Encyclopaedia Britannica's website (author John P. Rafferty.) 'The Wonder of the World' is an inscription that was used by the children's author and illustrator 'BB' (Denys Watkins Pitchford) at the front of his books, which my parents read to me, amongst many others, when I was a child.

Finally, for living so patiently with this book and for their encouragement and love, I'd like to thank my family: Mike, Charlotte, George and Archie.

www.sandstonepress.com

 facebook.com/SandstonePress/

@SandstonePress